LOVE ME NO MORE

Iris had lived an idyllic, sheltered life in Egypt, but when her father died, his final wish was that she be sent to England to live with her aunt. Determined to remain in her beloved home, Iris impulsively asked the mysterious Prince Usref to marry her ... little realising that British diplomat Stephen Daltry would soon arrive to sweep her off her feet!

Though she yearned to be with Stephen, her fear of Usref drove her to a fateful decision. For the insidious Prince would stop at nothing, not even murder, to make her his lifelong slave!

LOVE ME NO MORE

Love Me No More

by

Denise Robins

Magna Large Print Books
Long Preston, North Yorkshire,
BD23 4ND, England.

British Library Cataloguing in Publication Data.

Robins, Denise
    Love me no more.

    A catalogue record of this book is
    available from the British Library

    ISBN   0-7505-1721-2

Published in Large Print 2001 by arrangement with
Patricia Clark on behalf of the Executors of Denise Robins'
Estate

Magna Large Print is an imprint of Library Magna Books Ltd.

Printed and bound in Great Britain by
T.J. (International) Ltd., Cornwall, PL28 8RW

For
SILVIA AND GAWAINE

1

The midday sun beat down fiercely hot on the smooth white terraces and flower-filled roof garden of Lowell Pasha's villa on the Nile.

It was no ordinary villa, it had the noble proportions of a small palace. To the *fellahin* working in their fields on the delta it was called the 'Little Palace.' And Lowell Pasha – one of the few Englishmen to bear such an Egyptian title – was deeply respected, one of the wealthiest as well as one of the most brilliant of men, in a cultural sense, and an archaeologist of world renown.

The 'Little Palace,' glaring in the heat of such a day as this, glowed like a jewel, set in the restful shade of many tall palm trees. Its marble halls had been built around an open court which contained an exquisite fountain, and were enriched by borders and friezes of a design which Lowell Pasha had copied from one of the ancient temples he had excavated and preserved.

When the sun was at certain points in the zodiac the small carved domes of the building, which were decorated with wonderful tracery, wrought with blue glass and mother-of-pearl, could be seen flashing from a far distance. It was the wonder and delight of the native inhabitants of the small surrounding villages and of tourists. But nobody save certain privileged persons, well known to Lowell Pasha – and his retinue of Sudanese servants – ever got through the gates of the 'Little Palace.' The gate entrance was locked. On three sides the building was protected from the public by high white walls. On the fourth lay the glittering waters of the Nile.

Today the very Nile itself seemed turgid, oily with the heat. There was no sign of movement either inside the Palace or out, save from two magnificent white peacocks strutting slowly across the lower terrace.

The gardens and green lawns, religiously watered and tended by six Sudanese gardeners, simmered and steamed in the heat. A deep silence prevailed.

But high up on the flat roof, under a silken canopy, in a temperature controlled and cooled by electricity, a young girl, with a letter crushed in one slender jewelled hand, lay face downward on a low divan, sobbing as though her heart would break.

She was alone.

She had dismissed the servant who had just brought her the note. (It had been delivered by one of the great flying-boats which stopped a mile down the Nile, on the route between Luxor and Assuan). At a distance, half-hidden by a Moorish screen, there hovered a stout, grey-haired woman of Arab descent, wearing a black cotton gown and scarf about her head. She was anxiously watching the girl. Every now and again as those bitter sobs broke the hot silence the old woman, who was the girl's nurse, made a little wailing sound to herself and wiped away her tears. But she dared not approach the couch. When the Lady Iris told people to keep away from her, who would dare approach? The Lady Iris had a sweet and kind disposition but she was used to having her own way, and her word, when His Excellency the Pasha was away, was law. Nobody would argue with her, except the old English governess, Miss Morgan, of whose sharp tongue all the servants were afraid. And she, praise be Allah, was sick of a fever today and up in her rooms, unable to come down and interfere.

Let the Lady Iris cry ... it is good to loose the floodtide of grief, thought old Ayesha, the nurse. And why should she not weep, indeed, since this letter was to tell her that her revered father lay dying ... perhaps by now was dead ... in far-off Turkey?

Aiee ...aiee!... What a loss to all of them! Ayesha wept and watched the adored and beloved young mistress whom she had rocked in her cradle from the time she was

11

born ... twenty years ago.

Lowell Pasha's daughter turned now and lay staring for a moment up at the canopy which shielded her from the sun ... then looked through tear-swollen lids down at the garden ... and beyond to the desert ... far beyond towards a civilisation she had never known or seen. Turkey lay over there, somewhere ... Ankara ...whither her father had gone on a conference ... and from whence he would never return. It was almost unbelievable to Iris, who a week ago had seen him drive off in his car to Cairo, in what seemed the best of health and spirits. He had gone to meet and consult some well-known British engineer, who was on a visit there, about the installation of a new swimming-bath – for *her*. Iris loved swimming. The present bath, made in her childhood, was now too small. Dear, *dear* father, who had spoiled and indulged her slightest wish, always ... he had gone to Ankara on a mission for *her* ... but he had had a sudden stroke, so this letter said, in the 'plane, travelling to Ankara. He had been given only a few hours ... perhaps less ... in which to live. Lying in a hospital in the Turkish capital, he gathered together the strength to dictate some letters to an Englishman ... a new friend whose name Iris did not know ... and whose acquaintance he had made in Cairo the night before he flew to Turkey ... and beside whom he had been seated in the 'plane.

This man, Stephen Daltry, was described by Lowell Pasha as a young diplomat ... a fine type of Englishman ... whom one could trust ... in a world where values were shifting and integrity hard to find. Stephen Daltry had been exceedingly kind and helpful and finally gone with him to the hospital and stayed with him because Lowell Pasha said he feared his end was near. Because there were important words to be written ... Stephen Daltry had waited to write them down.

Iris, grief-stricken though she was, felt that she could remember every word of this letter, she had read it so many times before she had burst into tears.

I shall not be alive by the time this reaches you, my adored Iris ... whom I have felt always to be an incarnation of Isis, the great goddess of my beloved Egypt ... so I must hasten to send this letter and warn you that life as you have hitherto lived it can be lived no more. I have done you a wrong by bringing you up as I have done, sheltered and kept strictly away from the modern world. When your mother died in bringing you into the world I wished to protect you from that world ... and believed myself wise ... but now know that I was foolish. For I realise that when death overtakes me you will be unable to go on living alone in our beautiful home, blissfully ignorant of the sorrows and difficulties which beset human beings ... and that you must become one of them ... and go back to England ... to my sister in London who will guide and protect you.

I have lived only for you ... ever since your darling mother passed into the shadows ... but it has been madness ... a terrible mistake on my part, daring to hope that you could always escape reality... But you must be brave and obey what I am going to ask of you. I am sending instructions to you by Stephen Daltry, who will be in Cairo at the Legation next week, and will come to see you. I have entrusted him with your future. He has sworn to take you safely back to London to your Aunt Olivia. You know nothing of her ... nor she of you beyond what I am proposing to write to her if my strength holds out and I can dictate more to Stephen... The rest you can talk over with him ... good-bye, my beloved ... my Isis, daughter of earth and sky...

Daughter of Earth and Sky! That was how history described the ancient goddess of Egypt... Daughter of Keb and Nut. That, too, was what Lowell Pasha called his child.

Iris knew much about Ancient Egypt ... had studied the fascinating era with her father when she was still a child ... and was as conversant with the wonder and magic of

14

its history as she was with the Arabic language, which she spoke fluently.

She had always felt herself to be part of old Egypt. Outside these high white walls lay a world unknown to her ... a post-war world, occasionally described to her by old Miss Morgan, who had come, fourteen years ago, to teach her English subjects and remained, a faithful and devoted part of the household.

She lifted her father's letter in order to read it again but a voice interrupted her ... calling her from below.

'Iris ... my Lady of Moonlight, where are you?'

She sat up, pushing the long silken hair back from her wet, sad face. She knew that voice. It could only be Prince Usref, whom she called Mikhilo ... a young Serbian whom she had met through an Egyptian friend, Nila Fahmoud. Nila was the daughter of Fahmoud Pasha, one of the talented Egyptians working on a new temple excavation with Iris's father. She and Nila had been friends since babyhood, despite the utter difference in their characters and upbringing, for Nila had been educated in a university and was fond of the fashionable, social life of Cairo about which Iris knew nothing.

Nila was engaged to be married. Her future husband, whilst training for a special job in America, had met Usref there and he had come back to stay with the Fahmouds in Egypt. From the hour that the young Serbian Prince had set eyes on Iris he had been deeply enamoured of her.

He was handsome and amusing, and the only person so far to open Iris's large long-lashed eyes to the fact that a young, good-looking man can be more stirring to the pulses – and so much more interesting – than elderly grave professors! He called her his 'Lady of Moonlight.' It was his especial name for her ... and amused her so she had allowed it. It was the first touch of familiarity she had ever accepted. For she had grown up in these walls ... lived in the 'Little Palace' like a queen ... young though she was ... issuing her royal commands and expecting as well as receiving blind obedience – even subservience – from those around her. Nobody save her father and her English governess, whom she loved, ever dared thwart the Lady Iris.

'My Lady of Moonlight ... let me come to you...' pleaded the voice of Prince Usref, the Serb.

Old Ayesha shuffled nearer the couch.

'Shall I bid him depart, little mistress?'

'No, bid His Highness wait below on the terrace, and then come, do my hair and fetch my mirror and face-box,' Iris said in Arabic.

The old nurse hurried to do her bidding. It was well for the little dove to have young company and stop this grieving ... even though Ayesha had no great liking for the Serbian Prince, friend of the Fahmouds. He had found her in his way the other evening when entering the Palace and had caught her with his foot, tripped her up and laughed when she had difficulty in raising her big bulk from the ground. It had been mischievous and deliberate, and she had resented it.

But Iris felt suddenly glad because Mikhilo had come to see her. She could talk to him. He would help her. Nila said that he was greatly taken with her. He was cultured and had been in the modern world. He must advise her ... as old Miss Morgan could not do. She had been so long here, in the 'Little Palace,' that she had half forgotten English life and customs...

A few moments later Iris was downstairs in the upper terrace, where, beneath a great awning of blue-painted canvas, cool iced drinks were being served by Pilak, one of the Sudanese house-boys.

Prince Usref was leaning over the balustrade smoking, watching the great garden hose being sprayed in high silver jets of water over the parched grass and the scarlet carnations which fringed the lawns... He turned and flung away his cigarette as he

17

heard the soft patter of Iris's sandalled feet. He gave her an ardent look, then bowed. He had been warned by Nila never to take liberties with Lowell Pasha's daughter. And, ye gods, she was indeed like one of the goddesses of the past, he thought ... her slender beauty outlined against the jade-green painted doors through which she had just come. Alabaster-pale, her face was young and pure and of classic outline, with dark silken hair braided around her head. (Nila had told him that when Iris's hair was loosed it fell to her knees in a glorious cloud.) Her eyes held something of the changing colours of the Nile ... dark, amber-flecked under delicate narrow brows. The only touch of colour lay in the scarlet of her proud lips ... of her filbert nails.

She wore a long white gown, looped on one shoulder by a great scarab brooch of brilliant blue, and with a hem of blue and scarlet. She nearly always wore such clothes – designed from engravings she had seen of the women of ancient Egypt.

'My Lady of Moonlight...' murmured Mikhilo, 'I have heard of your disaster. News travels fast along the banks of the Nile. I have come to offer my services. My life is yours.'

Iris did not reply to this extravagant speech for a moment. She looked at him in a grave, searching way which she had, and which always disconcerted Mikhilo (fresh from easy conquests of the pretty American women). Then she said:

'Sit down. I have worse news for you, Mikhilo. I shall need your help.'

He allowed her to sink into one of the low, cushioned chairs facing the river. He stood watching her, fascinated as always by her marvellous beauty and the incredible atmosphere of a bygone imperial dynasty which she managed to create around herself. He said, speaking French, which was a language he knew better than English and which Iris spoke as well as Arabic:

'What can I do?'

Her big, mournful eyes looked up at him. She hardly saw the slim, well-groomed young man in his white linen suit ... so sleek, so handsome ... with the ebony-black head and big liquid eyes of his race.

She saw only the burning blue of the sky and heard the harsh plaintive cry of the peacocks on the lower terrace. This was her home; she could not, she *would* not, leave it, she thought desperately.

In a few brief words she told Mikhilo the contents of her father's letter.

A change came over the smiling face of the young Serbian Prince. He was aghast at the possibility that this most unique and exquisite girl might be removed from him. And at the very thought of the Englishman a bitter jealousy sprang to life within him.

Who was Stephen Daltry? A diplomat. An intruder who had no earthly right to control Iris's existence.

'But this is not to be tolerated!' he burst out. 'You must refuse to go away. He cannot forcibly remove you.'

Iris bit her lip. She was struggling with many emotions. Intermingled with her grief for her father was the desire to obey his dying wishes. He was sending Stephen Daltry to her and she knew that she must receive him. From him alone could she hear details of her father's end. But as she listened to Mikhilo's outburst, which continued on a note of passion, an uneasy feeling came over her. Perhaps he was right ... perhaps she *could* escape her fate and insist upon remaining here with old Miss Morgan. She knew nothing of the law, and Mikhilo was forgetting that Lowell Pasha's daughter was under age and might be forced to accept the guardianship of her aunt.

'Oh, Mikhilo,' exclaimed Iris, 'I knew that you would comfort and advise me. Say ... what *can* I do?'

'Refuse to see this man,' said the young Serb promptly.

She hesitated.

'I think I must see him if it is my father's wish.'

'When is he coming?'

'Soon, I understand – from Cairo.'

'Send for me the moment he arrives and I will deal with him,' said Mikhilo with youthful arrogance.

But as soon as he had spoken he regretted his words. He had forgotten that Lowell Pasha's daughter was not used to being given orders. She stood up, drawing her slender body erect, and said with a touch of coldness:

'No, Mikhilo, *I* will deal with him. I am mistress here now that my father...' She did not finish, but turned from Mikhilo, choking a little.

He kept a respectful distance.

So far he believed that he had gained her friendship and trust and that the rest would follow. It was only in moments like this when she 'froze' that he was less certain of himself and of her; made aware of the strange determination and strength of character in this extraordinary girl.

When he next spoke it was meekly.

'You have only to send for me, my Lady of Moonlight, and I will come. But I implore you, be firm with the Englishman.'

She looked through her black, glistening lashes at the waters of the Nile. Then she repeated in a low, slow voice:

'I will deal with him.'

There came the sudden sound of voices ...

of a disturbance unusual in the quiet gardens. Iris frowned and looked enquiringly in the direction of the gateway that led into the Palace grounds.

Mandulis, the Nubian who was Lowell Pasha's head *suffragi*, or servant, came running towards the terrace, his striped gown flapping, his broad ebony face betraying much indignation.

He spoke in Arabic to Iris. Mikhilo saw the girl's face flush a little. Then she drew herself into a position of incredible dignity for one so young.

'So!' she exclaimed. 'He has come already...'

Mikhilo said:

'It is Stephen Daltry?'

'Yes,' she said in a tense voice. But in spite of that colour in her cheeks and the slight quivering of her slender body, she remained cool and poised. She gave an order to the *suffragi*, who turned and hastened away. Then she said:

'They are trying to stop his coming to the Palace.'

'Why let him enter?' said Mikhilo eagerly.

'Because my father has sent him,' she said, her brows knit, and she caught her lower lip between her small white teeth in an effort not to betray any more emotion. She added, 'Leave me, please, Mikhilo. I must see this man alone.'

The young Serbian made a gesture as though to argue this point but one look from Iris's glorious eyes restrained him. He bowed and left her.

She walked out of the sunlight into the dim coolness of the house, there to wait the man who called himself her father's friend yet seemed to be the one and only enemy she had in the world.

2

Stephen Daltry was shown into the 'Little Palace' with slightly more respect than he had received at the gates. But he was hot, tired, and not in the best of humours.

He had come here on a difficult and delicate mission which he was already regretting. He had made up his mind to waste no time, but to give Lowell Pasha's daughter the instructions from her father immediately and carry out his own promise to see her safely to England.

Since Romney Lowell's death in the hospital at Ankara Stephen had made one or two enquiries about the old man whom he had first befriended when taken so critically ill. Lowell Pasha was reputed to be a little mad. Everyone said that he had brought his daughter up as a kind of goddess – and kept her a prisoner in her own home.

Nobody seemed to have seen Iris Lowell, except on rare occasions driving in a car, veiled, when she accompanied her father to their summer villa near Alexandria. There she was equally well guarded. And nobody seemed to think that she was kept 'in purdah' against her will. It seemed that she had never known any other existence and hankered for no other.

Stephen had received confirmation of these facts from Romney Lowell himself. But the old man, when he lay dying, had appeared to Stephen agitated, because of his fears for the girl's future. It had become obvious to him that Iris could not go on living alone in the palace with only an old English governess as chaperon.

'I have confidence in you, my boy,' he had told Stephen. 'My child shall be a sacred trust to you. She must be taken back to England, where my sister Olivia will look after her. She must have a chance to know her own people and country. Then when she is of age she can make her choice – return to our Palace and marry in Egypt – if she so wishes.'

It seemed to Stephen fantastic – more like a slice from a Rider Haggard novel than anything in real life. And the last thing he had ever imagined himself doing was acting as guardian to a beautiful girl of twenty.

At twenty-seven he had already distinguished himself in the Diplomatic Service; had just handed over his job as secretary to the attaché at Ankara and was now in the running for a new and important job as assistant attaché in Cairo.

Stephen liked Egypt. He also liked the

heat and sunshine, spoke a little Arabic, and got on well with the Egyptians.

He had a tremendous zeal for work, an unflagging enthusiasm for anything upon which he embarked. He was now on a fortnight's leave, and although he could not altogether look forward to his meeting with the girl, he wondered what he would find. What would she be like? How would she act? What the deuce would he do if she proved unwilling to fall in with her father's plans?

But the greeting which he had prepared died on his lips once he entered the room in which Lowell Pasha's daughter awaited him.

After the strong sunlight he stood blinking a moment, holding his smoked glasses in one hand. A swift survey revealed to him exquisitely carved walls and white graceful archways. The floor was pure mosaic. There were tall flowers everywhere. The atmosphere was fragrant and of refreshing coolness. Through the archways one could glimpse a green palm tree and a greener Nile.

Then Stephen saw Iris Lowell. She spoke in a cool, musical voice which seemed to him to have a faintly foreign inflection.

'You are Stephen Daltry?' she said.

For an instant he could not speak. He stared at her. He was an easy-going young man, the typical diplomat with all the social graces at his fingertips. He had met many beautiful women in his time, but he was literally struck dumb by the entrancing picture made by the remarkable daughter of Lowell Pasha.

She sat motionless in a chair which had a high back carved out of cedarwood and wrought with gilt Egyptian scrolls. The two arms were shaped like Sphinx heads and on each rested a slender hand. Stephen recognised the fact that the emeralds on those pointed fingers with their red lacquered nails might well have come from one of the coffers unearthed from a Pharaoh's tomb.

It was rather a shock, too, to see her in the classic white Egyptian gown which showed the exquisite lines of her lissom body.

Slowly he moved nearer her. Despite the beauty of her face, it seemed to him that there was a childish fragility about her, and he could only guess at the length of the black silky hair which was wound in three great plaits about her small head.

She repeated:

'You are Stephen Daltry?'

He felt a vague inclination to bow as though before royalty – so regal was her bearing.

'Yes,' he said. 'I have brought back your father's effects – and his instructions concerning yourself. I had the honour to be with the Pasha at the end. I would like to offer you all my sympathies...' He broke off in an embarrassed way.

Her head remained high, but he saw the slender hands grip the Sphinx heads tightly, and into those wonderful eyes of hers crept a desolate look. She said:

'Thank you. I am ... grateful for all you did for my dear father. Later, when you have had food and drink, I want to hear ... everything. You will stay in the "Little Palace" as my guest tonight. You will be well looked after. It would be my father's wish and there is much to settle.'

Stephen raised his brows. He was, as a rule, completely at ease with women, but this girl persisted in making him feel that he was merely being given an audience, and that at any moment he would be peremptorily dismissed.

He said:

'I have already booked a room in a hotel at Assuan and left my luggage there.'

'The room shall be cancelled,' she said haughtily. 'My servants will fetch your things. I know that my father would wish you to receive the hospitality of our home.'

Again Stephen raised his brows. He began to be a little amused. But the smile which hovered on his lips faded when he heard her next words.

'But I wish you to know right from the

start, so that there shall be no misunderstanding, that I shall obey my father in all
things except his order that I should go to
England. I shall not go. I shall never leave
Egypt.'

So the gauntlet had been flung down at
once and the fight was on, thought Stephen
wryly. Iris Lowell was not wasting time. He
had been prepared for opposition. The
Pasha himself had anticipated it. But he had
said: 'She must be made to see reason. I
could not rest if I thought of her living alone
in our Nile retreat. She must go to her Aunt
Olivia...'

Stephen said:

'I think we had better discuss that later,
don't you?'

He saw a sudden flash of anger stain the
camellia paleness of the girl's cheeks.

'Not at all. There's nothing more to discuss on that point. I have made up my
mind.'

Stephen's grey eyes regarded her gravely.

'But your father also made up his mind.
And I am here to carry out the promise
which I made to him and do not intend to
break.'

So unused was Iris to being thwarted in
such a fashion that for a moment she could
not speak but only stared at the English
stranger. And now for the first time she took
full stock of him and had to confess herself

extraordinarily interested in his appearance. She had never seen a man like this one before. In pictures, in books, or passing through the streets of Alexandria in her father's car on her way to their summer villa, she had glimpsed the occasional Englishman and had not been interested.

But she had to confess Stephen Daltry was as handsome and intriguing as he was unexpected – tall and beautifully built in his well-cut white linen suit, with his bright brown curling hair and a tanned, frank countenance. He bore no resemblance whatsoever to Prince Usref; and to Iris, accustomed to the dark hair and eyes of the swarthy Egyptians, it came almost as a shock to look into the light-grey of Stephen's eyes. There, too, she recognised a humour and quick intelligence, a spirit of daring. *He dared to dictate to her.*

She rose from her chair.

'I shall do as I think best,' she said.

Now that he saw her standing there in her matchless grace and dignity he caught his breath, but at the same time he was angered at her obstinacy.

'My dear child,' he said, 'forgive me – but you are only a child to me – and in the eyes of English law you are still an infant. Your father has instructed me, in company with Miss Morgan, your governess, to take you safely to your aunt...'

He drew a long document from the attaché-case which he carried. 'You can see that the seal of this is unbroken,' he added. 'It was your father's wish that I should read this to you and make you understand more clearly the reason for this decision which he has taken to put an end to your life in Egypt.'

He saw her eyes widen with an almost superstitious fear as she glanced at the papers in his hand. She seemed to struggle with herself and then sat down again, her slim body quivering with repressed emotion.

To accept pain unflinchingly and to be proud in the face of disaster were to Iris essential qualities for the 'Daughter of Earth and Sky.'

'Very well,' she said. 'Be seated, Stephen Daltry. If this is my father's dying wish I shall at least listen to you. Read what you like to me.'

Once more Stephen did not know whether to be amused or impressed by her dictatorial manner. But, curiously enough, now he was not amused. She took his breath away, and she was in deadly earnest. He was conscious, too, of a certain curiosity to learn more about her and her upbringing. While he stood and watched, she clapped her hands and gave an order in pure Arabic to the *suffragi* who entered. A chair was

31

brought forward for Stephen. Turkish coffee, a carafe of iced wine and a plate of spiced cakes were placed before him. He felt as though he were in some strange dream as he broke the seal of the document which he had brought with him, and then began to read...

3

Twenty-three years ago Romney Lowell – then one of the youngest and most brilliant professors of Egyptology and an archaeological expert – had been invited by the Egyptian Government to undertake one of the most colossal tasks of its kind on record: the excavation of an ancient temple in the desert not far from the Assuan Dam and considered the most important of the temples dedicated to the worship of the goddess Isis since Philae, an islet above the First Cataract, had been submerged.

It was a task which was to take years and necessitated enormous expenditure and all the knowledge as well as the enthusiasm which Romney Lowell had for ancient Egypt.

Before leaving England he had suddenly met Iris's mother, Helena. He described her as a 'pale, slender dream of a girl with dark hair and eyes, of a fragile loveliness,' which seemed to Stephen to be also a description of this lovely girl who sat here before him. After a whirlwind courtship, Romney and Helena were married and he brought her out to Egypt for their honeymoon.

During the process of the excavation of the Isis temple they lived in a luxurious houseboat on the Nile. Lowell described these days as being 'the most supremely happy' that any man in love could have desired, and then, two years later, when they knew that they were to have a child, that happiness was perfected. His work was going well, the excavation had unearthed mysteries and beauties of a fabulous nature. Every day Helena would wander with her husband through the great colonnades now revealed, and he would explain to her the meaning of the wonderful painted engravings and hieroglyphics, and translate for her some of the old papyrus taken from chests of gold and cedarwood.

Egypt and Helena, his love, his wife: these meant the world to Romney Lowell. But then came the unforeseen day when it was necessary for him to return to England. His old mother, for whom he had a great love, was dying and had sent for him. He did not wish to leave Helena alone in the 'Little Palace' which he had built for her and in which they now awaited the advent of their child. Neither did he wish her to travel, but Helena seemed to have some presentiment of disaster. He wrote:

'My darling clung to me. She implored me not to leave her and yet I knew that I must go, and

because of my mother I was torn between the two. Again and again I begged Helena to stay quietly in Egypt, for the birth of our child was only two months away. But she would come with me, and I can remember now the look in her wonderful eyes when she said, 'Who knows, if you left me here, Romney, we might never meet again.'... I tried to laugh away her fears but in a sudden panic decided to take her. I, who hate all modern things and this mechanical age, was glad that there were fast luxurious ships. We motored to Alexandria, embarked from there to Venice, and thence by train to Paris ... and so to England.'

Continuing his story, Romney Lowell told of their safe arrival in London. All seemed well because he was able to be with his beloved mother before she died, and Helena had stood the journey well. The fears he had suffered for her safety seemed after all groundless. But she had only one wish (which he shared): to return to their beloved Egypt as quickly as possible. She had the same absorbing interest in the temple excavations; the same uncanny feeling that they too were the reincarnation of Isis worshippers who had known and loved each other in Egypt in that bygone dynasty.

All preparations were made for their voyage back to Alexandria, but neither of them allowed for the dangerous change of temperature – Helena had been brought too suddenly back to the damp and cold. She was so used now to warmth and sunshine. On the very day they were due to travel, she was struck down with a chill. Romney Lowell cancelled the journey. In a hotel bedroom overlooking the Thames, Helena took to her bed never to rise from it again. The little Iris was born prematurely and the mother died in giving birth to her.

For a few days, wrote Romney Lowell, he was so stunned with grief, so besieged by despair, by the feeling that he should never have brought his wife back to England despite all her pleadings, he cared nothing for the unfortunate infant who was the cause of the disaster. But the finest nurses and doctors saved that frail life. The child lived. And Romney Lowell lived, too, but with one burning purpose – to return to Egypt ... to the country which Helena loved. It had been her own request to him that he should take her baby with him. He had given his solemn promise to do so.

Her very words were quoted in Lowell's document:

'Our daughter is like Isis, Daughter of Earth and Sky ... take her back to the sun – like myself she will not survive this cold, damp climate. We belong to Egypt. She, too, must belong to it, Romney.'

36

So he had started to take an interest in the infant – an interest which later became all-absorbing. He decided to hire a nurse and have the child conveyed to the 'Little Palace' on the banks of the Nile. She should be brought up as the Daughter of Earth and Sky; in *her* the spirit of the goddess would live again. Lowell went so far as to take the child to a church in London and ask that she should be christened Isis. Lowell wrote:

'The parson was an old, conventional man, shocked at what he called my pagan choice of a name, and, despite my protests, insisted upon christening my daughter Iris ... the nearest approach to the Egyptian.'

So Iris she was christened and remained.

As he read aloud the rest of the document Stephen saw why Romney Lowell, unhinged by his tragic loss, had become a fanatic after his wife's death. He had given the little Iris over to the care of Ayesha, the nurse, and resolved that she should never be allowed to make contact with that cold, cruel world which had killed his beloved.

The document told also of the coming of Miss Morgan to the household and of the careful upbringing of the little Iris and finally her initiation into the mysteries and splendours of the excavated temple. (This work completed, Lowell was rewarded by the government conferring upon him the title of 'Pasha.') He unearthed a fortune from that temple and Egypt was grateful to him. The museum in Cairo benefited by the many wonders, and Lowell Pasha benefited also. He and his daughter could live in luxury and continue their studies.

Only towards the end of this astonishing biography Lowell Pasha expressed a certain uneasiness about the manner in which he had brought up his child.

'I pray she will always be as happy as she is now and need never leave the Land of Sunshine and Mystery, but when she comes of marriageable age, what then? Steeped though we are in Egypt and Egyptian things, her rightful heritage is England. She is by birth an Englishwoman. Have I done wrong to keep her in ignorance of the progress of the world? The war has not touched her. She has only seen the 'planes and flying-boats that pass over our heads; driven veiled beside me in my car. I have told her a little about London but she dreads it even as I do. Oh, Helena, Helena, I have tried to keep faith with you, my darling, but sometimes I fear for our child!'

Stephen stopped reading and now he raised his eyes to Iris and saw that she was marble-pale as her Egyptian gown and that her large lustrous eyes were full of utter desolation. He was suddenly unbelievably sorry for her. Almost he felt that it would be a crime to uproot her – for was she not part of the old, mysterious Egypt in which she was steeped?

He was the first to break the silence. He stood up and came towards her uneasily. He was more moved than he would ever care to admit by the amazing story which he had just read to Iris. But he knew that he must be practical for Iris's sake, for she must face reality sooner or later.

'You understand, perhaps,' he said gently, 'why it is necessary for you to go to England now. But when you are twenty-one you will be free to leave your aunt if you wish and return here.'

He heard a gasping cry break from her. She sprang to her feet, both small fists clenched, and tilted back her head.

'No, no, no! I will not go! I will not! You shall not make me!' she said, her voice vibrating.

'My dear Iris,' he began, 'if I may call you that... I am so much older than you are... I understand how you feel, but I beg you because of your father–'

'Even for him I will not go,' she interrupted wildly. 'Oh, go away, please! I do not want you here. I was happy until you came. I shall never, never let you take me from Egypt...'

She broke off, choking, and turning from him ran out of the room.

He stood staring after her, then sat down again and poured out some wine. He felt hot and disturbed. Lord, he thought, what had he taken upon himself? How could any mere man deal with such a tempestuous creature ... a young woman completely ignorant of life as it was led today?

But, curiously enough, these few hours spent with Lowell Pasha's daughter had firmly decided Stephen that he would not go away without carrying out the old man's wishes. The girl obviously needed guidance and protection and he must give it. The best thing for him to do was to stay here. For all he knew, if he left the Palace one of her fantastic friends might come and spirit her away to a place where she might never be heard of again. And apart from his growing personal interest in her fate, Stephen had never liked the thought of failure in any mission he chose to undertake.

The next thing, he thought, was to see the English governess and attempt to make an ally out of her – but, damn it all! this reincarnation of the goddess Isis appeared to have unlimited authority in the Palace, and it was not going to be easy to treat her as 'an infant in the eyes of the law.'

And then there was Elizabeth...

It had been last winter at a party in Cairo

that Stephen had met Elizabeth, only daughter of Sir William Martyn, J.P., and become engaged to her.

He had a quick mental vision of her. He had thought her a delightful example of a real English girl with her abundance of fair hair, blue eyes and fair complexion. She had, too, all the social graces and an ambitious mother behind her. With a slight smile Stephen recalled how cunningly Lady Martyn had manoeuvred Elizabeth and himself into their engagement last Christmas. Stephen, ready and willing to fall in love in the glamour of a moonlight picnic by the Pyramids, had allowed himself to believe that Elizabeth was the girl he had been looking for.

She had returned to England with his ring on her finger. He had been happy enough about it at the time and they proposed getting married in the autumn. In fact, if his job kept him out here, they had agreed that she might join him and could have their wedding in Cairo.

All very satisfactory and – as had been usual in Stephen's life – he had so far encountered little opposition. He had always been lucky. He had a large circle of friends, and although there had never been anything serious before Elizabeth he had had one or two very pleasant 'affairs.' And yet ... whenever he thought about Elizabeth that uneasy feeling would creep in to disturb him ... the fear that he might find it hard to settle down ... that marriage *might* put a complete stop to the free and adventurous existence he had enjoyed leading since he had left Oxford and entered the Diplomatic Corps.

He wondered what Lady Martyn would think of him now, in this Arabian Nights dwelling of Lowell Pasha's, endeavouring to rescue the lovely Iris! Lady Martyn would not approve, and perhaps Elizabeth would not either. But he had let himself in for it now and there was no drawing back. For a moment he sat there fingering the document which he was still holding, then he looked up and saw that Iris Lowell had returned.

She had recovered her poise. There was no trace of softness or grief now in her face or bearing. She spoke to him coldly:

'I wish to thank you for coming here and for delivering my father's message to me,' she said. 'But I want you to understand that it is useless for you to remain. I have quite made up my mind. I have always obeyed my father, but this time I shall not obey. I am remaining in Egypt.'

Stephen's eyes narrowed. He drew near to her and with a quickening of the pulses looked down at that proud, white young face.

'But I, too, have made up my mind that you shall go to England,' he said. 'And the first thing I want to do is to see Miss Morgan.'

Iris stared and gasped. No man had ever dared override her wishes under this roof. She said:

'If I do not choose, you will not see Miss Morgan.'

'Oh, come!' he protested. 'Don't make things too difficult.'

It seemed then that all the hot blood in her was roused. She gasped at him:

'You shall *not* dictate to me! I shall have you thrown out of the Palace.'

Then he gave a short laugh. His own temper flared up to match hers.

'You have a lot to learn, my child,' he said. 'We are not living in the Thirtieth Dynasty of Egypt, I assure you. This is 1947, and it is high time you were taught something about life as it is lived today, and taught, too, that it is primitive to fling people out of houses as you suggest.'

Aghast, Iris stared up at him. Tears of sheer rage glistened on her lashes. It could not be true, she thought, that any man should speak to her like this. All efforts at maintaining poise and dignity failed. She panted:

'I hate you, Stephen Daltry!'

He did not answer for a moment but

shook his head a little, watching her with the expression of one who surveys an amazing phenomenon. And now his gaze rested on that red, passionate mouth, and as he watched the convulsive clenching and unclenching of her slender fingers he had the incredible sensation that a man might easily forget the modern age and modern woman and lose himself in the enchantment of old Egypt and of this glorious girl. Through that cool, logical brain upon which he prided himself swept the shattering thought:

'What if she had said *"I love you!"* instead of *"I hate you!"*? It would be with the same fire and determination ... and, ye gods, *it would be wonderful!*'

He stood there staring at her in the breathless silence. Outside, in the heat and glare of the late afternoon, the last ruby-red gold of the sun dipped into the shimmering Nile and the white peacocks called harshly, warningly, to each other.

4

The spell was broken for Stephen by the entrance of Pilak, one of the young *suffragis*. Immediately Iris regained her dignity and asked him what he wanted. Stephen's knowledge of Arabic was slight and colloquial, but he gathered that Miss Morgan, the English governess, had asked to see the Lady Iris.

The boy withdrew. Iris turned back and looked at Stephen.

'My governess has bad fever. If you will excuse me, I am going to her,' she said.

Stephen found it a little difficult to recover his own equilibrium. It had been a tense and curiously passionate moment when he had felt the unconscious provocation of this girl's incredible beauty and strength of will. It was like a challenge to his own, and Stephen could never resist a challenge.

He took out his cigarette-case and looked at it thoughtfully. Then he said:

'Will you come and talk to me again? Don't hate me, please. I assure you I haven't the slightest wish to make you unhappy. I am only a stranger to you, after all. I understand that you must resent my intrusion. It would really be easier for me to throw up the whole thing and walk away. But your father was so insistent that I should carry out his wishes, and I gave him my word. Do try to understand this and not let there be personal antipathy between us.'

Her large luminous eyes widened a little as though in some slight astonishment as she thought over his speech. Then an expression of contrition softened the haughty young face.

Deep down within her she was grateful to Stephen Daltry – would have been to any man who had helped to ease the last moments of the father she had adored. She still yearned to ask Stephen about the journey to Ankara where the two men had met. But she was so confused and disturbed by all that she had been told so far, and so terrified of being uprooted from her home, she could not think at the moment along reasonable or logical lines.

Her mind still whirled with the story that had been unfolded to her when Stephen had read to her her father's account of his meeting and marriage with her mother. One clear fact stood out among the rest: England had killed her mother. She had died there away from the sun and the warmth of her beloved Egypt, and she, Iris, had a premonition that disaster would overtake her if she ever went to her father's country. All that she most prized and understood lay here by the waters of the Nile.

But it was true that she had no real cause for antagonism towards Stephen Daltry and she was a little ashamed of her recent outburst. He was unlike any other man she had met. Mikhilo, the only other young European, was, she knew, ready to fall at her feet. Her father's elderly friends had all done homage to her. It was a shock, to say the least of it, to find herself being treated like a foolish child by the young Englishman. And she had not, so far, encountered much humour in her life, drenched as it was in the serious, even gloomy, atmosphere of ancient Egypt. It was a new experience to her to see that slightly amused look which came at times into Stephen's grey eyes when he spoke to her. And certainly they were handsome eyes. That was not to be denied.

Iris could be hot-tempered and difficult, but she could also be generous, and somewhere amongst her untutored emotions was a very human, little-girl longing for laughter, for joy, for a younger and more thrilling companionship than she had known with her father.

When she spoke to Stephen again it was without rancour.

'I will try to understand,' she said, almost humbly for her. 'Please stay in the Palace, Stephen Daltry, as my guest.'

He was surprised and charmed by her complete change of demeanour. This girl's moods were unpredictable. Why, he could have sworn he saw the hint of a smile tilting that exquisite, passionate young mouth.

But, swift as lightning, Iris added a sentence which destroyed his hope that she would be really tractable.

'Only it is better,' she said in her lilting, rather measured voice, 'that you take it for granted that I shall not leave my home in Egypt. Now please follow my head *suffragi* to your room. We will eat together on the terrace at nine o'clock.'

He stood, with the cigarette-case still unopened in his hand, staring at the archway through which the slim, white-clad form vanished. Ye gods! The young woman knew how to throw her orders about, he thought wryly. There was no question of asking him what *he* wanted. He had never come across anything like this. The set-up here was so unreal that it took him several moments to readjust his mental balance and remember such mundane things as the fact that he owed Elizabeth a letter ... *Elizabeth!*... He was not a little disturbed to think how far away his fiancée seemed from him at the moment. There was no place in these exotic surroundings for *her* ... poor little Elizabeth; so sports-loving and jolly and typically modern. He could imagine her comments on Lowell Pasha's daughter, too. She would think all this a big joke.

Mandulis took Stephen to his room. Without lighting the much needed cigarette he walked through the beautiful house with its high domed ceilings so richly carved and ornamented; it's marble steps and Moorish screenwork; its rich satins and tapestries and gorgeous rugs; and he could not begin to think very sensibly or even agreeably about Elizabeth.

Indeed, it did not seem to him possible that he had ever loved or wanted her for his wife. Not that he could excuse himself for feeling such a complete revulsion of emotion just because he had met this fantastic girl, Iris Lowell.

He was shown into a magnificent suite of rooms with wide balconies overlooking the gardens and the Nile. Iris had not been long in carrying out her projects, he thought. His luggage was already installed. Mandulis asked him for his keys. He gave them to the man and then walked on to the balcony and stood there smoking, wondering how long this mission would take him and when he would find himself back in Cairo.

It was as well, he thought, that he had a fortnight's leave. His work was important to him and he would have allowed nothing – even this absorbing adventure – to interfere with it.

He must write to Elizabeth ... *he must* ... her last letter had reproached him because he had sent so few letters home lately. And she was only waiting for him to say that the time had come for her to join him – make her home with him here in the Middle East. His work was centred here for at least another year.

But the letter to Elizabeth was not written.

Like a man shaken with a strange fever and excitement, Stephen bathed and changed into the dinner clothes with white jacket that Mandulis had laid out for him, and wondered if he would be dining with Iris Lowell alone.

In another wing of the Palace Iris sat by Miss Morgan's bedside.

She was not hurrying to dress nor even remembering, at the moment, that she had ordered dinner for nine o'clock. Iris lacked a sense of time. It seemed to her un-important; she did not belong to a modern world ruled at it was by machinery, by clockwork, by man's ceaseless effort to defeat time itself.

Mournfully, looking more like a sad child than the young queen of this Palace, she conversed with her old governess.

'You see, Morga,' she said, using her especial name for the Englishwoman who was dearer to her than anybody else within these walls, 'I know that Stephen Daltry is trying to carry out Father's wishes, but I cannot ... I will not be forced to leave all this...' – she made a sweeping gesture with one slim hand – 'and live with my aunt in London, with my cousin ... relatives whom I have never known and who would not understand me any more than I would understand them... You will take my part, won't you, Morga? You will see Mr Daltry and tell him I cannot go?'

Caroline Morgan did not answer at once. Propped up by pillows, nursing an aching head after a bad bout of malaria, she was a little confused and unhappy about the future of her beloved charge. The news of the Pasha's death had been a great shock to her. She had always deeply respected her employer. She knew, too, the devastating loss that it was to Iris. The two had been inseparable.

At the same time Miss Morgan viewed the possibility of the 'Little Palace' being closed down and of Iris and herself going to England with trepidation. She could see what a painful uprooting it would be for Iris. It would be so even for her ... an old woman. She had grown to love Egypt and her life here with the Lowells. It had seemed an extravagant and rather ridiculous life when she first undertook the care of the child and of the English side of her education. She had often disapproved of the way in which Iris

51

had been guarded from the world. It was not good for her to live in a bygone age, sublimely unaware of the civilised world which revolved around her. Of course, Miss Morgan was aware that Lowell Pasha had been an eccentric. And she was not really surprised now that he had regretted his daughter's upbringing and wished to do the sane and right thing when he lay dying.

But Iris in London... Iris in this post-war world to which she was a complete stranger!... Caroline Morgan's heart sank a little at that thought. Her own luxurious life in Egypt would be over too. She would be pensioned off ... she would maybe sit alone in front of a spluttering gas-fire in a Bayswater hotel (she was verging on sixty now and had no relations who counted)... Ugh! What a depressing outlook.

Nevertheless, Miss Morgan ever dutifully sought to uphold her late employer's wishes even while she thought it a little regrettable that he should have sent an envoy in the shape of this strange young man. Iris was not used to dealing with strange young men. Of course, he was at the Legation, good family, no doubt ... and the Pasha must have thought him trustworthy...

Iris's sweet voice interrupted her reverie.

'I don't want to go, Morga. Oh, Morga ... do not let him take me away!'

The old governess's face, lined and

52

browned like leather after years of exposure to the sun, wrinkled in compassion. She put out a hand and touched the girl's dark, braided head.

'I think you will have to go, my child. You have lived too long in this seclusion. I have known it for a long while, but your dear father realised it only at the last. There is another world, Iris. You have seen pictures of it, you have caught glimpses of it in Cairo and Alexandria as you have driven through. And London is the mainspring of the world. It is your birthplace. You have an English heritage, my dear. And soon you will be of age and you will want to marry. Who could it be but to an Englishman? And if you stay on here in this environment you will not be ready for an English marriage. You will not be able to take your place in the civilised world.'

The colour sprang to Iris's cheeks.

'From all I have heard and seen I refuse to accept that it is more civilised, or even as much so, as the world in which my father and I have lived,' she exclaimed. 'There could be no greater civilisation than that of the Pharaohs. What architecture in the modern world could be so sublime as the Temple of Isis?... What modern house could I live in in London that could be like my Palace?' She broke off, choking a little, and added: 'Oh no, no! If it is true that I sleep here like one in a dream, then I do not

53

wish to wake up. Keep me here with you, Morga. Let us send this Englishman away.'

Caroline Morgan, tempted though she was to sympathise with Iris, still felt it her duty to encourage her to obey her father. She sat talking to her of London and its advantages. She harped on the possibility of her marriage.

Iris listened uneasily. Marriage ... why, the subject had never so much as been mentioned between her father and herself. But now that she was made to think about it she *wondered* ... and she grew even more afraid of being torn away from this life with which she was so familiar and satisfied. She could not envisage herself living in intimacy with any man ... least of all one who had neither sympathy with nor understanding of Egypt.

Inevitably her thoughts turned to Prince Usref. Mikhilo, who was the first man ever to look at her with open admiration and barely concealed longing. Could she as a matter of interest marry a man like Mikhilo? If so she might remain here undisturbed. He wouldn't let her go away. He had expressed his horror at the mere idea of it.

But one must love the man one married, she pondered. To be a good wife it was necessary for a woman to be dedicated to love and the man of her choice, even as the priestesses were dedicated in their ancient temples and for whom the breaking of any vow meant dishonour and death.

She spoke openly of these things to the old governess.

'I do not love anyone,' she said. 'I cannot therefore think of marriage.'

Miss Morgan sighed.

Iris was so intense – far too profound and serious-minded for her age. And yet she was emotionally so immature. The girl would be lost in modern life among modern men. A casual flirtation would horrify her. Miss Morgan was afraid, more than a little afraid, of the various repercussions of the Pasha's death. She wished he had not made her, Caroline Morgan, and this man, Stephen Daltry, responsible for Iris's future. Indeed, she wondered if Mr Daltry realised what a terrific responsibility he had taken on.

At length Iris rose and left the old woman. They had come to no happy conclusion. Everything seemed at its gloomiest and worst. Iris realised that her dear Morga was on the side of this man who had come to uproot her from Egypt.

The only person who seemed to be in sympathy with her was Mikhilo. She felt a sudden desire to see him. She would send for him. He should come later and she would let him talk to Stephen Daltry. That might be a good thing. She would send Pilak with a note, bidding him come here later this evening.

5

She kept Stephen waiting an hour for his dinner.

He sat on the terrace smoking, drinking the apéritifs offered him. If Elizabeth had been an hour late he would have been annoyed, for he was a man who liked punctuality. But it did not seem to him either strange or annoying that Iris should be unpunctual. It was all in keeping with this timeless, unorthodox place.

A table had been laid for two on the marble terrace with gleaming silver and exquisite crystal glass. There were festoons of red roses spilling their fragrance and lighted candles in heavy silver candelabra. The tall wax candles burned without a flicker in the still heat of the evening. The terrace and gardens were bathed in moonlight. Light spilled through the open windows of the Palace. The faint sound of music drifted from a felucca on the Nile: the plaintive half-tones of an Egyptian song.

What a night, thought Stephen, and what an intriguing atmosphere!

The next moment he was on his feet and the blood rushed to his head as he saw Iris coming towards him. Fascinated, he stared.

She wore a long straight gown, burnt-rose colour, of exquisite Egyptian silk, with a design picked out in silver thread. It was caught up on the right shoulder by a heavy ornamented clasp. The silken hair, which had been braided when he saw her this afternoon, was piled high now in soft looping waves on her head. In the darkness glittered a single diamond star. As she drew nearer him he saw that she was pale and that the huge eyes were heavily shadowed as though she had been weeping. But those eyes devastated him. They were as deep and mysterious as the moonlit river. He experienced something approaching a shock at the unearthly beauty of the girl. She moved with an effortless grace on her small feet in their silver sandals which showed the red-lacquered nails.

She gave him the Egyptian greeting.

'*Saiida!*'

He answered, instinctively bowing.

'*Saiida!*'

Two of the *suffragis* stood behind the chair into which she sank. She motioned Stephen to his. For a moment he sat silent, and he who had dined at all the Embassies and always found small talk so easy did not know what to say. He could only look at the shimmering figure of what might indeed have been a reincarnation of a goddess on

57

this superb moonlit night.

It was Iris who spoke first.

'There are many things I wish to talk to you about, Stephen Daltry,' she said. 'But first we must eat. It is growing late.'

Stephen said:

'Won't you drop the "Daltry" and just call me Stephen? I do want you to feel that I am your friend.'

Gravely her heavily-fringed eyes rested on him.

'I, too, wish to feel that, Stephen.'

He felt relieved.

'Then we are friends, Iris? You know, you made me feel as though I were a mortal enemy when I arrived.'

'You did not come with good news,' she said, biting her lip.

'I am truly sorry about that, but you know the position.'

'Yes. We need not go into that again.'

He wondered but did not ask whether after all she had come to the conclusion that her fate was inevitable. It was not easy to read what was going on in Iris Lowell's amazing mind. But Stephen was sure that she held no conception of the inexorability of the English law. How could she even begin to see that the Pasha's dying decision to alter her whole life was nothing short of brutal? The girl was bound to suffer.

'You have talked things over with your

governess?' he asked hopefully.

Her lashes drooped.

'Yes. But let us enjoy our dinner now and speak no more of my future,' she said abruptly.

Stephen found himself only too willing to acquiesce.

Iris was a wonderful hostess, and the meal served by the two *suffragis* on that moonlit terrace was a miracle of culinary art. Stephen was a young man who liked good food and wine. And everything tonight was perfect.

It was not until they were drinking the strong Turkish coffee, served in tiny gold cups of Moorish workmanship, and Stephen had lit the cigar given to him by Mandulis, that Iris brought the conversation back to herself. Up to then their conversation had been entirely impersonal. She had wanted to know about his flight from Khartoum; had discussed with him affairs of the nations ... art, science, the classics ... a variety of things of which she displayed an astonishing knowledge and a genuine interest which he found fascinating. She was so many-sided, and not the least of her attractions was that almost pathetic childish ignorance of life as it was lived, for instance, by girls like Elizabeth. She knew all and she knew nothing. In theory she was as learned as some of her father's professors. In practice she was but a babe!

But now she asked him, at last, for the full story his meeting with her father and what had been said between them.

When Stephen finished talking she gave a heavy sigh and he caught the glisten of a tear on the long black lashes. She said: 'Why, why wasn't I there to hold his hand and hear him speak just once again to me? Why, why could I not have told him that it would kill me to leave my beloved home?'

Stephen said gently:

'He has done what he thought best for you, and I assure you it *is* best. You will get used to the change in your existence. It is all a question of time. You may even grow to love England.'

Now all the softness in her face was replaced by the obstinacy which he was beginning to recognise.

'Never!' she said. 'I am part of Egypt. Just as my mother was part of it. England will kill me as it killed her.'

'My dear, that is surely an exaggeration!'

'It is the truth!'

Stephen looked at the point of his cigar. Damn it, he thought, the girl was so intense that she could make one believe that what she said was true. She would make him feel like a murderer if he tried to enforce her obedience to her father's will and make her accept the guardianship of her English aunt.

Then suddenly she staggered him by asking:

'What is my position if I marry?'

Taken aback, he answered:

'Marry? Marry whom? I mean ... is there any question...?'

'I want to know if I am entitled to marry whom I wish.'

'I'm afraid you are not,' said Stephen awkwardly. 'That is, not without your aunt's full consent.'

This seemed to anger the girl. She rose and stood before him, all her tempestuousness of the afternoon returning in full force, the moonlight shimmering on her burntrose gown.

'It is iniquitous,' she said. 'I will not accept such tyranny!'

He looked up at her. What was in her mind? What man did she contemplate marrying? Lowell Pasha had not spoken of her in connection with any affair of the heart. Stephen awoke to new and even greater complications. Perhaps Iris had some secret love affair. She was young and beautiful and ... before he could restrain the impulse he put a blunt question to her:

'Is there somebody whom you wish to marry, Iris?'

For an instant their gaze met fully. For some inexplicable reason the man's heart had begun to race. And she, taken aback by his direct question, hesitated to answer. After all, she had merely toyed with the thought of Usref ... wondering if she could accept marriage with him and thus escape her fate.

But the whole idea was still entirely new and frightening, and there was something new and equally frightening in the way this young man, Stephen, looked at her. All through their meal together she had been growing more aware of his intelligence and charm. He was not superficial like Mikhilo. He did not weary her with flowery phrases of empty flattery. She had been enthralled by the manner in which he talked and the theories he expounded. He alone, of all the people she had ever met, had awakened her to the realisation that there could be companionship and humour between a girl and a young man. He had also brought her closer than she had ever been before to the essentials of English life.

He did not approve of her or the life she led out here. That, too, fascinated her. And yet when he looked at her with those strange, light-grey eyes ... when he made her aware of the strength and determination which Mikhilo lacked, she felt confused and uncertain of herself. She could no longer command. It was as though she waited for *him* to dictate ... something hitherto unknown to her.

Now he was speaking again.

'I beg your pardon, Iris. I had no right to enquire into your personal life. But you asked me about your marriage and so I had to tell you ... it is not possible until you are of age. Unless your aunt consents.'

She made no comment upon this, but he could see that she was angry and bitterly resentful. And then, after a pause, looking at him through her thick lashes, she said:

'And is the English law so powerful that it could force me bodily to England, even if I resist?'

Again she saw that slightly amused smile lift the corners of Stephen's fine-cut lips.

'Now you wouldn't do that, would you? It would make things most awkward for all of us.'

She stood up and turned from him, one small hand clenched against the palm of the other. Her gaze was fixed on the splendour of the stars and that deep-blue Egyptian sky which had an unearthly brilliance on nights like these. Those same stars were shining over the desert, over the Isis temple which her father had unearthed, she thought. And she loved it. She loved it all so much. She really could find it in her heart to hate Stephen Daltry for the power which he seemed to be able to exercise.

Stephen looked hesitatingly at the slender, rigid back of the girl. What could he say or do to help her? he wondered. So learned, so highly developed along mental lines, she was still something of a little savage at heart. Therein, perhaps, lay her fascination.

Mandulis came out on to the terrace and spoke to his mistress. Stephen saw her turn round and throw back her head with a suggestion of defiance. As the *suffragi* went away she said to Stephen:

'Prince Usref, my very good friend, is here.'

Stephen raised his brows. His silence was an interrogation.

Iris volunteered a brief outline of her meeting and friendship with the young Serbian.

'He will not want me to go to England,' she added naïvely.

'I'm sure he won't!' said Stephen, and was greatly inclined to ask her there and then if this was the young man she was thinking of marrying. But he decided that it would be more tactful to do nothing of the sort.

It took him only a few moments after meeting Mikhilo to size up that flamboyantly handsome princeling. One of the playboy types – many of whom he had met in his job as a diplomat; a little hysterical and womanish and without reserves – obviously deeply in love with Iris after his facile fashion, but likely to be of no value to her as a wise or sensible friend.

After they had been introduced the two men sat talking and smoking, their conversation fluent, and neither betraying the fact that each regarded the other with suspicion – even antipathy.

The beautiful girl who sat between them said little. She kept a sullen, brooding silence. But now and again she caught the full glance of Mikhilo's adoring eyes and her drooping spirits lifted a little. He was not against her, like Stephen Daltry. He did not want to exile her to a cold, cruel country. Perhaps he would think of a way out ... he must ... a way to elude the shadows which were threatening her life's happiness.

Stephen became aware that his presence was superfluous and that these two wished to be alone. Oh well, he thought, it was not his business. Iris must deal with her friends as she thought fit. But he wondered whether Lowell Pasha would have approved of Mikhilo as her counsellor or a future husband. In his, Stephen's, opinion Mikhilo Usref was not good enough for Iris.

When at length he rose and suggested that it was time he retired he could not fail to see the relief in Iris's beautiful eyes. He did not know whether to be amused or chagrined. He said:

'Tomorrow I hope to meet Miss Morgan.'

She knew what that implied. He meant to try to talk Morga over. Oh, she did hate

Stephen Daltry – she *did*. And yet as she bade him good night and watched his tall, well-built figure walk away, she was consumed by uneasiness. The Englishman with the light-grey eyes was strong, far too strong. And in his way vastly intriguing. She had never felt more confused or miserable.

The moment he was out of earshot Mikhilo turned to her eagerly.

'You sent for me, my Lady of Moonlight? I can be of use to you?'

'Sit down and let us talk, Mikhilo,' she said.

He wanted to fall at her feet, kiss the hem of her shimmering gown and pour out an extravaganza of passionate admiration. But he was wise enough to refrain. The time had not yet come, he told himself, for him to take Iris into his arms. He sat down beside her and waited for her to speak.

It was many hours later, up in his own suite, that Stephen Daltry heard a slight timid knocking at his bedroom door.

He was in bed, reading. The night was hot and he had been unable to sleep. He had made several abortive attempts to write to Elizabeth but each time had laid down his pen ashamed and yet conscious of the fact that the lovely, stormy face of Iris Lowell rose to banish the memory of the girl who was his future wife.

A quick glance at his watch showed him

that it was now one o'clock in the morning. Again came the knocking. He threw on a dressing-gown, walked to the door and opened it. He saw to his astonishment an elderly woman with a scarf tying up her head and a thick dressing-gown muffling her angular figure. A pair of short-sighted eyes peered at him anxiously through strong-lensed spectacles.

'Oh, forgive me ... I must apologise ... most unorthodox ... but I need your help, Mr Daltry,' stammered this nocturnal visitor.

'You are Miss Morgan?' said Stephen.

'Yes ... I've been ill. I regret I was not downstairs to welcome a countryman to the "Little Palace",' she said. 'But, Mr Daltry ... I am so anxious about Iris ... so very anxious...' She broke off, coughing.

Stephen said kindly:

'You still have fever. You ought not to be out of bed. Will you sit down?'

'No, I want just to speak to you for one moment about Iris.'

'Is there anything I can do?' he questioned.

Miss Morgan found him a most personable and courteous young man and at once allied herself to him. She said:

'You dined with the child, did you not?'

'Yes.'

'What time did you leave her?'

Stephen, wondering what this was leading up to, felt a slight thrill of apprehension.

He told the old governess that it must have been soon after eleven o'clock that he left his beautiful hostess with Prince Usref.

Miss Morgan clicked her tongue against her teeth. She did not like Mikhilo, but, in common with the rest of the household, she rarely opposed any wish of Iris's, and Iris seemed to like the Prince. But Miss Morgan had always secretly regretted that particular introduction made through Nila Fahmoud.

'Oh dear!' she said. 'Then it must have been the Prince who drove away at about a quarter to twelve, but the guards at the gate did not notice if Iris was with him. Mandulis questioned them for me...'

'Is Iris missing from the Palace, then?' asked Stephen.

Miss Morgan nodded. She had awakened, she said, half an hour ago, and with a sudden feeling of uneasiness about the girl had gone to her suite and found that she had not been to bed. She had then searched the place. But there was no Iris to be seen.

Stephen lit a cigarette. His heart beat a trifle fast. Remembering the girl's state of mind, and their conversation about marriage, he wondered if she had been mad enough to run away with the Serbian. And then Miss Morgan asked:

'There is only one possibility... Whenever

she was distressed as a child she would slip away to the Isis Temple and hide there. It was as though she gained comfort in the ruins, although to me they are grim and frightening. But what with the Pasha's death and all this talk of England, I know she is distraught. Maybe she is there, Mr Daltry.'

'What! Out in the desert alone at this time of night!' he exclaimed.

'She knows no fear. And she is very determined, as perhaps you may have judged,' said Miss Morgan apologetically.

'She should not be out alone in the ruined temple at this hour,' said Stephen abruptly. 'If you will allow me to dress, Miss Morgan, I will go at once in search of her.'

Miss Morgan looked relieved. She could direct him to the temple, she said. It was useless sending the *suffragis* as, even if they found her, she would merely order them to come back and leave her alone. And she herself was not well enough to go out in the night straight from her sick bed.

Ten minutes later Stephen Daltry walked rapidly through the deserted gardens down to the edge of the Nile. In accordance with Miss Morgan's instructions, he found a boat and rowed himself across the gleaming turgid water.

As he moored the boat on the other side of the river he saw another small boat there and presumed that Iris had indeed already

69

come this way. What a mad girl she was! But if he found her here, it would be a relief. He had not relished the thought of her eloping with Usref.

So it was on this magic night of darkness, pierced sharply by white moonlight and canopied by stars, that Stephen Daltry first saw the fabulous splendour of the Romney Lowell excavations.

He could not begin to take an intelligent interest in the architecture now. Only for a moment, in wonder, in amazement, he looked up at the massive black marble columns, and passing under the arches, which were of gigantic height, came into an almost perfect courtyard and then into a small temple which had been dedicated to the goddess Isis. The glorious mosaic floor was hardly impaired by the ravages of time. Only the roof had gone and the moonlight poured down on what had once been a sacred shrine unseen save by the priests and priestesses who had worshipped here thousands of years ago.

There on the cold marble steps before the chipped and ruined figure of the goddess he found Iris ... still in her burnt-rose gown, crouched in an attitude of complete despair. Her hair was unpinned. It gave him something of a shock to see the dark cloud of it tumbled about her slenderness, almost covering her.

Softly he called her name:

'Iris, my poor child...'

She looked up like a startled fawn. He caught a glimpse of a white, tear-stained face. Then she sprang up and in a choked voice answered:

'How dare you come here! You have no right. You've done enough harm already, but you shall not come here to my temple. You shall not!'

'Iris, this is nonsense,' he said. 'You have worried your Miss Morgan to death and set us all looking for you. Come back to the Palace, please. I assure you this is no place for you alone ... it is fantastic...'

He made a gesture with his hand, indicating the ruins.

She said stormily:

'You shall not interfere with my life any more. Go and leave me here alone.'

'Come back with me, please,' he said.

Without another word she ran down the steps. He put out a hand to stop her. She, trying to elude him, missed her footing, but his arm caught and steadied her. For a moment she struggled with him, teeth clenched, eyes full of angry tears.

'Let me go!' she said again.

He had a confused sense of the slim, graceful figure in the circle of his arm, and of her perfumed hair falling across his face. In all his life he had never known a more

71

unguarded moment. It was as though civilisation as he knew it ceased to exist. This was primitive Egypt and he was primitive man with but one desire in his heart ... to conquer, to tame this wild, beautiful creature. Propelled by an irresistible force, he caught her yet closer and pushed the silken hair back from her flushed, angry young face.

'Iris!' he whispered. *'Iris!* You mad, lovely thing!'

And she, hearing her name, conscious of his strength, of his mastery, ceased to struggle and was suddenly quiescent, pliable in his arms.

6

Never before in all her life had Iris been held in the arms of a man. Her first inclination had been to protest indignantly, and then some strange delirium shook her, followed by a hitherto undreamed-of happiness. She had not been meant for loneliness – for that segregation from all human contacts save her father, her governess and their retinue. She had not been meant for the isolation which belongs to the great. She was not Isis, the Daughter of Earth and Sky. She was Iris, a young girl who needed the thrill of love and being loved. And suddenly without warning she wanted to win the approval and admiration of the Englishman of the light-grey eyes. He no longer seemed her enemy but a god-like man, this Stephen who had been sent to her by her father.

Suddenly she no longer wanted to fight with him but to be humble and submissive, even to wait upon him – she who had issued royal commands ever since her childhood. She still would refuse to go to England. But she would bend Stephen now to her will; she would make him feel as Mikhilo felt. He should become her devoted admirer, out-standing among the other men, and she would say: 'Do not take me from Egypt but stay with me here, Stephen!' and he would promise not to take her and he would stay.

This great idea welled up in the girl in a sudden and illogical manner. Stephen, totally unaware of it, was meanwhile fighting one of the biggest temptations of his life: the desire to take advantage of this moment and kiss the red, exquisite mouth which was so surprisingly raised to his.

He gave one confused look at the long silken lashes lying like little fans against the soft, pale cheeks, then drew away from her. His heart beat madly. His pulses were on fire. He said:

'Come, Iris, let me take you home.'

He expected a violent antagonism and protest. But Iris, still in the throes of her newly-discovered ecstasy, gave a long, quivering sigh, opened her large, lustrous eyes and looked into his. She whispered:

'Not yet. We have so much to talk about. I have much I wish to show you here in my beautiful temple.'

Taken aback, he stared at her.

'My dear child, this is scarcely the time for discussion or sight-seeing,' he said bluntly.

She gave a little pouting smile. She began to be amused by his manner. How different he was from Mikhilo. He was intriguing and he was strong – so spiritually strong – it roused all her admiration. She began to understand why her father had liked and trusted this man. She could also see how wonderful it would be if he would take her in his arms and keep her there. Ah, she would teach him to love Egypt as she did! Yes, the Nile would put her bitter-sweet spell on Stephen and he would never want to leave Egypt or her, Iris, again.

'I am not a child, Stephen,' she said in a more gentle voice than he had ever heard from her. 'Mikhilo thinks that I am a very beautiful woman. He has said so many times.'

Again Stephen was completely taken aback by this new aspect of Lowell Pasha's daughter. He took a quick look at her, wondering what this change from hostility and hauteur on her part signified. From an English girl, her last remark might have sounded arch and conceited, yet coming from Iris it was charmingly candid and inno-cent. And heavens! he thought, she could not know how infinitely desirable she looked with that incredible dusky hair tumbling in thick waves to her knees, and with her long lashes still wet with tears; the brooch that caught up the burnt-rose gown on one bare shoulder glittering in the moonlight.

Quickly he turned his gaze from her.

'Look here, Iris, Miss Morgan is ill and

worried, and it is time you were home,' he said.

But his head was whirling and he felt a vague, uncomfortable sense of disloyalty to Elizabeth. He was finding it more than hard to keep any sense of proportion under these circumstances or to remember that he was supposed to be in love with the girl at home.

His very feeling of guilt made him irritable, unresponsive to Iris's allure. Now that he had command of himself again he turned and began to walk away.

She looked after the tall figure with wonderment and fresh admiration. For the first time in her life she was being made to realise that her wishes were of no avail and that all men were not ready slaves like Prince Usref. She found herself following the Englishman through the great colonnade of the Outer Court, and down to the banks of the gleaming river where she had moored her boat. Stephen turned and looked at her.

'I'll row you back,' he said. 'You can send one of the *suffragis* for the other boat.'

'Very well,' she said obediently.

He put out a hand to help her into the craft. For a moment he felt the thrill of her cool slender fingers curling about his. Taking up the oars, he quickly rowed across the water. He avoided her gaze and looked frowningly over her head at the black shadow of the ruined temple sharply etched against the opalescent sky. Iris's great eyes were fixed on him. Heaven knew, he thought grimly, what thoughts were flashing through that unpredictable pagan mind of hers! But he felt more than ever that a great wrong had been done her by Romney Lowell. For what possible peace or happiness could there be for this young girl torn away from her fantastic background? He heard her softly calling his name:

'Stephen!'

Now he turned to her. She was lying back against the cushioned seat braiding her hair into a single rope which lay across her breast. How young she looked, he thought. Young and beautiful and curiously sad. She was smiling at him.

'Tomorrow will you talk with me, Stephen? Will you let me show you this country which I call mine, so that you will understand why I do not want to leave it?'

'I understand that now, Iris. But you also must try to understand why you must do as your father wishes.'

Still the expected outburst did not come from her. Still with strange new humility she said:

'We will not talk any more of that, Stephen. There is so much beauty and magic in Egypt; I want you to feel, to recognise it. Let us talk only of Egypt.'

He remained silent, pulling strongly at the oars with a rhythmic movement. In a strange way he felt more baffled by her softness than he had been by her open hostility.

He had been tired when he went in search of the girl. Now he was wide awake, his body full of feverish restlessness. He would like to have turned the boat again and rowed a long way down that moon-silvered Nile away from civilisation, alone with this fascinating 'Daughter of Earth and Sky.'

He admonished himself.

'You are letting yourself be bewitched by a lot of damn-fool nonsense, and the sooner you snap out of it the better, my boy.'

He did not speak again until they reached the other bank. Then they walked together through the deserted grounds of the Palace. He said:

'Tomorrow we must cable your aunt in London and see about a passage for you and Miss Morgan, Iris.'

He did not see her expression, but heard her draw a sharp breath.

'Perhaps you would rather go by sea than air,' he added. 'There's a very pleasant route from Alexandria to Venice, or if you would like flying as an experience–'

Now her voice interrupted him, a broken little voice full of trouble and fear.

'Oh, Stephen, please do not speak of these things any more.'

His irritation returned. When now he forced himself to look at her he saw to his horror that her huge eyes were full of tears again.

'Oh, for heaven's sake don't cry!' he said violently. 'And don't make my job impossible. Now good night. We really must all get some sleep. Here is Miss Morgan. She ought to be in bed, poor old thing. You'll be losing her next if you're not careful.'

He had not meant to be so brutal but his nerves were unaccountably in shreds and the mere fact that Iris Lowell affected him so acutely made him worse.

He was thankful that the old governess appeared at the terrace and he could hand Iris over to her. He knew that the girl was weeping. With a muttered 'good night' he left her and walked quickly away from the two women up to his own suite.

He shut the door, sat down on the edge of his bed and pulling a packet of cigarettes from his pocket lit one and smoked steadily, his brows drawn together, his body shaking a little.

What in God's name had he let himself in for? The less he came in contact with Iris Lowell the better. Be damned if he was going to see Egypt through her eyes. Tomorrow he would get on with his job and then get back to Assuan.

Iris walked slowly with her governess up to

her rooms. The tears were still rolling down her cheeks and she listened mutely while the old woman lectured her.

'It was cruel of you to run away and give us all such a fright... You are behaving badly, my dear. I know this is a bitter experience for you, but you must be brave...'

The old woman rambled on. When she had finished, Iris gave a long-drawn sigh and said:

'I'm sorry, Morga, particularly sorry that I got you out of bed. It was thoughtless of me.'

'You got that nice young man out of bed too,' grumbled the old woman.

They were in Iris's bedroom now. It was a beautiful big room with three french windows opening on to a wide balcony. A great low bed with a head-board shaped like the outspread wings of a swan made of gold stood on a dais in a cage of gossamer mosquito netting. It was covered with an exquisitely embroidered silk spread of that Nile green which was Iris's favourite colour. On the floor there were white fur-skin rugs. Light spilled from tall alabaster jars. The ceiling was jade green inlaid with gold. There was a soft amber glow over everything and a scent of roses. There were flowers – great bowls and jars of them – everywhere.

Iris yawned and began to unhook her gown.

80

'Go back to bed, Morga,' she said. 'I will not run away again.'

Miss Morgan lingered.

'What did Prince Usref come here for? What mischief are you up to?' she asked with a suspicious look at the girl.

Iris bit her lip. But she had always spoken the truth to her governess and she spoke it now.

'I had thought of marriage with him, Morga, as a means of staying here in spite of my father's last will and testament.'

The old woman wrapped her shawl closer about her and, shivering with ague despite the warmth of this luxurious perfumed bower, clicked her tongue against her teeth.

'Tch, tch, you're crazy!'

'Yes, I know that now. I merely discussed with Mikhilo the possibility. Of course, he was most willing. I asked him to consult a lawyer and tell me what I might do. But now I shall not marry him,' she added with a strange note in her voice.

'I do not like that Prince Usref,' said Miss Morgan. 'And neither did your father particularly. He was received here only because he was a friend of the Fahmouds, who are your oldest friends. But in any case you cannot marry any man without your Aunt Olivia's consent until you are twenty-one.'

Iris half closed her eyes. Slipping on a thin

white wrapper, she tied the girdle around her small waist. She said:

'When Stephen told me that earlier today I was angry. Now I am not angry any more.'

Miss Morgan regarded the girl with renewed suspicion. Nobody knew Iris better than she did after the years she had been with her. She was aware that Iris was in a dangerous mood. And by 'dangerous' Miss Morgan meant this was one of the times when Iris let her heart rule her head; at such times the young 'queen' became a tender-hearted, submissive child. In Miss Morgan's opinion she needed careful handling. Iris was a dual character with an extravagantly loving and generous side in conflict with the cool and logical one. She seemed to have no happy medium. She had once, for instance, peremptorily dismissed a *suffragi* for laziness and had him severely punished. Yet on another occasion when she saw a young Egyptian woman with a baby half-dying of starvation and exhaustion outside the Palace gates, against everybody's advice she insisted upon bringing her into the Palace and having her nursed and cared for, ignoring the general fear of disease or infection.

On Nila Fahmoud, whom she loved, she would shower presents and affection. Another high-born Egyptian girl who had once been her friend offended her, and Iris refused to receive her again.

What was she thinking and feeling now? What lay at the back of that strange young mind?

Then suddenly Iris glided across the room and took the old governess's arm between her slender hands.

'Darling Morga,' she said in her softest voice, 'are you glad that I am not going to be angry with Stephen any more?'

Miss Morgan blinked.

'My dear, I don't know why you should ever have been angry with him for trying to do his duty. Indeed, it is really no duty of his coming here to assist us, but a great kindness to your poor father.'

'I know, and once he seemed hard and cruel and I resented it,' murmured Iris. 'But I respect him for it now. Morga, do you not think he is wonderful?'

Hmm! thought Miss Morgan. So that was it! The child was beginning to find the young Englishman attractive. Well, *that* would do no harm, and the more kindly disposed she was towards Mr Daltry the better, because heaven forbid that she, Caroline Morgan, should alone have the task of getting Iris to London.

'I consider Mr Daltry to be a very nice and dependable young man,' she said at length.

'I am going to make him love Egypt as we do, Morga,' said Iris in that dreamy voice which had worried Miss Morgan because it was such a change from her earlier attitude. 'He shall stay with us here. I shall make him stay.'

Miss Morgan's heart sank. So *that* was the next thing! Iris meant to wheedle Stephen Daltry to abandon the project on which he had come; in other words, as usual, she was going to try to get her own way.

The old woman felt far too indisposed to probe further tonight or even attempt an argument.

'Oh well, we'll all meet tomorrow and discuss things. Good night, my dearest child,' she said.

Long after the old woman had gone Iris stood in her long white gown, with the lights out, on the balcony staring across the moonlit river, that same dreamy look in her eyes. She had forgotten Mikhilo Usref and their conversation; forgotten that she had, through asking him to gain information for her about the marriage laws, raised in him the wildest hopes.

No word of love had passed between them. She had, in her usual cool, haughty way of dealing with him, forbidden any approach of love on his side. With her complete ignorance of men and life in its true meaning, she had discussed marriage merely as a means of remaining in Egypt, and with a complete lack of emotion. Now she had forgotten even their talk and his plans to help her. She could think of nothing but Stephen and of the miraculous emotion that he had unmeaningly aroused in her as he held her close in his arms in the Isis Temple.

7

Stephen slept fitfully that night and he was awake early and out on the balcony of his suite trying to write that letter which he owed to Elizabeth.

He began it many times.

Well, Angel, I hope it won't be long now before you and Lady Martyn will be back in Egypt...

That was what he *ought* to feel but didn't. All of a sudden he was not in love with Elizabeth any more, which was a dreadful discovery for a man to make – and especially a man of integrity like Stephen Daltry who prided himself on sticking to a bargain.

He began again:

So sorry I haven't written much lately, darling, but since my return from Ankara I've been pretty rushed...

But he tore that up too. It wasn't really true that he had been so rushed that he could not write to Elizabeth. It was just that he did not know what to say. He supposed things like this happened. He was by no means the first person to find, after an engagement, that he had fallen out of love. One read in the papers every day notices of broken engagements. But he used to take a poor view of it; to think that a chap should know his own mind before he proposed to a girl. What in heaven's name had come over him, then? Most certainly he had thought he loved Elizabeth when he had first taken her in his arms and kissed her fresh, eager lips.

He flung down his pen and stared moodily down at the gardens. The sun was mounting higher. Soon it would be too hot to sit out here. The gardeners were spraying the emerald grass and the giant red poinsettias that grew so profusely out here. A fragrant steam rose from the warm, bedewed earth.

Stephen had a quick mental flashback of that night at Mena House when he had taken Elizabeth to a dance and afterwards they had strolled out towards the Great Pyramid; on one of those perfect Egyptian nights of black and silver, of romance which goes a little to one's head. She had looked radiant in her evening gown with its white *bouffant* skirt and a white flower in her shining fair hair. She laughed a lot and had a charming dimple in one pink cheek. She had stood there laughing at him in the moonlight and he had thought suddenly what an engaging young woman she was and that it would be nice to give up his bachelorhood and the loneliness which at times depressed him and to have her for his wife, and have a home and children.

Then the thing was done... He had said, recklessly:

'Let's get married one day, Elizabeth...'

And later, with linked hands, they had walked back to the hotel and Lady Martyn pounced on them. There were a lot of kisses and congratulations and toasts in champagne ... and he had been proud and pleased because Elizabeth was a popular girl and he felt a lucky man. He had missed her quite a lot later on when the hot weather came and she went back to London and he to his job in Ankara.

What had happened to him? It was all through that meeting in the train with old Romney Lowell ... all through that stupid soft spot which he had for the old and sick and dying ... and he had got himself hopelessly involved... Then last night ... *Iris*. His mind and heart had been on fire and emotions of which Stephen had never thought himself capable had been roused. And now he no longer wanted to marry Elizabeth.

'It's damnable!' he said aloud.

He refused to hurt Elizabeth or to allow wild ridiculous feelings like these to subjugate him. No! The sooner he finished his job in the 'Little Palace' and got away from Iris and her incredible fascination, the better.

So that letter to Elizabeth was never written. But Stephen was a harassed man when, after he had finished breakfast, he went down to the lower terrace and stood smoking, waiting for somebody to appear. Except for the gardeners and the *suffragis* there was no sign of life.

At midday he was still alone and his temper and his nerves were frayed. Where the devil was the girl? How long did she sleep in the morning? Miss Morgan was ill but there was no excuse for Iris to sleep so late, he told himself rather pompously. She was wasting his time. The devil of it was he could not even settle down to write business letters, let alone personal ones. But he must organise some kind of letter to Lowell Pasha's sister.

Soon after midday he rang a bell and asked for the head *suffragi*. Mandulis appeared, bowing and smiling. Curtly Stephen told him that he wished to see Miss Lowell.

Mandulis looked horrified.

'Her Excellency is not yet down–'

'Then tell Her Excellency that I have been waiting here two solid hours with nothing to do,' Stephen snapped.

Mandulis, looking even more horrified, bowed and departed.

Another interminable wait and then out into the sunshine came Iris wearing one of those fresh white linen embroidered gowns which made her look so incredibly virginal and slender; cool as a lily. She came towards him with that peculiarly graceful gliding walk of hers, and he was furious because of the way his pulses leaped when he looked again into her unfathomable eyes.

'Oh, Stephen, how can I apologise?' she said with a swift sweet smile. 'But I was so tired and I thought much about my father when I woke early...' she gave a little sigh, 'and then about you, Stephen, and why you have come here, and I did not sleep again. But I read a book of philosophy which helped me. Time went by and I did not realise how late it was.'

Exasperated, he turned from her.

The maddening girl! Reading books on philosophy and hugging her thoughts to herself, then coming down here and smiling at him in that angelic fashion. He did not know whether he wanted to snatch her into his arms and kiss that red mouth until she begged for mercy, or tell her that he was thoroughly annoyed.

'Would you like to spend the rest of the morning looking at the excavations, taking with you my father's history of Isis, and of her temples?' added the lilting voice behind him.

He swung round, his mouth and chin firm.

'No, Iris. We have no time for that ... much as I would like it.'

She stared, like a surprised child.

'But Stephen, it is early. We need not eat until after two.'

'We need not, maybe,' he said drily, 'and it is not a question of food. I have business to do. The business on which I came. We must write this morning without fail to your aunt in London.'

Iris stood immobile. It struck Stephen that he had never before seen any woman stand so still when she wished. Iris seemed unconsciously able to fall into the pose of some ancient lovely statue; slim arms and hands straight down at her sides; dark braided head tilted. She did not speak for a moment. It was as though she struggled with her feelings; that she controlled a natural inclination to protest angrily. Then she said:

'Let us not talk of this aunt whom I have never seen nor wish to see, Stephen.'

'I am sorry, my dear. It is essential that we should talk of her. Come along, take me to some quiet room where we can write, and read some of these papers which your father signed. He drew up a deed, you know, Iris, before he finally lost his strength and faculties, and made your aunt your guardian and Miss Morgan and I the executors of his last testament.'

A slight colour rose to the girl's cheeks now and her brows drew together as though what Stephen had said hurt her. Still she surprised him because she did not protest. She was quite changed from the haughty, violently self-willed Iris of yesterday. But a curiously stubborn look replaced the sweet, friendly one which he had noticed when she first bade him good morning. She appeared to capitulate.

'Very well. We will go to my father's study together and talk.'

Relieved, he followed her into the house. But any hope he had entertained that this was to be an easy victory vanished at her next words – which baffled.

'Oh, dear! This is indeed a waste of a glorious morning.'

Stephen snapped:

'Nonsense! You forget I came here for this purpose.'

A graceful little shrug from Iris. Now they were in a big cool room, the walls of which were lined with books. At right angles to the tall open windows, framed by striped silk curtains, stood a large, flat-topped desk, beautifully carved and polished. Upon it were a bowl of magnificent roses, freshly cut, and many papers, books and sheets of foolscap, half-covered with small writing.

'My father was just beginning a new history of the Thirtieth Dynasty,' said Iris in a mournful voice. 'I was helping him. It is hard, Stephen, for me to believe that he will never come back to complete this great work.'

Stephen nodded but did not answer. He did not want to feel too sorry for her. It was all too easy to sympathise with Iris; to want to spoil and indulge her as everybody else in the Palace appeared to do. But he knew perfectly well that if he did he would only make a fool of himself ... as he had so nearly done last night. No! He was going to remain hard and absolutely impersonal.

Iris pointed to a large oil-painting which hung over a tall, carved fireplace on the right. Stephen's gaze followed her slender hand and he was at once entranced by the beauty of this painting. It was the portrait of a woman reclining on a low divan in the classic indolent, graceful pose adopted by great beauties of the past, one cheek resting on a long thin hand. The richly-coloured painting showed the fair glory of her hair and exquisite complexion. Her green, flowing gown was of a similar design to the one Iris had worn at dinner last night. Stephen knew at once that this was Helena, her mother; it answered so completely to the description in Lowell Pasha's document.

In respectful silence Stephen gazed at the

portrait. He had an uncanny feeling that Helena Lowell was here in the room.

'What a wonderful painting!' he said at length.

'Yes. It is all I have ever had of my mother. But she seemed very real to me,' said Iris.

Impulsively Stephen added:

'*You* should be painted like that.'

And now he saw that she was smiling in a secret, almost happy, way. She said:

'I had intended sitting for this same painter, who is an Italian and lives in Rome. I had meant to give the portrait to my father for his birthday. However, I shall send for Luigi Connetti and he shall paint the portrait for you. Will you like it, Stephen?'

He was staggered for a moment into silence. Subtle Iris might be, with her feminine wiles, and yet there was a shining honesty about her which was almost disconcerting. Man of the world though he was, he found himself stammering:

'My dear child ... I appreciate the honour, but such a portrait would naturally belong to your aunt and–'

Now she interrupted and he could see that this time he had made her angry.

'Aunt! Aunt! Can you never stop talking about my aunt? I hate her!'

He shook his head at her. Here she was the refractory child again. Well, it was easier to deal with than the beguiling woman, warm and yielding to his touch.

'We've wasted enough time, Iris, my dear. Let's sit down and look through these papers. I see Mandulis has put my case on the desk. What an excellent *suffragi* he is! So intelligent.'

But Iris's large eyes were stormy and her breath came quickly. She was not listening to his praise of the servant. She was being made to see that her schemes for avoiding exile to England by winning Stephen Daltry over to her side were not going to succeed with any ease. Oh, if only he would do as she wanted ... fear to displease her, worship and praise her like Mikhilo! That would be wonderful. *But would it?* Wasn't his very strength, his complete difference from Prince Usref, one of the things that had first caught and held her attention? It was her turn to be baffled. Like a sulky child she let her lashes droop and muttered:

'Very well. Proceed.'

A half-amused smile lifted the corners of Stephen's mouth. She would have been ridiculous if she had not been so wildly attractive, he thought, with the uneasiness of a man who is not sure of his own ground.

He made her sit down by the desk and listen while he read through some of the papers Lowell Pasha had given him, in particular the deed which assigned her to the care of the hated aunt.

She had hated him when he first came, his brain began to remind him ... then furiously he pushed aside these personal feelings and continued with his work.

Patiently he pointed out and explained all the things which he thought might confuse her.

'I presume you know something of your aunt,' he went on. 'Mrs Claude Cornwall ... you know she was married to a well-known doctor who died some years ago ... that she still has her home in Wimpole Street and that she and your cousin, Daphne, who is the same age as yourself, occupy the upper half of it, as it was converted into flats and...'

He stopped. He did not believe Iris had heard one word. She sat in that motionless way of hers, the long, silky lashes veiling her eyes.

'Iris!' said Stephen.

The lashes lifted. The big eyes were full of tears.

'Oh, damn!' thought Stephen. 'If she's going to cry I can't stand it. She really is an impossible girl to deal with.'

Then came her voice, low and reproachful.

'You seem bent on wishing to hurt and distress me, Stephen. You know that I have no intention of going to London to live in this Wimpole Street. It sounds horrible. My aunt and my cousin sound horrible...' She broke off, choking.

Stephen did not know whether to laugh or lecture her. At length he compromised and with renewed patience pointed out that neither the flat nor her relations were necessarily 'horrible'; she had not seen them; they might be charming; that she had loved her father and that there was no reason why she should not love his sister, who was only in her late forties and, according to the Pasha, had been a gay, good-looking girl. Of course, the Pasha had not seen her for years nor had he ever met his niece, Daphne, but Daphne was twenty... Iris's own age, and they might become great friends ... they might even come back here to the 'Little Palace' with her for a long stay ... etc., etc.

This appeared to be an unfortunate suggestion because Iris sprang to her feet and all her docility vanished.

'I shall never allow such people to come to the "Little Palace" ... never! They would not understand my Egypt ... they would bring discord where there has been harmony, and battle where there has been peace!'

She caught Stephen's gaze as she uttered the last words and saw his brows lift. She added through her teeth:

'Yes, there was peace here until *you* came.'

He pulled out a cigarette-case and snapped it open with an irritable gesture.

'I fully realise that I am breaking up your peace, Iris, and that you dislike me for it, but you know the invidious position I am in.'

'I do not dislike you,' she said in a voice which was calculated to wring any man's heart. 'But I am very unhappy and I cannot make you understand. I want you to be my friend. I want...' She paused, shaking her head as though she found words difficult. 'Oh, don't let us talk any more. You have said all you need to say. You have told me what you were asked to tell. Let that be enough.'

He stood up.

'My dear child–' he began to protest, but she broke in:

'I will hear no more today. Either we are friends or enemies, Stephen, and oh, *Stephen,* I want us to be friends!'

'You cannot keep avoiding the issue like this,' he exclaimed.

'I will never leave the "Little Palace",' she said in a low voice of concentrated passion, and turned and walked out of the room.

Stephen spent the rest of the morning alone, somewhat ruefully admitting that he was making a failure of this more than difficult task and trying at the same time to stifle his inclination to go in search of Iris and tell her that hurting her was almost more than he could bear and that there was nothing he wanted more than to enjoy her friendship and be wooed to forgetfulness of his job in this glorious retreat from the world.

At lunch-time Prince Usref arrived.

Mandulis showed him out on to the terrace where Stephen sat alone, moodily drinking an *apéritif*. The two men greeted each other coldly. Usref looked what he was … annoyed to find the Englishman still here. Stephen felt that he was in no mood to exchange polite small talk with the Serb.

'Has my Lady of Moonlight not yet come down?' asked Mikhilo.

'Damn' silly name!' thought Stephen, and snapped:

'Yes, Miss Lowell and I have been talking over her father's affairs.'

Mikhilo's eyes narrowed.

'So! Are preparations still being made to break her heart, and uproot her from this country which she loves?'

In sudden anger Stephen said:

'I do not think that is your affair.'

The Serbian's handsome face flushed a dull crimson. Then he showed his white teeth in a smile which might have indicated anything, but the menace of which was not lost upon Stephen. He bowed and murmured:

'I think you are mistaken, Mr Daltry. But it will be for my Lady to decide.'

Stephen picked up his glass and drained it. He was angry, but anxious not to show it. For why, after all, should it matter to him so vitally if Usref adopted a possessive attitude towards Iris?

Mandulis reappeared.

He spoke in Arabic to the Prince, whose smile broadened as he listened. Then he turned to Stephen.

'You will pardon me if I leave you for a few moments, Mr Daltry. My Lady has sent for me.'

He clicked his heels together and made a graceful exit which could not have annoyed Stephen more. Insolent young puppy, he thought. He could have knocked him down with the greatest of pleasure and it was not to be denied that he was furious because Iris had sent for Usref. What was in her mind now? Must there be more of this nonsense about marriage laws? One never knew where one was with that fantastic girl.

But one thing ... he firmly made up his mind ... he was not going to retire defeated either by her or by the Serbian whom she had so unwisely chosen as a friend. The more he saw of the latter, the more he felt that Iris needed advice and protection.

With set lips, Stephen sat down again. He was determined not to leave the 'Little Palace' until he had got Iris safely away and across the Mediterranean with her governess. He would stay even if it meant days and weeks – and an extension of his leave!

At this precise moment, could Stephen have been able to see her, his promised wife, Elizabeth Martyn, emerged from the Air Travel Terminus in Victoria on one of those cold wet days which we call summer in England and joined her mother, who was sitting outside in a saloon car.

Lady Martyn had been kept waiting half an hour. She was cold and cross. She eyed her daughter with disapproval.

'Well, after all this, have you got your own way?'

Elizabeth stepped into the car, and as the chauffeur drove them down Buckingham Palace Road towards Knightsbridge, where they lived, she said:

'Yes, I have. Ticket in my bag, passage on Friday, Cairo on Saturday night. So it's no good grumbling, Mummy.'

'Well, I think it's a wild-goose chase and most unseemly,' said Lady Martyn. 'When I was a girl one didn't fly to Egypt without an invitation from one's fiancé. Besides, Stephen might not be in Cairo and–'

'Oh, we've gone into all this before, Mummy,' broke in Elizabeth. 'Stephen's last letter from Ankara said he would be in Cairo this week, and if he isn't I shall be with the Wilsons – they said I could stay with them as long as I liked. So I shall just wait there until I *do* see Stephen.'

Her mother relapsed into silence. She had Elizabeth pretty well in hand at most times, but she realised that the girl had a stubborn streak and that when she chose to exert it there was no use arguing.

Elizabeth Martyn sat looking at the ticket for which she had just paid sixty-five pounds. Thank goodness, she thought, Daddy was in sympathy and had let her have the money. He had agreed with her that she could do no harm by going out to Cairo to stay with friends and to see Stephen, since they were so soon to be married. And he seemed to realise more than Mummy how worried she was because Stephen had not answered her recent letters. She did not believe it was the fault of the post. It was something to do with Stephen. She *must* see him. She could not stand this uneasy feeling that he had changed his mind since their last meeting.

But she would soon settle that doubt ... and her blue eyes saw not the grey wet streets of London but the green and gold of Gezirah Club ... the glittering sunshine; the tall palms, and *Stephen* ... and the surprise that he would get when she arrived in Egypt, without warning him, at the end of this week.

8

In the wing of the 'Little Palace' in which Romney Lowell had built a special suite for his idolised and idealised daughter there was a small boudoir in which Iris had done most of her studies as a growing girl and which she now used as her private writing-room. Like the rest of them it was lofty and cool and designed especially for hot weather. The walls were exquisitely panelled in pale polished wood; there were rich Persian rugs on the parquet floor, the furniture had been specially made to match; the curtains were of striped crimson and grey Damascus silk. Let into the walls on one side were shelves full of Iris's favourite books. On the other side stood a magnificent radio-gramophone and cabinets containing records of classical music amongst which Tschaikovsky was the outstanding choice. Ever since she was a small girl Iris had loved the wild, sad stirring music of the Russian composer.

It was obviously the room of a thinker, a student, beautiful but austere. And many were the long hours and days that the child Iris, and later the grown girl, had spent here alone. Not that loneliness ever worried her, for she never hankered after the petty excitements and amusements the average modern girl longs for.

Indeed, Iris, imbued with so much Eastern philosophy, was able to extract pleasure from solitude and contemplation; but the death of her father and the coming of Stephen Daltry into her life had had a most disturbing effect. Loneliness no longer seemed desirable.

She was changing ... her whole outlook was changing through this and because of Stephen. He had changed the vista of her world. She had accused him of disturbing her peace and in more ways than one he had done so.

As short a time back as a week ago she had thought herself secure. Now it was as though a volcano had erupted under her, and always she was afraid of this new arch-enemy, the English law, against which she seemed powerless.

When she sent for Prince Usref it had not been from any personal wish for his company. She would have preferred to talk to Nila, her pretty, vivacious, Egyptian friend whose worldliness and vanity and sense of fun (the antithesis of her own) nevertheless amused Iris. But Nila was still away. Iris had nobody outside the Palace to whom she felt she could talk or trust, except the devoted Mikhilo.

She sat in one of these straight, high-backed chairs which seemed her natural background, with her slender hands lying still upon the carved arms, and looked at Mikhilo with large, grave eyes.

Debonair and smiling as usual, he bowed to her.

'What can I do for my Lady of Moonlight? I rushed when you called... I would fly from the four corners of the earth to do your slightest bidding.'

Iris frowned. It was peculiar, she reflected, morbidly interested in her own metamorphosis, how quickly one could change. Usref's flatteries threatened to irritate her. Yet he was the same Usref. But downstairs was a grey-eyed Englishman who would most certainly not 'fly from the four corners of the earth' to do her bidding; on the contrary, he continually frustrated her. She said:

'I wish that you could do for me one thing that I really want, Mikhilo.'

He drew nearer her.

'But I can!' he exclaimed eagerly. 'There is nothing Mikhilo could not achieve for his Lady of Moonlight.'

Her large stunned eyes continued to scrutinise him but her red pouting lips twisted.

'I wonder! You do not know the English law, Mikhilo, I am beginning to learn a little about it.'

Mikhilo smiled, but that smile had a

105

menace to it – the same menace that Stephen had noticed downstairs.

'You have been listening to Mr Daltry. May I dare to say that that is a mistake, most Beautiful of All?'

The slender fingers gripped the arms of the chair more tightly.

'I am not mistaken, Mikhilo,' Iris said sharply.

Afraid that he had offended her, he quickly added:

'The error is Mr Daltry's, not yours. *He* is mistaken if he has been trying to prove to you that you must agree to this lamentable project to send you to England.'

She turned and looked at a photograph of her father which stood in a beautiful shagreen frame on her writing bureau beside a vase of tall cream roses. Romney Lowell in his early forties had been very handsome. The classic features were not unlike her own, although he had always declared passionately that she was the living image of her lovely mother.

Oh, she thought, with a deep yearning sadness, *if only Father had not been stricken down and died before I had a chance to tell him that I could never leave my home and the Egypt which he taught me to love. If only I could have convinced him that he was mistaken in thinking it the best and kindest thing to send me to my aunt.*

If only he could come back for one moment, with one stroke of the pen to erase his signature from that awful deed!

So many times since Stephen had unfolded to her the contents of that deed she had argued with herself that were she a good daughter she would do as her father had asked; that it would be her privilege to grand his dying wish. Yet always it seemed that that wish had been the one and only mistake she had known him to make; a fantasy of the dying; and that he would retract it could he realise that it threatened to break her heart.

'Dearest father!' she murmured to the pictured face. 'Forgive me if this is the only thing I cannot do even for *you!*'

Turning back to Mikhilo she said:

'Have you seen the lawyer again?'

'I have seen two,' he said. 'One from Cairo and one from Alexandria. They were flown to Assuan at my special request and I interviewed them at the Fahmouds' villa this morning. Both confirm that it is indeed the inescapable law of England that you cannot marry until you are of age without your guardian's consent, but both also approve of my plan to circumvent this ridiculous jurisdiction.'

'It is not only the marriage laws which I wish to hear about,' she said impatiently. (Mikhilo winced.) 'I asked you to find out if

I could be forcibly taken to England against my will.'

Usref smiled again and spread out one thin brown hand.

'My Lady – what an unthinkable idea!'

'Unthinkable to you, but not to such men as Stephen Daltry,' she said in a low, significant tone.

'I would like to pick up this Englishman and fling him into the Nile,' said Mikhilo in a grandiose manner.

Once again Iris felt irritation rather than an appreciation of Mikhilo. In her coldest voice she said:

'Do not swerve from the point nor waste breath in abuse of Mr Daltry.'

With a hurt look on his handsome face Mikhilo bowed.

'I can only look on him as my Lady's enemy.'

'That is for me to decide!'

Mikhilo's fingers twitched. He would dearly like to have thrust them into the night-black masses of this girl's hair, dragged it from its pins and half-strangled her with those glossy braids before he closed her lips with kisses. Did she not know how frantically he loved her? he asked himself. And how insane was his jealousy of Stephen Daltry and the privileges accorded him by Lowell Pasha? And were not all women as illogical and changeable as the phases of the moon? When Stephen first came Iris herself had called him 'enemy.' Now he, Usref, was not permitted to use the word. For a moment he sulked in silence. Iris looked beyond him, completely indifferent to his emotions, although she spoke again:

'I repeat my question. What do your lawyers say about my leaving Egypt?'

'That it can be forced, but they do not think it would ever come to that if you persist in remaining here.'

An enigmatic smile played suddenly about her beautiful mouth. He did not know Stephen. She could well believe that if she refused to go he might have her forcibly lifted into an aeroplane – yes, taken by physical force – to London. She intimated so much to Usref, who again looked sulky but bowed.

'Very well, my Lady. This being so, my lawyers maintain your only course is one of marriage, for, although this is illegal, by the time the case has been fought you will already have been a wife for weeks and months, and by then you would have come of age and could decide for yourself.'

'I see,' said Iris. The silence that followed was tense. Mikhilo's agate-dark eyes sparkled with renewed hope. He added in a beseeching voice:

'My Lady of Moonlight, will you not take this way out? Trust in me! As my wife,

Princess Usref would be under my protection and safe. I will take you to the Fahmouds' villa. There we should be married by special licence in the Egyptian manner. I would then charter a private 'plane to fly us to Paris and—'

'Wait, Mikhilo,' interrupted Iris, frowning. 'You go too fast. I have no wish to go to Paris. Nor do I intend to leave Egyptian soil. Besides, such a marriage would only be a temporary escape from my poor father's will. I would be in no way a real wife and I would require a divorce according to Egyptian law as soon as I was twenty-one.'

That was far from what Usref wanted. Under his façade of friendliness and respect the Serbian was capable of treachery and dishonour. After his own flamboyant fashion he loved this girl, but love for him was a selfish thing. Once having persuaded her to become Princess Usref he had no intention of letting her go again. He had developed an almost murderous dislike of the Englishman. He would stop at nothing to defeat Stephen Daltry. He stayed talking for some time with Iris. She asked many more questions; probed deeply into the whole subject, carefully listening to everything Mikhilo quoted as having been said by the lawyers. But she gave no promise that she would go through with such a marriage. She was not to be moved, as he hoped, by

110

impulse alone. She baffled him. He was sure that all kinds of plans were forming in that unfathomable young mind and he was furious because he could not even guess at them. When she dismissed him he retired gloomy and dissatisfied. He could see that it was going to be extremely difficult to make Iris agree to *his* plans of escape. She had merely said that she would think things over. She would let him know her decision.

He left the Palace without seeing Stephen, for he was in a mood which he knew only too well to be dangerous; and if he was too insolent or overbearing to the Englishman Iris might banish him for good and all, and he could not begin to understand the respect which Iris appeared to have suddenly developed for Stephen Daltry.

Iris spent the next hour at the bedside of her governess who once more had a rising temperature. With that rush of natural affection and kindliness innate in the girl, she busied herself about the room although the *suffragis* had cleaned and tidied it; sent Ayesha for fresh perfumes and a bowl of ice, and bade her return instantly to bathe the invalid, to apply bandages soaked in ice cold lotion to the aching head and keep the green shutters drawn so as to shut out the hot sun. Stroking the old woman's hand, she said mournfully:

'I hate to see you ill, my poor Morga. But

you must lie still and not attempt to get up again until you are quite well. Mandulis shall bring Dr Ibrahim again this evening.'

The old governess groaned. She was heartbroken, she said, that she should be laid up now just when her darling child most needed her. The fever seemed to have lasted much longer than usual. No doubt it was due to her advancing years and her health would improve when she returned to England. She was too ill to see the look of fear that dilated the beautiful eyes of the girl beside her. Iris whispered:

'England; now it is a name which is full of foreboding for me.'

Miss Morgan blinked at her painfully.

'Have you been talking to Mr Daltry again? Have you made plans? Are you being sensible, my dearest child?'

Iris patted the feverish hand and then rose.

Her reply was noncommittal. She soothed the governess by telling her she was being as sensible as possible and was on terms of friendship with Stephen. But there was not yet any definite talk of how or when they would go to England.

'First you must get well, Morga,' she added. 'I implore you not to worry about me. I promise you I will not do anything drastic and that you need have no cause for alarm and despondency.'

After this she went downstairs to find Stephen again. Once again she felt deeply depressed at the awful uncertainty of the future. At least, she thought, whilst poor Morga was ill there could be no talk of rushing them into a ship or aeroplane. The young girl who was outwardly so poised and autocratic with Mikhilo was inwardly a troubled, anxious girl. She had a sudden burning desire for the strength and support that only a man of character such as Stephen could give her.

When she joined him he had already started his lunch in the cool dining-hall – it was too hot at this time of the day to eat on the terrace. Mandulis and Pilak moved noiselessly around, resplendent in their striped satin gowns and scarlet turbans which they wore at meal-times.

Stephen stood up as the slight, white-clad figure of Iris approached. What mood was she in now? he wondered. He had got tired of waiting for her again, and was still strangely annoyed because she had, he supposed, been talking all this time to Usref. Rather coldly he apologised for commencing his lunch and explained that he had not been certain when she would come down again and he had been hungry.

She did not seem annoyed by this but gave him one of those surprisingly frank smiles which he found so enchanting.

'You must never wait for me, Stephen. In my life time is of no account. But I know that in your country all things are scheduled and every moment accounted for. It sounds horrifying.'

She took her place at the head of the table and he sat down opposite her, one eyebrow raised.

His country. So the little witch was not even going to admit that it was hers. What mischief was she up to now? What plot was she and that highly unsuitable friend of hers, Usref, hatching together?

He watched her as, with the delicate grace which he had never before seen in any woman, she ate the tiny roast quail which Mandulis placed in front of her. The *suffragis* served her as they would do a queen, he thought, and like a queen she received their homage. She spoke to him quite frankly about Usref while they drank their coffee.

'Mikhilo is in touch with some important men of law from Cairo and Alexandria. I am interested in what they said about my father's deed.'

Stephen mentally prayed for patience.

'My dear child, I can tell you all that you want to know, and I assure you that these learned men who are airing their knowledge on the Prince will find no loophole of escape for you. You are wasting your time and theirs.'

She lifted her gaze from her cup and gave him a long, unfathomable look.

'We shall see, Stephen.'

'Well, I am certainly not going to waste my time by endless repetition,' he said bluntly. 'You know what I've told you and facts remain.'

She thought, 'How strong he is ... indomitable ... mistaken but truly marvellous... As one of the Pharaohs of ancient Egypt he could have conquered the world. With him there could never be half-measures nor bribery and corruption; nor recapitulation.'

And once more a veritable fire of admiration for Stephen burned in her young heart, but with it there burned that other fire ... the desire to make him yield to her, alone... She would not go with him to England, but he would stay in Egypt with her. She, too, could be indomitable. She would prove it to him. Her heart beat quickly, nervously, and with a renewed confidence in her own supremacy.

9

Nobody was more surprised than Stephen Daltry himself a week later to find that he was still Iris Lowell's guest at the 'Little Palace.'

During those seven days he had lived like a man in a kind of trance; one who he thought bore little resemblance to the level-headed practical Stephen that he had been before Fate flung him across Lowell Pasha's path. Every morning when he woke up he resolved to leave his work undone and escape from Iris's all-too-intriguing personality and go back to Cairo. She was being utterly tantalising, refusing to say anything about her removal to England; fencing and hedging. She never now showed hot temper or disdain which he had witnessed when he first came here; in fact, she was proving herself a most charming, agreeable hostess in every way. She seemed to want to sit at his feet and learn; the proud 'Daughter of Earth and Sky' became a wistful-eyed child thirsty for knowledge, meekly willing to take his help and advice. Then, when he thought he had 'pinned her' and suggested she should give him a definite date for departure from Egypt, she became nebulous and elusive again. And all his talking, his efforts, appeared wasted. They were back where they had started.

It could not go on. Stephen faced that fact. It could not go on for several reasons, amongst which the main one was his ever-growing interest in the girl; an interest that was fraught with danger. She might be a spoiled, stubborn little wretch, but she was also a *woman* and adorable – made for love – the very breath and essence of poetry, of beauty, and of romance. And there had always been a strongly romantic streak in Stephen, a thirst for beauty and poetry, deep-hidden though it was under the veneer of the worldly-wise experienced diplomat.

Miss Morgan's health was slowly improving. She was able to come down and sit on the terrace in the cool of the late afternoons. She, Stephen found to his relief and satisfaction, was his firm ally. She would talk to him lengthily about England and English current affairs. He could see that the poor old thing was frankly scared of being uprooted from Egypt and sent back to face her last few years – rather bleak and austere ones – in a damp, cold climate. But she made a valiant effort to paint a rosy picture of London life to Iris. He noted, also, that when such conversations took place Iris sat silent, in that calm, detached way of hers, her incredible lashes veiling her eyes. And he wondered, sometimes, if she deliberately closed her ears to what they were saying.

Assuredly it was not going to be easy to take her away from Egypt. And Stephen knew it.

His mail was sent regularly from Cairo through Assuan. Two letters came from Elizabeth; the usual light-hearted, cheerful, unsentimental letters she always wrote. There was an almost schoolgirl shyness in her ... a typical reluctance to show deep emotions, or perhaps she was incapable of expressing them very well on paper. But that she was in love with him he was certain. And once he had prized that knowledge. But today he read her letters with a growing unease and sense of guilt.

Why don't you write, Steve darling ... too busy, I suppose. But I know you are thinking of me...

(How little he had thought of her ... poor Elizabeth!)

You are an old meanie ... no post again. Who's the new girl-friend? I'm going to sue you for breach of promise if I don't get news from you soon. Darling Steve, it will be a thrill when we don't have to have all these miles between us... Just read the new thriller by Francis Gerard.

118

Jolly good. I'll send you out a copy...

Dear friendly Elizabeth! She wrote as she thought and felt, without subtlety, brimming over with good-humour, but underlying her words lay a note of anxiety and frustrated affection which did not escape him and filled him with remorse.

He wished to heaven he had not changed ... that he could feel for and about her as he had done at Mena House that night when he had rushed into their engagement...

'Who's the new girl-friend?' she had asked in jest. Oh God! he thought, it was no jest. What was he doing? Why was he allowing Iris Lowell to keep him here? *She* was the woman of his dreams ... she, not Elizabeth. *She* alone could hold his heart between those slender, lily-white hands of hers. In those dark, unfathomable eyes, in the curve of those wonderful pouting red lips lay heaven (or hell) for any man.

Elizabeth's letters were read, noted and locked away in his attaché-case. Sooner or later they must be answered. Meanwhile he allowed himself to drift ... yes, that was the word ... to drift on the too-strong tide of feeling that Iris aroused within him.

Mikhilo Usref had not worried him lately. He had called, but not been admitted to the 'presence.' To Stephen and Miss Morgan Iris expressed a disinclination to see the

119

Prince at the moment.

'He bores me. I shall make him wait,' she said one morning when Mandulis brought a note from the Serbian, and she looked at Stephen as she spoke, with a softness, a richness, in her eyes that made his heart plunge wildly. After which he had tried to tell himself that it was pleasant to be in this exquisite, wayward creature's good books ... but a man might break his heart if she was indifferent to him (Not that he minded about Usref's heart-aches!) But he was not sure whether or not the Serbian was a danger to be reckoned with. The longer he stayed here, the more he saw of Iris and gauged the full extent of her innocence and candour and lack of knowledge of modern times, the more troubled he became for her. And the more certain that she must not be left here in the 'Little Palace.'

The Pasha had been right. If old Miss Morgan died ... Iris would be utterly alone ... a prey to anyone like Usref who managed to come here and influence her.

And next week ... unless he asked for an extended holiday ... he must take up his duties at the Legation in Cairo. And that was hundreds of miles away from the 'Little Palace.'

He knew so much about the whole place now – and loved it. She had shown him every room, every treasure, every book. She

120

had taken him through her beloved temple ... shared with him her secret knowledge there ... half awakened in him some of her own enthusiasms and love for the day of the Pharaohs ... for the splendours that were dead.

She had almost bewitched him, he told himself drily, into believing that she was indeed the reincarnation of the goddess herself.

She was incomparably lovely in her beautiful, exotic clothes. He was never tired of being with her, watching the graceful movements of the braided head, the expressive hands. And always he remembered poignantly the Iris he had seen that night in the moonlit ruins, with that glorious hair tumbling to her knees. *And he wanted to see it again* ... to hold her ... in mad passion ... with the beautiful hair sheltering them like a cloak.

From such thoughts he occasionally fled like a man possessed, but they returned to haunt his fevered fancy.

Day after day he came downstairs determined to tell Iris about Elizabeth. He did not suppose it would have any particular effect on her ... she would not mind whom he married ... she was not sufficiently interested. Yet somehow when he came to speak of his English fiancée the words died on his lips. And that seemed to him, when he thought it over, his most flagrant disloyalty. *He did not want to tell Iris about Elizabeth.*

But that could not go on...

Iris, all this time unaware of the struggle in the mind and heart of the Englishman whom she believed to have an iron will, went on in her own dreamy, insular fashion, playing a waiting game. Deliberately she avoided the issue about going to England. Morga was still too ill to travel anyhow. And soon, after Stephen had been here with them a little longer, she hoped he would have fallen completely under the spell of her beloved Egypt ... that he would understand ... and not ask her to go away.

Day after day Iris drifted, as was her custom, on that tide of glamour and un-reality ... and she was happy with Stephen ... for intellectually he had taken her father's place ... and he also afforded her a companionship she had never known before ... something so unique and thrilling – so wonderful that she was intoxicated by it. She refused to think about the past or the future. She lived entirely for the present. She had abandoned even her project of forming any kind of alliance with Mikhilo. She did not think it would any longer be necessary. She was too sure of winning Stephen to her way of thinking.

The old governess gently chided her one

morning when they were alone.

'When will you write that letter to Mrs Cornwall? It is time you did, my dearest child. Mr Daltry has written ... but you, too, must get in touch with your aunt.'

Iris gave her enigmatic smile.

'Soon, perhaps. Don't trouble me about it, Morga...' was her answer.

'But Mr Daltry will soon have to go to Cairo. He said so last night. He has his own affairs to attend to as well as yours, Iris. And he is waiting for you to act.'

Iris bit her lip but continued to smile.

'He will wait a little longer, Morga...'

Miss Morgan knew better than to carry on with the argument. But she was full of foreboding; a feeling that this pleasant interlude with Stephen Daltry and his present control of Iris and the situation would end ... and end in disaster of some kind.

That night it was particularly still and hot. A full moon hung like a great silver lamp in the deep-blue sky. There was a blaze of stars.

Miss Morgan had retired early to bed. Stephen, as usual, dined alone with Iris – one of those long-drawn-out meals with excellent food and wine, served on the terrace. So still was the night that the unflickering candles in their great sconces pierced the darkness like little golden spears.

Stephen looked at the girl opposite him.

123

Always observant of feminine attire, he saw that she wore a new dress tonight. It was more exquisitely designed than anything he had seen her in before; of black, pleated chiffon over silver with a wide, jewelled belt confining her small waist. Sun-golden throat and shoulders were bare. A wide, heavy collar of semi-precious stones of Egyptian design, glittered around the long, slender neck. There were big ear-rings to match in the tiny ears. Her face, as usual, was perfectly made up. Tonight the dark braids were interwoven with silver ribbon. He found himself staring at it fascinated and likening it to moonlight playing in and out of the shadows of the night.

As he drank his strong Turkish coffee and smoked his cigar Stephen felt more restless and troubled than usual. *It must end,* he told himself, for this was madness. Tonight he would tell Iris about Elizabeth. He would say, *'You must meet my future wife ... perhaps you two will become friends...'*

But nothing could sound more ridiculous, or, he knew, be more improbable. Few modern girls, and least of all his prosaic Elizabeth, would understand or care for Lowell Pasha's daughter.

Iris watched him through the curtain of her lashes.

He was brown from the sun and very handsome, she thought. She liked that white

124

drill smoking-jacket and the whiteness of the collar against his bronzed neck. But why was he so silent tonight? He made a few of those blunt and sometimes cutting remarks which amused and intrigued her. He did not laugh or talk easily. He even looked cross.

She accused him of this. He turned his gaze from the fascinating black-and-silver figure and gave a short laugh.

'Nonsense!' he said. 'But I may as well tell you here and now, Iris, that although this has been a very charming week and you have been more than hospitable, I must return to Cairo the day after tomorrow. I want you to promise me that tomorrow morning you will allow me to make definite plans for your journey to England.'

An icy little thrill of fear ran through the girl's veins. She caught her breath sharply.

'No!' she said. *'No!'*

He was in a state of being easily exasperated. Angrily he broke out:

'Oh, yes, my dear! There can be no more dissembling and delay. Make up your mind that this thing has got to be done and do it, no matter how unpleasant it is to you.'

A tense silence. He dared not look at her. Then he heard a little rustling movement and was forced now to gaze at her. She had risen and stood before him very straight and pale. Her eyes were enormous.

'I will not listen!' she said in a low voice.

125

'It is a beautiful *beautiful* night. All around us is beauty and perfection. I forbid you to spoil it for me, Stephen.'

He, too, stood up. So it was to be a fight between them again! The amenable, sweet companion had become the difficult young autocrat again. Well, it was time they had a showdown, he thought savagely.

'Listen, young woman,' he said. 'You're going back to London next week. I shall take you and Miss Morgan as far as Cairo and then...'

He stopped, for Iris had turned and he saw her suddenly running away from the candlelight on the terrace, down the wide, marble steps and into the shadows of the garden. A sudden unaccountable fury of feeling engulfed the man. A refusal to be defeated ... to be kept dangling like this on the string of a spoiled girl's whim. He put down his cigar and ran after her.

She was well ahead of him, moving noiselessly on her light, sandalled feet down to the edge of the gleaming Nile. In and out the bushes he caught occasionally the gleam of silver in her draperies and her hair.

He called to her.

'Iris! come back, come back, you little fool!'

He caught up with her by the water's edge. For one horrifying moment he thought she was going to dive into it. She stood there on the edge, poised like a slender statue in her classic favourite attitude, arms straight at her sides, head tilted back. Breathing hard, Stephen came up and caught one of her arms between his fingers. It was cool and firm to his touch, but the face she turned on him was stormy and passionate. She panted:

'You shall not make me go, Stephen. I tell you I would die if I went to England. Leave me here. Let me live and die here. You shall *not* destroy me, Stephen.'

'Little fool, you're trying to destroy yourself,' he said.

She tried to draw her arm away from him. Her slender body was shaking.

'Let me go...'

'Come back and talk to me reasonably, Iris.'

'No.'

'Well, I'm not leaving you here to swim across the Nile and spend the night in that confounded temple of yours, you mad child.'

Her great eyes blazed at him.

'I shall go to my temple if I wish. You cannot stop me.'

But Stephen's blood was up. With a sudden laugh he picked the slender figure up in his arms and held her suspended in the air. Light-grey eyes flashed down into dark ones. He said between his teeth:

'It's time you learned to do what you are told...'

For a moment she struggled. Then it was as though the fevered dream which had been haunting his imagination for so many days and nights came true. The loosened waves of hair poured like a cascade from her head across his eyes, half-blinding him. The fragrance of it completely broke down his resistance. Suddenly he was holding her madly, closely to his heart. One hand touched her slim throat and felt the pulse beating there like a captured bird. She was all woman in his embrace now ... yielding like a flame ... a warm sweet flame in his arms. Her pouting lips were close to his mouth. A low, tremulous voice whispered his name.

'Stephen! *Stephen...*'

And then he closed her flower-like mouth with one long kiss. He set her on her feet and they stood together there with straining arms and lips in the tense hot beauty of the night. For Iris it was a revelation, a complete surrender of heart and soul ... a woman's victory; that triumph which goes hand in hand with admission of man's mastery. But for Stephen Daltry it was defeat; un-imagined bliss and bitter regret. For even while his senses reeled and the moonlit world spun about them, he knew that there must be a reckoning and that there was still ... *Elizabeth...*

10

Iris, during that long and passionate embrace, felt that now at last she understood the real meaning of life, and was following her destiny. She had been born to love and be loved by Stephen Daltry. It was predestined ... written in the stars a thousand thousand years ago. For this purpose fate had led Stephen across her father's path and so to her, and whilst with straining arms and lips she clung to him, gloriously content in the revelation of this marvellous love, she thought how ridiculous it was that she had ever regarded him as an enemy or wished to order him peremptorily out of her sight.

She loved him. She loved him with all the fire and purpose, all the tenderness and passion, in her make-up. In her dreams – remote and formless until now – love had always existed. She had read of it. She had been made aware of it through her very studies. Had not Cleopatra loved Antony here in this very Egypt by the waters of the Nile? Had not her own father and mother loved greatly, until death separated them?

In the same way she would love Stephen.

There would be no further battles between them – no more clashing of wills. For Iris had her own theories about love between a man and a woman. It was her belief that when a woman met the one and only man who was to be her husband she should be submissive. She should not attempt to lead but should be led. In love and in friendship they would be equals, but his wish should be her law.

With this white-hot idealism unfolding like the petals of a flower under the touch of Stephen's lips, under the caress of his strong fine hands, Iris dedicated herself to him.

But the man drew back. So much older and more experienced – so far removed, really, from the mysterious and unique world in which this girl had been brought up – he was a prey to apprehensions and doubts which she would not begin to understand. True, he was conscious that he had fallen most deeply and hopelessly in love with Iris. But there seemed every obstacle in the way of that love and he tried desperately to keep his head; to regain mastery of himself.

She lifted the heavy shadow of her lashes and looked up at him with eyes of such beauty he hardly dared look into them. They were far too soft and disturbing – almost too much for his strength. She saw that he was as white as death and that there were little beads of moisture on his forehead.

'Stephen!' she murmured. 'What is it?'

Gently he let her go and drew the back of one hand across his brow.

'Oh, God!' he said under his breath.

'Stephen – dearest...' The word fell rather shyly from lips that had not used such an endearment to any man before. 'Are you ill? What is it?'

He tried to pull himself together.

'Let us go back to the house, Iris,' he said.

'If you wish,' she said.

He gave her a despairing look. She could not know, he thought, that she was temptation itself – all the black and silver, the ivory and rose, the exquisite beauty of her. He had guessed from the response of her lips that she loved him, and that in her youth and innocence she was all too assailable; the battle on her side was over. He could control her life and her wishes if he so chose. But the whole thing was impossible. An hour ago he had had complete control of the situation. But now, having held and kissed her and realised his own incredible change of feeling, his state of mind was chaotic.

She had been all woman in his arms. Now, again, she seemed just a child with that heavenly hair tumbling to her waist. Rather shyly she shook it back from her face and tied it loosely with the silver ribbon which his feverish fingers had unwound.

He did not want to go … to bring this glorious hour to an end and face facts. He wanted to sail with her on one of those feluccas down the gleaming waters of the Nile, holding her close to him again. He wanted to forget the world, with her alone.

The very vehemence of his feelings made him speak harshly to her.

'This sort of thing cannot happen between us, Iris. We must both be sensible.'

For a moment she did not understand and the astonishment in her eyes told him so. He added:

'I had no right to make love to you, Iris. I'm sorry my dear. You must forgive me. You're far too lovely and attractive … it really isn't fair to any man.' He gave a short, miserable laugh.

'No right?' she repeated. 'But you love me and I love you. It has been written. It is in our stars. I have read, Stephen, that love and death are inescapable. So why – if we love – should we wish to escape?'

He did not answer for a moment, but turned and began to walk back to the 'Little Palace.' She walked with him and he knew that she watched him, waiting for his answer. He knew, too, that this was no mere moment of 'careless rapture' … of light-hearted lovemaking … the sort of thing the modern girl would understand and forgive and forget. Iris was one of the most serious-minded girls he had ever met. She had also struck him, when he first met her, as being the very epitome of proud, unapproachable womanhood. Never for a moment had he dreamt that she would fall in love with him. But she had just said it in that calm, detached way of hers. He knew her well enough to see how her mind worked. Those strange, philosophic words of hers rang in his ears:

'Love and death are inescapable.'

Did he want to escape from love? No, not from the love of Iris, which would be a rare thing – a miracle to be experienced by only one man in a million.

But it was not for him ... he was going to marry Elizabeth Martyn. At the very thought of Elizabeth a fresh shock assailed Stephen and brought him down to earth again.

He did not speak to Iris until they were on the moonlit terrace once more. Soft amber lights shimmered through the tall windows in the lower hall of the Palace. Upstairs, no doubt, old Miss Morgan was asleep. But Stephen knew that sleep would be impossible for him until he had been honest with Iris and with himself.

He turned to her and said:

'We must talk, my dear. Shall it be here or indoors?'

Iris felt a faint thrill of dismay suddenly run through her. It had been an effort on her part to still the wild, passionate beating of her young heart and follow him back here when all of her had clamoured to be taken in his arms again. Truly, she thought, the ways of the grey-eyed Englishman were incomprehensible! She said:

'As you wish, Stephen.'

He tugged at his collar. He felt hot and stifled.

'Let's sit down out here – it is cooler than indoors.'

'Very well,' she said submissively.

When they were seated and he had lit a cigarette, he kept his gaze from the tantalising loveliness of the slender figure in the chair opposite him. He knew that he must be frank, brutally so, for both their sakes and because he owed it to Elizabeth.

'There is so much I want to say to you, my dear, and none of it must be said. I should have told you this before, but somehow the occasion has not arisen. We have both been concerned with your father's affairs. I came here as his friend and yours. Now everything is altered. You see ... there is another girl ... I'm engaged to be married ... that's it in a nutshell.'

He broke off stammering. He knew that he must reproach himself bitterly for having allowed this situation to arise, but one did not bargain for these things ... they just happened. Perhaps he had been a fool not to have more foresight, but he honestly felt that he had been given little warning of such an emotional catastrophe. He had imagined that Iris disliked and resented him, and he, in blind superiority and self-confidence, had not thought it possible that he would fall precipitously in love with her.

He went on doggedly:

'I'm engaged to be married to a girl ... Elizabeth Martyn ... back in England ... we're supposed to be getting married quite soon.'

And now the sweat broke out on his forehead again. He pulled out a silk handkerchief and wiped it away. Leaning forward, he looked not at Iris, but at the red point of his cigarette. He hated himself. Damn it, one couldn't laugh off a situation like this. One couldn't say, *'This is all very charming but it meant nothing to either of us and now we must call it a day.'* It meant far too much to him and he dared not begin to think what was passing through Iris's mind.

He might have been surprised if he had realised that that strange and unpredictable mind of hers was less confused than his own and working quite coolly and logically. He *was* surprised when he heard her next words, spoken with the dignity which he had first found so astonishing in her.

135

'I see! So you are betrothed, Stephen. A marriage has been arranged for you between your two families. No doubt you do not love this girl. Is that it?'

His brows drew together. He gave a short, unhappy laugh. Iris made it all sound very mechanical. She was living in her world of books again. She had, of course, little knowledge of modern romance.

'That is not exactly so, Iris,' he said. 'It is scarcely what *you* imagine a betrothal to be – and it was not arranged by either of our families. In England one just meets a girl and falls in love and you decide to get married. It was a mutual agreement.'

'Then you do love her? If it is not arranged, it must be something you have chosen voluntarily, and so you must love her,' said Iris in her cool voice.

'God!' he thought. 'This is going to be harder than I imagined...'

'I thought I understood,' she added. 'But now I do not. You cannot love two women at the same time. If you want to marry this ... other girl ... you will not wish to marry me. Why then did you kiss me? What does it all mean?'

In all his life Stephen had never been more nonplussed. Such pitiless reasoning must be met with truth. It would be an insult to dissemble or prevaricate. Right from the start he had recognised the extreme candour which went hand in hand with this girl's innocence. Such qualities all the more endeared her to him. He wanted to throw himself at her feet. He wanted to say, 'Darling ... *darling* ... how adorable you are! Let us forget everything and everybody except each other...'

But that was no way to deal with such a problem. And he knew it. Now he forced himself to look at her. How calm she was! In one of her statue-like attitudes she sat there scrutinising him with her grave, shadowed eyes. He said:

'Iris, you must forgive me if I seem confused and stupid. But this sudden love which has sprung to life has shaken me to the core. I was not prepared for it. If I didn't love you so much I'd feel pretty much of a cad, but I do love you, so I excuse myself on the grounds that I was swept away by my feelings before I could control them. Will you try to understand and accept that as the truth?'

'Yes. But what about Elizabeth?'

'I thought that I loved her, Iris. But it was not the same as this. It does not begin to be the same. I can assure you of that, although I cannot analyse or attempt to excuse it. It was just not the real thing. This is. Such things do happen and it has happened to me...'

He bit hard on his lip and added:

137

'Now all I want is to make sure that I do the right thing ... for all of us.'

Iris sat very still. Her heart was sinking. The glory of this night's awakening was fading slowly but surely, she thought, like those stars would fade with the breaking of the dawn. Stephen looked so unhappy ... it hurt her. Her own wish to reason and be logical was fast vanishing too. She yearned for the warmth and comfort of his arms and lips again. She wanted to banish the ghost of this *other girl* who threatened to destroy her happiness.

Stephen spoke again:

'Try to believe, dear, that I didn't mean this to happen.'

'But, Stephen,' she said slowly, 'you could not help it. You know ... I have told you before ... my father and I both believe utterly in predestination and, as I have said to you before, what happened this night was written and could not be escaped.'

'I don't altogether believe that,' he said with a short laugh. 'I think one can control one's fate up to a point.'

'We can control the manner in which we behave, but the fact that we met and we meant to meet and love each other was as inescapable as life and death,' she said.

'Oh, Iris, my adorable darling!' he groaned. 'That may be so. Let us admit that it is. But an engagement is a contract that one cannot break lightly or easily. That is the serious side of this thing. My engagement and the fact that I know Elizabeth is very fond of me.'

'How fond?' asked Iris in a low voice.

He swallowed hard. It was not easy to talk about Elizabeth to this girl. He said:

'Well ... as far as I know ... fond enough to want to marry me...'

'Does she feel that you are the beginning and the end ... the sun, the moon and the stars ... the very breath of her existence?'

Stephen reddened. Somehow poor little Elizabeth did not fit in with any such extravagance. He was only too well aware that she was incapable of the depths that were in this girl. But how many women understood love as Iris Lowell did?... Or were willing to surrender so completely and be so refreshingly honest about it? It was not fair to make comparisons. There were no years of concentrated study of philosophising behind girls like Elizabeth and her kind. In dealing with Iris Lowell, a man was dealing with a unique phenomenon, and therein lay the danger. She was almost more than any man could resist, Stephen thought in justice to himself.

'Tell me, Stephen, does she love you like that?' persisted Iris.

'I'm damned if I know, darling,' he said.

'But that is how *I* love you, Stephen. And

once having said so it is for ever.'

He flung his cigarette-end into the shadows.

'I think that is how I love you too,' he said impulsively. 'But I've got to think of Elizabeth. I've got to play fair.'

'Play?' She repeated the word in a puzzled voice. 'What has play to do with this?'

Now with some relief he felt some of the old humour return to help him over this most difficult moment in his whole life. He had to laugh.

'Oh, my darling, that's a very English term. We talk a lot about fair play. An Englishman's sense of honour and integrity is enormously important to him, you know, but heaven forbid that I should be a hypocrite. I can't kiss you one moment and talk about Elizabeth and fair play the next. I'm not going to do it. I'm going to say here and now that I realise that my affection for her has changed and that I want to marry *you*. I never want there to be any other woman in my life as long as I live. Do you wish me to tell Elizabeth that, and to ask for my freedom? Would you marry me, Iris, if I asked you to?'

A great surge of new, wild joy arose within her. The colour came back to her face. She said:

'Yes – yes – and yes! And you will do what is right, Stephen. I know that. I do not

140

understand much about this "fair play" but I believe in loyalty and the keeping of a promise. On the other hand, if you love me, you cannot marry Elizabeth. She would not want you to. I, personally, could never marry a man who loved somebody else. And surely she will feel the same?'

'I hope so, Iris,' he said.

Suddenly she caught her breath.

'But suppose she does not! Supposing her love is selfish and she still wants you for herself, not caring how you feel. What will you do then, Stephen?'

'Oh, darling,' he said, 'don't lets go that far. It's been more than enough for me to discover how much I love you. Let me think it all over and decide what is best to do. I'll write to Elizabeth immediately. It's only fair. When we get her reply we will think again.'

Iris stood up. She was pale and he saw that her slender body was trembling.

'Oh, Stephen,' she whispered, 'I'm afraid. The way is not so clear as I thought. Oh, Stephen, why must there be this shadow between us? I thought you were mine and that I was yours. But you belong to somebody else. You love me and yet may not be permitted to love me. Stephen, I could not *bear* it if you married another woman now.'

He was stricken for her. He, too, was filled with forebodings – useless to wish now that this thing had not happened. It was too late.

141

Whichever way he argued about right and wrong, he knew that the love that had grown into being between this girl and himself was undeniable – too deep to eradicate.

He could not bear to see her standing there before him pale and trembling. But he controlled his longing to take her into his arms. In that way madness lay. Until he had seen or heard from Elizabeth he must deny himself the exquisite happiness that any man who loved or was loved by Iris would attain.

'I must say good night to you, my dear,' he said. 'It has grown very late.'

She did not speak but looked at him with large eyes full of fear and grief. Such an expression threatened to unnerve him.

'Don't be unhappy, my darling,' he added huskily. 'It'll all work out. I know it will. And Iris, I do love you. That I will swear. The trouble is that I love you too much.'

The corners of her red, pouting mouth lifted suddenly in an entrancing smile. She held out one slender hand.

'You could *never* love me too much. And now good night, my Stephen – *mine* if only for this little while.'

He took the slim, fragrant hand and pressed it to his lips. She could feel them burning against her palm. Then he moved quickly away and the black-and-silver figure was left alone in the drenching moonlight.

11

In the Wilsons' cool, spacious flat in a big modern block facing Gezirah Club – the famous sporting club of Cairo – Elizabeth Martyn found herself, almost as soon as she arrived, plunged into an important cocktail party.

Elizabeth adored cocktail parties. She had her mother's unquenchable enthusiasm for social gatherings and, having no particular brains or interest in an intellectual life, parties or dances were the essence of good fun to her.

But for once she felt depressed and *distrait,* encircled though she was by a crowd of young men eager to bring her drinks and all the lovely nuts and caviar and *pâté* sandwiches which were such a luxury after the rationing at home.

Elizabeth had only arrived by aeroplane in Cairo late last night, since when she had been receiving one disappointment after another.

The main blow, of course, was finding that Stephen was not in Cairo. She had only half expected this, despite Lady Martyn's warnings. But she had felt sure that she

143

would trace him easily. Sam Wilson was in the American Embassy and knew everybody at the British Legation. Eleanor, his wife, a young and attractive American girl, had become a friend of Elizabeth's when she was out here before and was only too delighted to have her to stay and to help her. But neither Sam nor Eleanor seemed able to find out where Stephen had gone.

The most Elizabeth could deduct was that he had reported to the Legation here two weeks ago, since when his mail had been forwarded to a hotel in Assuan.

Sam Wilson, cheery and helpful, had at once telephoned the hotel, but the management there knew nothing of Stephen's movements beyond the fact that his luggage had been removed on the same day that he had arrived. Since then his mail was collected daily by a *suffragi* but that was all they knew.

Elizabeth confessed herself baffled and not a little anxious. The Wilsons' theory was that he was staying with friends.

But they couldn't think who ... and it was all vague and unsatisfactory, and Elizabeth was beginning to feel resentful as well as disappointed. Where *could* Stephen be? What right had he to disappear like this just when she had come out to surprise him?

It was hot at this time of the year in Cairo. Many of the Wilsons' guests at the cocktail party tonight strolled on to the wide balcony and looked down at the glittering lights of the city. From here one could see the outline of the Great Pyramid of Gizeh. Elizabeth found herself surveying the exotic scene in the company of a tall Egyptian, Heluan Bey, who was in the Ministry. He had been educated at Oxford, spoke excellent English and was being polite and charming to the fair-haired, blue-eyed English girl who looked (as Elizabeth always did in the heat) a little pink and flustered.

'You are very thoughtful, mademoiselle...' He smiled.

Elizabeth sighed and suddenly turned to the Bey and said:

'Do you know Assuan very well?'

'I have been there many times,' he answered. 'I have an uncle who has an estate on the Nile up there. What makes you ask?'

Elizabeth blushed. Really, she thought, she could hardly start telling the Bey that she was trying to find her fiancé. After all, it *was* making herself a bit cheap. Stephen was on leave and had every right to go where he wished. But she was anxious, all the same, and mainly, of course, about his attitude towards herself.

'Oh, it's just... I'm interested. I wondered what sort of people live round there,' she stammered.

The Bey looked round and indicated an

exceedingly pretty, dark-eyed, dark-haired girl. She was dressed in a somewhat *outré* black-and-white dress, a chic Paris hat and veil, and wore a lot of expensive jewellery.

'There is my cousin, Nila Fahmoud,' he said. 'She lives on this estate near Assuan which I have just mentioned. Perhaps you would like to meet her?'

Elizabeth made a suitable reply.

The Bey called his pretty cousin out on to the balcony. A moment later the two girls were chatting vivaciously, for Nila Fahmoud, like the Bey, spoke very good English and had travelled extensively in Europe. It did not take Elizabeth long to turn the conversation to Stephen. She explained to Nila that her fiancé had gone to Assuan and was staying with friends of his but that she was not quite sure whom, or how to get in touch with him.

'Maybe you have met him if you have just come from Upper Egypt,' she asked Nila hopefully. 'His name is Stephen Daltry.'

A change came over Nila's olive face. Her big black eyes narrowed.

'Oh, *la, la!*' she said under her breath. '*Stephen Daltry!*'

'Do you know him?' asked Elizabeth a trifle suspiciously.

The amiable sports-loving English girl of Stephen's choice was rapidly becoming a jealous and possessive young woman.

146

Nila Fahmoud was silent a moment. But her shallow little mind worked rapidly. She had been away from her Nile home for over a month now but she had had two important and revealing letters from her brother's friend, Mikhilo Usref, and those letters had been very full of the name Stephen Daltry. *Mon Dieu!* Nila thought. *I know plenty about this English girl's fiancé, and I know exactly where he is, but the question is, shall I tell her?*

There was no malice in Nila Fahmoud. She was just a charming butterfly; as a character the very reverse of Iris Lowell, for whom she had a great admiration and with whom she had played as a child. But she had always been sorry for Iris and thought it dreadful that the crazy Romney Lowell should have kept her so incarcerated from the world. Nila had been hoping that Mikhilo's arrival on the scene might change all that ... indeed, she had been busy matchmaking in her gay, thoughtless fashion, quite ignorant as to whether Mikhilo and Iris were suited or not. They were a handsome pair and that was enough. Nila never bothered about analysing people's characters. She had always found Iris too serious and thought it time she came out of her 'gilded prison' and led a gay life.

According to Mikhilo's letters, Stephen Daltry was an ogre who had been given the right to pounce on poor little Iris and take her away to England. Apart from the fact that this would be a personal blow to Mikhilo, Nila did not want Iris to leave Egypt. She had looked forward to showing Iris off to Cairo and Alexandria society one day. There was no jealousy in her make-up and she was a wholehearted admirer of Iris's extraordinary beauty.

Now here was news! Stephen had a fiancée and she was trying to find him. On one of her impulses Nila decided to do Elizabeth and good turn and at the same time Elizabeth might intervene and persuade Stephen Daltry not to force Iris to leave the country.

She heard Elizabeth's somewhat gloomy voice:

'I don't suppose you've come across my fiancé, have you?'

Nila's black eyes sparkled.

'No, but I can tell you exactly where he is this moment,' she exclaimed.

Elizabeth's eyes opened wide.

'You can?' she asked incredulously.

'Yes,' said Nila with her tinkling laugh, and added (always with a sense of the dramatic): 'He is staying at the "Little Palace" as the guest of one of the most beautiful and unusual women in the world ... known in Egypt as the "Daughter of Earth and Sky".'

Elizabeth's reactions to this were negative.

She looked and felt a trifle stupid.

'I don't understand,' she said.

In a few brief words Nila described Lowell Pasha's daughter, her strange upbringing and her present plight. She added:

'My friend, Prince Usref, was a little vague about Mr Daltry's connections with the Lowells, but it seems that he is a sort of guardian to Iris and that he has been asked to take her back to England.'

Now it was as though a bombshell had exploded at Elizabeth's feet. She grew very red indeed and not a little angry.

'It just isn't true! Stephen *can't* be this girl's guardian...'

'Well, really,' said Nila, 'I'm not very sure of the facts. I'm a little confused myself about it and am also concerned about my friend. I am going back to my home tomorrow because Mikhilo thinks that Iris needs me...' She paused, and her big black eyes gleamed with a happy thought: 'Why don't you come with me, Mademoiselle Martyn?' she added. 'But yes, that is a wonderful idea! We shall go together. I will take you to the "Little Palace." Mr Daltry will be so pleased and surprised. Yes?'

For a moment Elizabeth said nothing. Her heart was pounding. She was literally dumbfounded, and as she pieced together the story the Egyptian girl had just told her all the suspicions and doubts and fears returned in full force and overwhelmed her common sense.

She had already chased Stephen across the Mediterranean and now she knew she would be lowering her pride still further by following him to Upper Egypt. She ought not to accept this invitation. She ought to be proud to stay here with the Wilsons and wait till Stephen came back to Cairo.

But it really was a bit too much to arrive here and be told by a complete stranger that Stephen was staying in a fantastic palace with a fabulously beautiful English girl who had been brought up as a sort of Egyptian goddess. What *would* her parents think? How *could* Stephen have become involved with this girl? Her guardian indeed! What nonsense!

'Do come with me'; the pretty foreign voice of Nila Fahmoud interrupted Elizabeth's confused reflections.

Then, rashly, Elizabeth replied:
'Very well. I will. It is most kind of you to invite me. What time do we leave?'

Yet another two days and nights had gone by at the 'Little Palace' since Iris and Stephen had become aware of their overwhelming love for each other.

For Iris two days of undreamed-of happiness; to love and be loved by a man like Stephen and have him here beside her was an incredibly happy experience.

The morning after Stephen had first taken her in his arms she had confided in her old governess.

'Tell me that it isn't wrong to love him, Morga, and that it would be wrong for him to make this marriage which he does not now wish to contract.'

But Miss Morgan had doubts on the subject and expressed them. The longer Stephen stayed here and the more she got to know of him, the more she liked him. She was convinced that Lowell Pasha would have welcomed him as a son-in-law. He had everything to commend him and Miss Morgan was sure the aunt would agree. It was also a tremendous pleasure to the old governess to see her darling so deeply in love ... so ecstatically happy ... almost pathetic in her anxiety to please Stephen and no longer fight for her own way.

But there was still this girl Elizabeth. And Stephen was engaged to her.

'It is not so easy as you think, my child,' she told Iris.

'Mr Daltry is a man of integrity. No matter how much he loves you, he will not find it easy to break with this girl.'

Iris argued:

'Oh, Morga, she must not refuse. It is unthinkable. Surely she will not want to marry a man knowing that he loves me.'

151

Miss Morgan looked at the girl's face: it was pale with emotion; the beautiful eyes looked enormous. Iris whispered:

'I never meant to take him away from another. It just happened before either of us could prevent it.'

Miss Morgan thought:

'She is different from other girls and I am afraid for her. If things do not go well, she will suffer terribly...'

But Iris refused to doubt that Elizabeth would release Stephen. He had sent an airmail letter to London, telling his fiancée the whole truth. When her answer came they would both know where they were. Meanwhile they had much to learn about each other and to Iris it was heaven indeed. She was beginning to understand his quick wit. His touch of authority and strength appealed vastly to her. His culture and love of beauty were the complement of her own. She loved him so much now that she was willing, she said, to go to England with him.

He found her enchanting, and for all his experience of women he, in his turn, could learn from her. He had never known such tenderness, such sweetness, in any woman, and found each new mood in her adorable.

He seemed to be living in a dream ... a brilliant dream from which he never wished to awaken. Their joy in each other was uninterrupted. Usref had called at the Palace

152

several times but had been refused admittance. Stephen and Iris wandered alone at will through the beautiful rooms and the exotic gardens – hand in hand like young idyllic lovers.

But Stephen had not kissed her again. He had vowed not to take that beautiful figure in his arms nor touch those exquisite, passionate lips again until he was free to do so. Nevertheless, love was there, burning like a white-hot flame between them. The merest thing they did, reading a book, examining old treasures, eating or drinking, was touched with magic. Their spirits seemed fused into one.

On the third afternoon of this perfect companionship a storm broke over the 'Little Palace.' Torrents of rain fell, drenching the grounds. Stephen had a headache and suffered from unusual depression. Iris was pale and nervy.

Stephen wished to heaven that Elizabeth's answer would come. Usually her letters reached him through the Diplomatic bag, but even if her answer was flown to Assuan it would be at least a week before it arrived. Unless she cabled ... and a week was a long time when one was in a restless mood.

He had quite made up his mind to ask for an extension of leave and fly with Iris and Miss Morgan to London. If Elizabeth would release him he would take Iris to her aunt and ask permission to marry her at once.

But this afternoon he was filled with new apprehensions. He sat on the terrace with Iris. The storm was nearly over but lightning still played across the sky, which was streaked with vermilion and orange. The Nile was the colour of gunmetal, swollen and angry-looking.

He turned to Iris. He was shocked to see how white she was – like the straight linen gown she was wearing.

'Would you like to go in and rest, my dearest?' he asked her.

She reached out a hand. He took it and felt her slender fingers close convulsively round his.

'No, I could not rest. I am not myself, Stephen. Sometimes I feel it is as though we are threatened by a mental storm as sudden and violent as the one which broke over us today.'

He smiled. He was growing used to her strange psychic fancies. She was still 'the goddess' living in a world of her own. But he also knew the other side of her … the woman in love, dependent upon him. He felt the grave responsibility of it. He thought grimly that he had little dreamed anything so volcanic could turn his life upside down.

The whole situation was perilous and difficult, and, apart from Iris and himself, he was loth to hurt Elizabeth.

He pressed Iris's hand quickly, then let it go. Rising, he lit a cigarette and walked a little away from her, frowning at the darkening sky.

He was beginning to feel the strain. It was almost more than he could bear to look into Iris's great shining eyes and not snatch her into his arms and feel once again the mad throbbing of her heart against his own.

Mandulis came on to the terrace and spoke to his mistress.

Stephen heard an exclamation from Iris. He turned and saw that she was smiling radiantly.

'Oh, Stephen,' she said, 'my great friend Nila Fahmoud has come to see me. She has been away so long. I want you both to meet: She has brought an English girl – a new friend – with her. I have told Mandulis to show them out here. Perhaps they will dine with us.'

12

Stephen frowned. He was not in the mood for meeting strangers and had no great wish to share Iris with anybody. He had heard a good deal about the Fahmouds and the very fact that they were friends of Prince Usref made them undesirable in his eyes. For he loved Iris as he had never thought it possible to love any woman in the world, and hand in hand with so great a passion there must always walk the spectre of jealousy. He would be jealous of any man who so much as touched those slender hands; the beautiful hands which inspired him once to quote to her a few lines of the famous Kashmiri song:

Pale hands, pink tipped,
Like lotus buds that float
On those cool waters where we used to
  dwell...

He was never tired of watching Iris move her exquisite fingers. He had often thought, during these wildly romantic, incredible days with her, that he might in truth finish that verse, even though it was exaggerated:

I would have rather
Felt you round my throat
Crushing out life than waving me fare-
  well...

Yes, it would be intolerable now to imagine
life without the 'Daughter of Earth and Sky'
beside him.

Iris was watching him a trifle anxiously.

'You do not mind my friend joining us for
an hour or so, Beloved?'

With a jerk Stephen returned to the
present and practical.

'Of course not! I shall be delighted,' he
began.

Then the words and the smile died on his
lips. He stood like an image, white under his
tan, staring at the two girls who were following the head *suffragi* out on to the terrace
towards them.

He could scarcely credit his own sight.
The shorter and darker girl of the two,
smartly dressed in white, he did not know.
But that tall fair girl in pale blue ... good
heavens, it was Elizabeth! *Elizabeth!*

But it couldn't be true. He must be
dreaming; or have a touch of the sun.
Elizabeth was thousands of miles away in
London. It was just somebody uncannily
like her...

The sweat broke out on Stephen's forehead. But now face to face with the apparition he knew that he was neither mad nor dreaming. Elizabeth ... very much the familiar Elizabeth with her warm pink face and a reproachful look in her blue eyes ... was speaking.

'Hullo, Stephen...' (That was Elizabeth's voice all right and she gave the little nervous laugh which was a habit with her when she was upset.) *'At last* I have found you. I thought you'd vanished or been murdered or something.'

She laughed again.

Nila Fahmoud, busily embracing Iris's slender figure and pouring out a torrent of words which she spoke in her pretty English, accompanied by much gesticulation, exclaimed:

'Yes, now, isn't this a surprise for you, Mr Daltry! I met your fiancée at a party in Cairo last night. We caught the night train to Assuan, and have driven the rest of the way. I am so thrilled!'

Stephen could find no words. He was absolutely flabbergasted, and looked it.

The 'thrill' seemed to be Nila's alone. Elizabeth did not even offer him a hand. She stood staring back at him in that queer, suspicious way which belied the polite smile on her firm young mouth. And Iris, having embraced her friend, stood aloof, her gaze wandering from Stephen to Elizabeth. She, too, was deadly pale.

Long afterwards Stephen wondered how he ever managed to pull himself together sufficiently to break the ice and make formal introductions. Diplomat though he was, he stammered and coughed. He heard his own voice on a strained note saying:

'This is certainly a terrific surprise, Elizabeth. Iris ... this is Miss Martyn. Elizabeth ... this is the daughter of Lowell Pasha. Miss Iris Lowell...'

He paused, pulled out a handkerchief, wiped his forehead and watched the two girls – the one with whom he had fallen so desperately in love, the other who was his promised wife – coldly acknowledge each other. They did not shake hands. Each inclined her head and murmured something under her breath.

Nila chattered on. For once Stephen was thankful for what in normal circumstances he thought a silly, artificial creature who talked too much. She was so *thrilled,* Nila repeated, to have been able to manoeuvre this meeting. The *poor* Elizabeth had been distraught, not knowing where Mr Daltry was to be found. It was so *lucky* that Mikhilo Usref had written and told her that Stephen was staying at the 'Little Palace' ... such *fun* the two of them coming up here together last night. But she mustn't let her high spirits run away with her like this and forget

159

that poor, sweet Iris had just lost her darling father ... what a *disaster* ... what a *dreadful* loss to Egypt – the brilliant Lowell Pasha who had done such fine work out here ... and there were rumours that Iris was going to England ... but no, she mustn't *dream* of going. She would be too grievously missed...

On and on chattered the Egyptian girl. Iris stood like a mute, pale image, scarcely heeding what was being said, for like Stephen she, too, had received a violent shock. A quick glance at his worried face and she realised that he had never anticipated this meeting. And now Iris was learning the intrinsic meaning of the word jealousy. Outwardly calm, she inwardly blazed with conflict of feeling. *This*, then, was the girl of Stephen's choice ... his first choice ... the English girl to whom he was engaged.

The big dark eyes of Iris examined with a most painful curiosity every detail of Elizabeth's appearance. Proud, almost imperialistic as she was in her own ideas and because of her extraordinary upbringing, she was nevertheless without vanity or malice. Impartially she made her judgment. She saw what was attractive in the other girl ... the fine athletic young figure with the straight legs and good ankles, the fine wrists and long supple hands of a born horse-woman; the agreeable combination of light-gold hair brushed crisply into thick waves, forget-me-not-blue eyes, rosy cheeks and dimpled chin. Hers must be, Iris thought, the typical English beauty likened by centuries of poets to 'a rose.' Instinctively Iris judged and guessed aright. But that was all. There was nothing more behind it. Here was a nice pretty creature who might easily turn a man's head in the Egyptian moonlight. But there was nothing of the *'femme fatale'* about her. Nothing deep or devastating; in fact she had none of the 'allure' which is as ageless as it is provocative.

Stephen might well tire of such a girl, Elizabeth would not know how to keep him.

Yet tangled with Iris's thoughts was the awful fear that Fate had let Elizabeth Martyn cross Nila's path in order to reunite the engaged pair. The awful dread that she, Iris, stood suddenly on the brink of personal disaster...

Something of horror completely unnerved her. She turned from her scrutiny of Elizabeth and took Nila's arm.

'Come with me into the house a moment,' she whispered... 'I suddenly feel faint.'

Nila, looking concerned and sympathetic, at once encircled her friend's waist with one arm and they walked away, Nila doing all the talking.

Stephen and Elizabeth were left alone.

Some of the rosy colour was fading fast in

Elizabeth's healthy face. Gloomily she regarded her fiancé. She found him changed. He looked positively thin and ill. What on earth had been happening to him? This wasn't the gay, debonair young man who had proposed to her last Christmas at Mena House; who had always made her feel at ease when they met again after a short separation. He would put an arm round her and say something sweet, such as, 'You're looking marvellous, angel!' Or, 'How's my Liz?' and murmur that he was longing to kiss her again.

All that seemed like the long-forgotten past. The memory of years back instead of weeks. This Stephen was a stranger ... distant and unrecognisable. Elizabeth said:

'Well, I suppose this is a shock to you, Steve.'

'I certainly didn't expect you,' he said with an effort. 'When did you leave England?'

'Thursday,' she said.

He made a rapid mental calculation. This was Saturday. Then his cable would never have reached her. She had not come in answer to that. She did not yet know he had asked for his freedom. God, what a position for a chap to be in! What had brought her out like this, without warning? He was made fully conscious now of the absolute change in his sentiments, for whereas this should have been a delightful surprise, it had all the

162

aspects of disaster.

'I can't say you look very pleased to see me, Stephen,' he heard Elizabeth's voice on a hurt note.

Compunction seized him. He held out his hand.

'I'm sorry, Liz. A hell of a lot has happened since we last met. Look here, my dear, come and sit down and let's talk. Will you have a drink?'

'No, thank you.'

He was conscious of her blue, searching eyes, so full of suspicion and resentment. Once more he wiped his forehead. They sat down. He offered her a cigarette which she accepted, and he lit it for her. He did not smoke himself. His mouth felt dry and hot, and his heart was pounding. In all his experience he had never known such an awkward moment as this. And now Elizabeth began to explain why, because he hadn't written, she had decided to come out and stay with the Wilsons and find him, and he was aware of fast approaching doom for Iris and Elizabeth and himself. He began to see that one could not change one's feelings and fall madly and hopelessly in love as he had done with another and hope for an easy solution. If Elizabeth had stayed in England and received his cable and letter it might have been better. And always he had hoped to avoid hurting her or Iris. But Elizabeth's decision to come out here without warning ... the damnable stroke of luck that had led her to make Nila Fahmoud's acquaintance ... was producing a crisis which he had not the slightest idea how to tackle. With a sinking heart he had watched Iris move away with her friend. This sudden encounter with Elizabeth must have upset her too. He had seen it in those large, expressive eyes of hers. *Damnation*, what was he to do next?

Elizabeth was saying:

'I just don't understand what goes on, Stephen. But I knew something was wrong when you didn't write. You've changed, that's obvious. When I was in London Mummy said I was mad to come out here ... she said I was chasing you...' Elizabeth gave one of her nervous laughs ... 'but I suppose I was pig-headed and thought everything would be all right. Then I got more worried when the Wilsons didn't know where you were. But after my meeting with Miss Fahmoud I think I understand. I think I understand *completely*...'

Stephen saw that she was on the verge of tears – Elizabeth who was always so cheerful and casual ... why, he never connected her with tears... When he had first become attracted by her he had thought her good spirits and amiability so engaging. Yet this evening when he saw her again, after

164

knowing and loving Iris – he was aghast at himself. He could see how completely he had been trapped by life; the desire to get married and have some home life, a temporary infatuation which bore no resemblance to real love (the sort of love which he knew had sprung to life within him for Iris), and by an astute and designing mother ... i.e. Lady Martyn. It was a sad irony, he thought, that if he were not engaged to Elizabeth he would be quite pleased to see her. He would like to know all the latest news from London, instead of which her presence embarrassed him almost to a degree of wishing her a thousand miles away again. Poor Elizabeth! What an absolute cad she made him feel.

'Oh, look here, Liz,' he broke out huskily, 'I'd give anything for you not to have come all this way out to see me. It was grand of you, but you oughtn't to have come, my dear...'

He broke off, leaning forward, hands clenched over his knees, face contorted.

She eyed him in that new resentful way which was so different from the old Elizabeth. She was not an hysterical person. She was very rarely emotional. In her way she was in love with this man, but love was not to Elizabeth Martyn as to many women, the beginning and end-all of existence. She had not that kind of nature. She had her 'moments,' her natural passions, but she took love as she took other things in life ... in a rather boyish way, just as a pleasant part of it. She could really get just as thrilled about the purchase of a new horse, or the winning of a tennis championship, as over a romantic affair.

But she had cared for Stephen ... quite a lot in her way...

In the main her vanity was suffering. It was not nice for a girl to find her fiancé had changed towards her. And she was asking herself: *'What will everyone think? Mummy will say, 'I told you so!'* ... *My friends will find it queer and it is humiliating for me. Stephen doesn't love me any more. That's obvious. And what's even more obvious is the reason ... that girl ... that incredible-looking model of the early Egyptians. I've never seen anything like it in my life...'*

She said aloud:

'Well, I think you'd better start some explaining, hadn't you, Steve?'

He looked uneasily at the 'Little Palace.' Darkness was falling. There was no twilight out here ... only the swift transition from day to night... From brilliant sunshine to radiant moon. In the Palace lights began to burn softly and steadily.

Stephen, who had begun to know the workings of this household, realised that Mandulis and Pilak would soon be bringing out *apéritifs,* and preparing for a dinner-party on the terrace. His spirit recoiled at the thought of a party which included both Iris and Elizabeth. Yet he knew that Iris, who had an exquisite sense of hospitality, was sure to offer a meal to her unexpected guests, and damn it all, Elizabeth had come a long way to see him...

On the other hand, this scarcely seemed the best moment for explanation and discussion on a subject which virtually affected the lives of all three of them.

Now Elizabeth seemed to read what was passing through his mind. She spoke again.

'You may as well tell me and get it over.'

He turned to her.

'Very well, if you wish it. I cabled and wrote to you earlier this week to ask you if you would release me from our engagement.'

He saw her flush red. He hoped that she wasn't going to burst into tears. But she remained calm. And he was soon to learn a new unsuspected side of Elizabeth ... the rather mean, petty one which was a legacy from Lady Martyn, and which had lain very well concealed under the cheerful 'sports-girl' façade.

'I thought as much,' she said. 'And I suppose you think you've really fallen for that extraordinary creature in the long white what-not. Well, all I can say is you must be raving mad.'

It was his turn to flush.

'You are free to think what you wish, Elizabeth. And as you've insisted on the truth – all right! I have fallen in love with Iris and I don't think if you knew more about her you'd call her a "creature" in that derogatory fashion.'

Elizabeth sniffed.

'H'm ... well ... I've no intention of getting to know her any better. And I'm not going to take this seriously. You're just suffering from some sort of mental derangement, my dear old Steve.'

'I'm not in the least deranged, thanks, Elizabeth,' he said curtly. 'I have never been more serious. As I told you in my letter, I ran across Iris's father in Turkey ... he was taken ill in the train going to Ankara and...' he proceeded briefly to outline the history of his meeting with Romney Lowell and his subsequent promise to come here and get Iris and her English governess safely to England.

Elizabeth listened, growing more and more annoyed. She was not so much jealous as worried about public opinion. She couldn't bear to be made a laughing stock. People at home *would* laugh ... behind her back... Fancy Elizabeth Martyn losing Stephen Daltry, the 'catch' of the season ... to a twenty-year-old girl who had been

168

brought up in Egypt as a goddess and never been out in the modern world. It was fantastic.

Stephen finished his story with a firm and repeated assurance that this was 'the real thing,' and that, deeply though he deplored his conduct and hated to hurt Elizabeth, he felt it best to be true to himself. She would not, he presumed, want to marry him knowing that he was in love with somebody else.

'My real regret,' he added with genuine feeling, 'is that you should have come all this way only to be told all this, my dear.'

Elizabeth sprang up.

'I'm very glad I did come. It's plain to be seen that someone ought to save you from making a fool of yourself and me.'

Stephen also rose, his heart sinking. He had anticipated almost any kind of reception of his news but this. He could scarcely recognise the nice amiable girl to whom he had proposed. And that last remark of hers was a painful echo of Lady Martyn. How often had he heard her ladyship discuss what she called the 'imbecilities' and 'indiscretions' of those around her. At all costs *Lady Martyn* wouldn't wish her daughter made a fool of.

'Oh, God' said Stephen in a hopeless voice.

Elizabeth swung round at him.

'Well, you don't expect me to just hand back my ring and say, *"Okay … I'll fly home and you marry your goddess and jolly good luck to you…"* do you?'

That struck him as being a trifle vulgar. He was prepared to excuse Elizabeth much … after all, the poor girl was very upset, and he was the culprit. But he was amazed at such a selfish and predatory outlook.

'Do you mean to tell me that you wish to bind me to our engagement, knowing how I feel?' he asked incredulously.

Her eyelids dropped. She chewed her lower lip.

'I'm quite sure Mummy would say I oughtn't to be in any hurry to break it off.'

It was all that Stephen could do not to snap, 'What's it got to do with your mother?' but he restrained himself and said:

'This is your affair and mine, Elizabeth, not Lady Martyn's.'

'All the same, she wouldn't want me to break our engagement until you've had plenty of time to think things over,' Elizabeth said stubbornly. 'You may imagine you're serious about this girl, but I don't.'

'I think that's for me to say,' exclaimed Stephen, conscious now of an ice-cold rage.

They were still arguing when Nila Fahmoud came out on the terrace and joined them.

13

Iris paced up and down her bedroom, clad in her flowing white wrapper, her hair unbound, her lips quivering with suppressed emotion.

'I cannot go down and sit at the head of my table ... watch him with *her* ... I cannot!' she was saying.

Miss Morgan stood by, leaning on the stick which she had used lately owing to her weak state of health. The old woman was dressed in the faded shade of mauve silk which she favoured, and, hearing that there were guests, had put on some of the ornate Egyptian jewellery which from time to time had been presented to her.

Worried and sad for Iris, she regarded her.

'My dear, this is where you must learn self-control,' she said, 'never losing sight of the fact that you are the mistress of this house, and that it is your place to entertain those who come here. Nila Fahmoud is an old friend. Miss Martyn...' she paused and sighed... 'Miss Martyn, whether Stephen loves her any more or not, was once dear to him, and she is English and in a foreign land. You are English, my darling, do not forget it no matter how much you love Egypt.'

Iris stood still, one hand against her breast, which was rising and falling with agitation.

'Oh, Morga, it is always hard for me to remember it. I am so closely knit with Egypt. Stephen understands me. I could grow used to his English ways and share his beliefs ... it is because we love each other so much. But I could never get used to English people like Elizabeth Martyn. How she stared at me! She made me feel ... oh, I don't know ... but I felt that she was contemptuous of me ... as though I were something to be ridiculed. It was horrible...' She broke off with a sob.

Miss Morgan went to the girl's side and put an arm round the trembling figure.

Face to face with the realities of life at last she was beginning to know the meaning of pain and fear. What a tragic legacy from the father who had wanted the world at her feet! His poor little 'goddess'!

She reasoned with the girl gently. Iris must try to understand Elizabeth Martyn's outlook as well as her own, she said. Elizabeth had a shock coming here in search of her fiancé and finding him in love with somebody else; it must be a considerable blow to her pride if nothing else. It behoved Iris to be gentle and kind to her.

Iris looked at her old governess with stricken eyes.

'But do you think she truly loves my Stephen? Will she try to get him back? Will I lose him? Lose the glorious love which I have only just discovered? Oh, Morga, how could I bear it?'

Miss Morgan reasoned with her.

'Now is the time to remember all your philosophy, my child, and apply it to yourself. Happiness cannot be found by ruthlessly walking across the grave of another woman's hopes ... hopes that you have taken from her. Happiness is gained only through sacrifice and suffering. In the history of the Temple of Isis these things are written – you know that, my child. It is an inexorable law both of the ancient gods and of our Christian times that those who do wrong must walk in darkness–'

Iris cupped her burning cheeks with both hands. With a fatalistic expression in her eyes she looked at the old woman who had so many times in the past discussed these things with her. For Miss Morgan, in her way, was a woman of great culture and wisdom. Yes, she was right! She must endeavour to do the right thing. Stephen did not belong to her. Love was not a law in itself. First, Elizabeth must set him free ... not because she was forced to do so but because she knew it was for the best ... and then, when the way was clear, and no harm could come of it, she, Iris, could fulfil her glorious destiny as the woman Stephen loved.

'Take your bath and dress, my dear,' said the soothing voice of her old friend, 'and then go downstairs and be your gracious, lovely self. In this way you will retain your dignity and no one will ridicule you. Is it not so?'

'Very well,' said Iris in a low voice. 'I will do as you say, Morga.'

But her heart was heavy as she clapped her hands for Ayesha to run the water in the bath and perfume it with her favourite carnation scent.

It was whilst bathing, lying in the foamy, scented water, the dusky braids of her hair pinned high on her head, eyes still heavy with unshed tears that she brooded over the crisis that was taking place in her life. Instinctively, try though she would to overcome the aversion, she disliked Elizabeth. She disliked seeing Stephen upset and unhappy. They had been so gloriously content in each other's company these last few days. Why, why couldn't it have lasted? But she must do her best, as Morga said, to appear cool, proud and unconcerned until Elizabeth Martyn chose to act. Meanwhile, why should poor Stephen sit at dinner with so many women? There must be other men there. It would be less of a strain if she could turn tonight's dinner from a small *intime* affair into a party. Acting on one of her impulses, Iris summoned the old nurse and gave a sharp order to send a *suffragi* immediately for Prince Usref and ask him to dine here and bring a friend, a man whom she had heard was staying with him. That, surely, would relieve the embarrassing position.

An hour later Stephen found himself flung into a kind of vortex which was almost as sudden and unexpected as Elizabeth's arrival.

A dinner for six had been mysteriously arranged and served at ten o'clock that night on the terrace with all the accustomed Arabian Nights' colour and glamour which could make a meal at the 'Little Palace' such a dazzling affair.

Delicate lace cloths, gleaming candles in heavy gold sconces, great bowls of scarlet roses and trailing fern, and tonight – to mark a special occasion – the pure gold plate, which had once belonged to a Pharaoh, was used. It was of such magnificence that even Stephen was startled and Elizabeth opened her round blue eyes wide and her mouth too. It also reduced her to a state of dumbness. With the lighted Palace on one side, and the moonlit Nile and desert on the other, the scene seemed to her like a film affair. She had anticipated that she and Iris would sit glaring, daggers-drawn, at each other. But nothing of the sort; a festive spirit prevailed.

Two other men arrived. Stephen had not the least idea how or why Usref should be here, but here he was, accompanied by a slim, olive-skinned youth of Persian extraction, with whom Nila as well as Usref was acquainted. He answered to the name of Omar and was the son of one of the big wealthy Alexandrian families ... handsome, lazy, and about as lacking in moral fibre as Usref himself. But he made a pleasant and decorative guest. Both Usref and Omar were immaculately clad in white dinner jackets, and with smooth ebony heads they were gay, talkative and witty. Only afterwards Stephen learned that his poor Iris had sent for them in order to try and break the ice.

Certainly Stephen, diplomat as he was, found it easier to behave normally in a crowd than had he and Iris and Elizabeth been *à trois*.

Iris's appearance that night took his breath away. She came down to that dinner in all her proud beauty, outwardly cool, courteous and smiling, and wearing a long tight gown of gold tissue which shimmered with every step she took. The darkness of her hair was relieved only by a single golden rose.

The sun-kissed shoulders and arms were bare. But around the slender neck there was a high collar of turquoises ... startlingly blue ... and huge ear-rings of gold and turquoises glittered in the tiny ears. Her eyelids were painted blue. She looked, he thought, extraordinarily Egyptian tonight, and moved and spoke with such royal grace that even the most sceptical critic could not have robbed her of her dignity. He was filled with pride in her, and asked himself, humbly, why it should have been given to him to receive the love of this wonderful girl. For love him she still did ... he knew it ... the shock of Elizabeth's arrival had not taken *that* away. Although she treated him during dinner as she treated the other guests, without favour, she had given him one deep look with her ardent eyes when she first came out on to the terrace. And he had thought, *'I love her; she is mine ... I can never give her up, never. Elizabeth must be made to see reason.'*

But he was deeply anxious, because so far it did not look as though Elizabeth was going to be reasonable. Before Nila Fahmoud had put an end to their discussion Elizabeth had shown him quite plainly that she meant to go on regarding this thing as a temporary infatuation on his part, and that she had no intention of giving him back his ring.

How he had disliked that smooth fellow Usref, *and* the look in his eyes when he glanced in the direction of their dazzling hostess. It became apparent, too, as the long meal dragged on, that Mikhilo was putting himself out to be nice to Elizabeth, beside whom he had been seated. Now and again Stephen, who sat between Iris and Nila, heard a few of the things Usref was saying. He caught the words:

'Delightful for you to find your fiancé here—'

And:

'When are you going to be married, Miss Martyn?'

And Stephen felt his blood boil, although he avoided speaking to Usref and with polite smiles tried to be entertaining to Nila.

There was one decidedly awkward moment while Pilak was handing around the great dish of peaches, figs, mandarins and melon... Omar leaned across the table and, in his broken English, asked Elizabeth how long she was staying at the 'Little Palace.'

Silence fell. The rest of the party seemed to wait for Elizabeth's reply. She cast a covert look at Iris and another slightly malicious one at Stephen.

'It's so thrilling here, I shan't ever want to go,' she said.

Stephen set his teeth. He dared not look at Iris, but he heard her voice, like a draught of sweet, cool water:

'The "Little Palace" is yours for as long as you wish to remain in it, Miss Martyn. I'm glad you like it so much.'

Stephen dug the silver point of a fruit knife savagely into a piece of melon. He thought he had never attended a banquet he enjoyed less. Oh, God, if this were only yesterday and he and Iris were alone as they used to be on this same terrace, undisturbed by the world. Last night peace and content, and the bittersweet pain of love suppressed, had been their position. But tonight, at this glittering dinner, among these chattering people, they sat under a dark cloud – of malice, of impending catastrophe.

Nila suddenly relieved the strain by giving one of her tinkling laughs.

'Omar has just said something so clever. He's a real poet,' she said to Stephen. 'Did you hear him?'

'I'm afraid I do not speak Persian,' said Stephen.

'I will translate it for you,' said Nila. 'He has just said that, as Mikhilo calls Iris the Lady of the Moonlight, which suits her so well, you should call your fiancée 'Daughter of the Sun,' for she has hair of gold and eyes the azure of the noontide sky... There! is that not charming?'

'Charming!' echoed Stephen mechanically.

But he thought:

'If they go on coupling our names together in this way, it will give Elizabeth fresh hope and take from Iris and myself all that hope means. I wish they'd all be quiet!'

Elizabeth, pleased and flattered, began to be more cheerful and talkative.

Now the table was cleared save for the candles. Turkish coffee was served in tiny crystal glasses of exquisite workmanship. Mandulis came round with cigars and cigarettes. Everybody laughed and talked. And at last Stephen felt that he must look at Iris.

As he turned to her his heart seemed to jerk violently. She was looking at him. Each held the other's gaze for a long, spellbound moment. The passionate adoration in the man's grey eyes was reflected in the great dark ones under their shadowed lashes. How straight and still she sat, he thought, with the candlelight reflecting the gold of her dress and the violent blue of the high turquoise collar. He thought, *She might indeed have stepped straight out of one of her ancient temples tonight. She is as inaccessible and as unreal as an Egyptian queen whom some Pharaoh loved thousands of years ago...*

He felt a sudden overwhelming longing to take her away from all this – to take her out there into the desert, stripped of her jewels and her glory, and with all barriers broken down between them. He wished madly that she was his wife, that they were a couple of wandering nomads who would pitch their tent out there on the moon-silvered sand. His arm would pillow that dark, sweet head. Her lips would respond to his insatiable desire for her kisses. They would forget the world and by the world be forgotten.

The interminable meal went on...

Later, the guests seemed disposed to wander through the gardens which were so full of enchantment and starlight, and heavy with the perfume of the roses which lived for a day, then, in the heat, languished and spilled their sweetness.

For one palpitating moment Iris and Stephen found themselves alone for the first time since Elizabeth's catastrophic arrival.

He moved close to her.

'Forgive me ... I had an idea that this was going to happen. I feel that a thousand apologies are owed to you,' Stephen whispered with a look of supplication on his face.

She drew so near him that he could smell the familiar and intoxicating perfume that was her aura. He could see the melting, mournful tenderness in her liquid eyes. Just for a bare second her cool fingertips closed around his warm ones and pressed them convulsively.

'My poor Stephen. It is terrible for you as

well as for me … and for *her*,' she whispered back.

'We can't talk now,' Stephen said hoarsely; for the voices and laughter of the others seemed all too close. 'But tomorrow the position will clarify itself. It *must* … oh, my darling!'

He saw Iris turn and look towards the Isis Temple, so sharply, blackly etched against the luminous sky. He heard her indrawn breath.

'Inshallah!' – just the one Arabic word fell like a sigh from her lips. Then she was gone and he felt immensely alone standing there in the velvet night. He could hear Elizabeth's familiar, schoolgirl laugh followed by Nila Fahmoud's giggle. The sounds jarred every nerve in him. He flung his cigar-end into the bushes, turned and walked into the house, feeling an irresistible desire to get away from this party, look for that nice, sane woman, Miss Morgan, and talk to her.

Elizabeth, meanwhile, had been manœuvred by Mikhilo Usref away from the others and down towards the edge of the Nile. It was not that he was in the least interested in her personally. This plump, fair, English type held no appeal for him, enslaved as he was by his thwarted passion for the daughter of Lowell Pasha. But he had an ulterior motive for wishing to get on the right side of Miss Martyn, and he felt

182

that tonight his lucky star was in the ascendant. First of all Nila's return, bringing with her Stephen Daltry's fiancée of all women in the world; secondly the unexpected invitation from Iris herself to dine here tonight.

He knew Nila Fahmoud well enough to be sure that she had no malice aforethought but was merely trying to do him a good turn by bringing Elizabeth to the 'Little Palace' and making things awkward for Stephen Daltry. But there was far more than that at the back of Usref's cunning and unscrupulous mind.

These days of exile from Iris's presence, and the knowledge that the Englishman was staying here, had driven him almost to a frenzy of jealousy. He hated Stephen now as he had never hated any living being. He hated him almost to the pitch of *murder*.

But *murder* was an ugly word ... and death, thought Usref grimly, could come in other forms easily out here in these days of intrigue, of swift retribution, of hostile demonstrations.

He decided to play his own game.

'You look sad, you whom my friend Omar has christened the Daughter of the Sun,' he said to Elizabeth in his silkiest voice. 'You should dwell in sunlight. Would it be impertinent of me to suggest that you are walking in the shadows – that you have not found the happiness for which you were seeking in Egypt? And would you forbid me to say that I admire you enormously and would like to serve you if I can?'

Elizabeth gave him a thoughtful look. She had seen Stephen and Iris touch hands and whisper together a moment or two ago, and had become suddenly depressed, feeling like a fish out of water in this place. But now her spirits rose. She smiled hopefully at the handsome Serbian. He was a prince (that would please Mummy, who adored titles) and was obviously highly cultured. Why shouldn't she make a friend of him? She had never needed a friend more. And she was immensely flattered by his speech.

'Shall we walk and talk a little?' he added in an encouraging voice.

'Yes,' said Elizabeth on an impulse. 'Yes, Prince Usref, I think I should like to very much.'

14

But that 'little talk' was not particularly encouraging to either Elizabeth or Usref. The English girl was shy of airing her feelings too intimately to the foreign stranger – even though he *was* a prince and exceedingly polite and amiable to her. And Mikhilo, listening to her, was soon disappointed and impatient – aware that whatever she did feel was luke-warm and without any particular depth or passion.

She confided in Mikhilo up to a point.

'Of course it was an awful shock to me to arrive in Cairo and find Stephen had more or less vanished, and my friends unable to trace him,' she said as she walked with the Serbian along the path fringing the moon-silvered river. 'And a bit of luck meeting your sweet little friend Miss Fahmoud, and being brought here. But it has only confirmed my suspicions about my fiancé. He is obviously infatuated with this extraordinary Lowell girl.'

Mikhilo, with a thin, pointed finger, traced an invisible moustache on his upper lip. His eyes narrowed.

'You think it is infatuation?'

'Oh, certainly – it can't be love. He hardly knows her,' said Elizabeth confidently.

Mikhilo kept his thoughts to himself. What an imbecile the girl was! No psychology; no real understanding of the strong tide of human emotions and passions that can swamp men and women. He knew; he had been in and out of love lightly so many times. But one did not fall lightly in love with the Lady of Moonlight. Her fascination was far too strong; her beauty and appeal too unique. When a man loved *her* it was for ever. It was as a madness, a fever in the blood, a fatal malady. Was not Mikhilo Usref dying of it? He had made up his mind days ago that the Englishman was suffering the same anguish. But with that belief was coupled the secret dread that Stephen did not love Iris without hope. She had excluded all her other friends from the 'Little Palace,' including *him*, her chosen friend ... and kept Stephen Daltry here, alone with her ... alone with her ... alone save for that old harridan Miss Morgan, whom Mikhilo detested (mainly because he read dislike in her watery eyes). Yes, Mikhilo was mortally afraid ... that Iris, for the first time in her life, returned a man's love. And now Elizabeth was confirming his suspicions. In her casual, senseless way she recounted all that Stephen Daltry had told her. Mikhilo ground his teeth with rage as he listened.

'Oh, Steve is a fool ... just because the girl has flattered him... Of course, she's awfully attractive ... I admit it. But very theatrical, don't you think? And so different from Steve and the sort of women he's used to. I mean, she couldn't take her place in Society as a diplomat's wife. Everyone would giggle at her... She's never had a chance, poor girl... I mean, all that stupid upbringing... I'm rather sorry for her. But Stephen's a fool ... to lose his head. So unlike him. And it's jolly hard lines on me ... I can't think what my mother and father would say...'

She rattled on. The fresh, artless chatter, the ingenuous blue eyes and pink blush which had once captivated Stephen Daltry held no kind of attraction for Prince Usref. Her figure was good, he admitted; her blonde, shining hair and fair skin might even have moved him to make love to her in a meaningless fashion. But he could see for himself that Stephen Daltry had made a bad mistake ... and must be regretting it bitterly. What was Elizabeth Martyn but a pretty nonentity ... with nothing to commend her but the fact that she came of a good English family and could play a fair game of tennis, ride a horse well – and giggle? Good *heavens!* ... when compared with Iris ... Iris, with her grave, wonderful beauty, her profound knowledge of Egypt ... her philosophy, her strange, mystic charm ...

Elizabeth was nothing. Usref could hardly refrain from breaking into a torrent of hot, resentful words as he listened to what he called her 'crass stupidity' when describing Iris ... daring to suggest the Diplomatic circle would laugh at her. Ye gods! they would fall down and adore her ... all of them ... as *he* did ... *as Stephen Daltry was doing.* It was that final reflection that drove Mikhilo to a frenzy.

'Surely,' he said in a slow, careful voice, 'you will not allow another woman to take your future husband from you?'

Elizabeth shrugged her shoulders.

'What can I do ... if he really wants to break it off with me? I've told him he's got to think it over and not rush into anything silly. That's all I can do. Isn't it, Prince Usref?'

'She is like a glass of milk...' the Serbian thought contemptuously. But aloud, with a smile, he said: 'Ah, you must be firmer than that. I am sure it is you for whom he really cares. I agree with you ... he is merely infatuated. As for my Lady of Moonlight – she belongs here, in her own atmosphere ... she should not be taken to England. You must prevent that at all costs.'

'But how?' asked Elizabeth in an aggrieved voice. 'I can't control Steve, and he seems so stubborn about it all. It's simply damnable that this English Pasha should have chosen to make Steve his daughter's guardian or executor or whatever he is.'

Silently Mikhilo echoed that last remark on an even stronger note. His own wild hopes of winning Iris's regard had been dashed to the ground by that fateful meeting between Lowell Pasha and Stephen Daltry in Turkey.

He continued, as smoothly and subtly as he could, to persuade Elizabeth Martyn that she must on no account give Stephen up easily.

'He must get away from here,' he said. 'They must be separated ... and if ... shall we say ... a little infatuation *has* sprung up between them...' Mikhilo winced as he said the words ... 'they will return to sanity once they get a proper perspective. Yes ... you must stay with Nila Fahmoud ... and refuse to return to Cairo unless Mr Daltry goes with you.'

Elizabeth considered this. Rather gloomily she recalled all that Stephen had said to her before dinner. He had been so *determined* to get his freedom ... so *certain* that he wanted to marry Iris Lowell. It was really rather dreadful. Just supposing he *wouldn't* give their engagement another chance ... and *insisted* on breaking it?

Elizabeth's lips took on a stubborn twist which strongly resembled an expression which she had often, personally, encountered on the face of her strong-minded mother. She said:

'Well, I'll try my best, Prince Usref, and you must try to make Miss Lowell see reason. You say she used to be awfully keen on you?'

Mikhilo winced again. *Keen* ... what a vulgar word! The schoolgirl slang of some of these English and American misses was intolerable, he thought. But he gave Elizabeth an encouraging look from his black, liquid eyes.

'Yes, indeed. And I know that it was always the Pasha's wish that my Lady should one day become my wife. You will see ... all will be well again ... for all of us.'

'Oh, do you think so?' said Elizabeth hopefully. But her expression suggested that the hope was mixed with considerable doubt.

Mikhilo, in his silky voice, added:

'But you must stand firm. You must not release him. As a gentleman ... a man of honour ... I am sure he will keep his bargain ... if you insist.'

Elizabeth sniffed. She was not at all sure she wanted Stephen if he didn't want her. But anyhow, she'd do as the Prince suggested and try to stop this folly ... at least until she had time to get in touch with Mummy and ask her advice. Mummy might, of course, tell her to give back her ring at once and show some pride. She'd have to see, and perhaps try to have a talk with Iris Lowell herself ... make *her* give Stephen up.

'I think we ought to go back to the others now,' she said primly to Usref.

He bowed and gave her his arm. They retraced their footsteps through the Palace grounds back to the terrace. Elizabeth felt rather tired and 'fed-up,' as she mentally classed it; so fed-up indeed, that she didn't even want to see Stephen again tonight. She wanted to go home ... to bed. These Egyptians kept outlandish hours. It was long past midnight.

Usref whispered to her as they reached the other guests, 'Stand firm. I beg you–'

But he had no conviction that Elizabeth was capable of standing firm either in her love affairs or anything else. She was far too weak and casual and superficial. No ... *she* would never get Stephen Daltry back from Iris Lowell. Mikhilo Usref decided to face up to that fact without further waste of time. He must act ... and act without scruple ... or watch his Lady of Moonlight spirited away to England by that damned English diplomat under his very nose.

The guests were saying good night ... Usref and Elizabeth joined them. For each Iris had a graceful and gracious word, standing on the upper step in a golden glow of light that shone through the open long windows of the Palace. She looked tired and pale. Stephen was talking to Nila Fahmoud. The Persian boy, Omar, kissed Iris's finger-tips and made one of his most poetic speeches in parting.

Elizabeth went up to Stephen. He looked at her in an embarrassed way. Deliberately she said:

'Good night, Steve. I'm going to ask you to take me to Cairo. Back to the Wilsons, tomorrow, if you will.'

He frowned uneasily.

'My dear ... I don't know if I can ... you shouldn't have come, you know. You've put me in a very difficult position. I have work to do here. I've got to carry out the promise I made–'

'To me – or to a stranger who happened to die beside you?' she cut in sarcastically.

He flushed.

'You have every right to reproach me. I'm more than sorry about this ... as I've already told you. But it will be better ... make things much easier ... if you'll only accept facts, Liz ... no matter how hard.'

'I'm not going to make it easy for you to chuck me and marry your goddess,' she said with sudden anger. 'Neither do I intend to leave Upper Egypt and crawl back to the Wilsons – jilted and humiliated.'

'For heaven's sake!' he protested, his face

a dark red. 'It was the last thing I ever intended. You know I have no wish to humiliate you. I didn't dream you'd come out to Egypt.'

'It's as well for you that I did,' she jibed.

He made a gesture of despair. He did not recognise the girl he had once wanted to marry. He could see how easy it was for men and women to deceive each other ... and themselves ... how mistaken they could be in each other. He had never known the real Elizabeth ... although he had always had a vague distrust of his future mother-in-law. He knew that Lady Martyn was 'a cat.' Well, it seemed the daughter was the same. Elizabeth was justified in being angry with him, disappointed, bitter, because he had changed his mind. But nobody was justified in being malicious. And what was an engagement between two people for but to enable them to get to know each other, then decide if marriage was the best thing? Marriage was sacred ... a binding tie. But an engagement could surely, with decency and no lack of respect, be broken? Elizabeth was showing herself at her very worst over this.

'I'll see you tomorrow ... you'd better come over to the Fahmouds' place,' she was saying.

He forced himself to answer:

'Very well...'

Their gaze met for a moment. She saw a steely look in those light-grey eyes of his which frightened her for a moment. Stephen was not to be talked over or cajoled; he was adamant, she reflected, and a strong feeling of a frustration and injured pride overruled completely her sense of good sportmanship. She added under her breath:

'I won't give you up. I just *won't*...'

He did not answer, but dug his teeth into his lower lip. He felt himself shaking. He saw Elizabeth's pink, mulish face through a kind of mist. He had stood almost as much as he could take today, he thought. The long-drawn-out strain of that banquet ... with both Iris and Elizabeth there ... had been the last straw. Now he felt as though all his tremendous love and longing for Iris Lowell was culminating into a mighty torrent which would shortly break its borders and submerge them both.

He turned his gaze to Iris. She had said the last 'good night' ... to Elizabeth. He fancied he saw an almost scared, appealing look in those great eyes of hers as she spoke to the other girl. Elizabeth thanked her for the 'party' in a formal, indifferent sort of way, then added:

'We must have a talk some time...'

Stephen ground his teeth together. Savagely he thought: 'No ... I won't have

Iris hurt and bewildered by Elizabeth's malice. She wouldn't understand it. I can hardly tolerate it myself. It's *damnable*.'

Iris stood immovable ... her slender hands clasped together as though in mute supplication.

Now at last everybody had gone. Nila, with a last fond kiss, whispering: 'We must have a long talk, dearest...' Omar, flattering .... Mikhilo begging for an hour alone with her ... and the girl Elizabeth ... she, too, wanting to 'talk.' They all wanted to talk. What about? Stephen, of course ... about Stephen and *her*. It all terrified Iris. She had never before known persecution, or come up against such human characteristics as evil, jealousy, greed ... all the base emotions which seemed to have broken loose in her beautiful peaceful Palace. She had never known a day's unhappiness until her father died. But now ... suddenly she was confronted with it. It seemed like a huge dark monster waiting to spring; to crush her. None of these guests was her friend. Even Nila had assumed the aspect of an enemy ... wanting, with the rest, to get Stephen away from her. As for Elizabeth ... oh, heavens! *she* would never give Stephen up ... it was written all over her face... She was determined to hang on to him no matter what he felt about it. That was not love. *It could not be*. If Stephen told her, Iris, tonight that his

195

happiness lay with Elizabeth she would vanish from his life as rapidly as she had entered it.

A low cry broke from her ... and suddenly she turned to the man with outstretched hands.

'Stephen ... Stephen ... my beloved ... they want to take you from me – or me from you. Oh, *Stephen,* what shall we do?'

It was a cry of such pain and fear that it wrung the man's heart. It appalled him to think that he, personally, was partially responsible for bringing this lovely, sensitive creature, so unschooled in the world ... in contact with such misery.

Here they were alone on the moonlit terrace ... while in Iris's suite Ayesha waited to undress her lady ... and in her room Miss Morgan read, for the hundredth time, her cherished, much-used edition of *Jane Eyre* ... listening for Iris to pass her door ... and look in to whisper 'Good night,' which she always did, no matter how late it was.

Iris and Stephen were alone ... with the magic of the deep Egyptian night bathing them in a glitter of starlight ... of tense, hot silence ... broken only by the occasional harsh, sad call of the white peacocks disturbed in their nests.

Stephen sprang towards the girl's golden, shimmering figure. And the next moment she was in his arms. The barriers of the day

... of the last few days ... crumbled. In that poignant moment, fraught with a dozen varying, bittersweet emotions ... nothing could keep them apart. They were together ... his arms crushing her close to him ... her hands locked about his neck ... her face lifted, pale and rapt, for his kiss. In a wild delirium of feverish love, of hunger that came from the depths of their beings ... they clung, kissing, as though in a mad, hopeless effort to assuage the desire that had been so long leashed...

Between the long, deep kisses they murmured brokenly to each other.

'I love you ... Iris, my darling, darling love ... I want you more than anything in the world. I can't let you go.'

'Stephen ... Stephen ... I never knew that love could be like this. Beloved, hold me closer ... closer ... never let me go again...'

'My dear ... my sweet ... my lovely one ... I shall never let you go. You're dearer than my own life to me now.'

'Stephen ... say it again. Tell me that I am the one you love ... that there will never be anybody else.'

'Never, never anybody else, darling. It is you – now and for always. Oh, Iris, Iris, if only I had known you were coming into my life ... no other woman would have had even a fragment of my love. Forgive me for not knowing ... not waiting.'

'I forgive it ... beloved, I understand. And I think the gods were kind to me ... for I waited for you. You are first and last with me. Stephen, you will not let anything separate us now? Swear it.'

He drew a deep breath, looked dazedly down into the big gazelle-like eyes ... kissed the blue-stained lids and curving lashes ... the smooth cream and gold of her throat ... just above the rim of the turquoise collar ... lifted the slender hands and kissed each fragrant palm in turn ... then turned, hungrily, again to her lips.

But he did not answer her ... and suddenly the ecstasy of passion died a little in her. She caught his arms between her slim, jewelled fingers.

'Stephen ... what is it? Are you afraid that something ... *somebody* will separate us now? Stephen ... will you go to *her* if she refuses to release you?'

Passion in the man, too, had cooled. Love remained ... an insatiable hunger ... and a tenderness such as he had never known possible. But he was a prey to doubt, to a dozen anxieties, and could not keep the fact from Iris. He cupped her face between his hands and looked long and deeply into her eyes. Then he let her go. He stared beyond her at the distant Nile. His face was grave and concerned.

'My sweet Iris ... I shall never give you up

now. I could not. You are my life now ... just as I am yours. But it isn't going to be easy. Elizabeth as I knew her was a kind and gentle sort of girl who would always demand fair play herself ... and give it. She has changed out of recognition. Or else it is that I am only seeing her now as she is ... and always was – but it isn't a pleasant discovery.'

Iris drew a deep breath. Doubts were flitting like little sinister moths in and out of her mind ... threatening to settle there ... to destroy the delicate fabric of her peace and contentment. She put a hand up to lips that were still stinging from Stephen's passionate kisses. In a low voice she said:

'It frightens me ... very much, Stephen. Can human beings change so? Is all love transient ... are all affections impermanent ... all beauty and appreciation a delusion? Oh, Stephen ... but for our meeting you would have married *her*. Will you one day wake from this dream that we are dreaming to find *me* no longer what you imagined?'

The immaturity and pathos behind that cry brought Stephen back to her side. He gathered her close in his arms again, kissing every lovely feature of her face, and burying his hot lips against her dark, heavy hair. The golden rose pinned to the silken waves broke. The petals fluttered down to her bare shoulders. And there his lips, too, rested for an instant in caressing tenderness.

'Oh, my love, my wonderful Iris, don't be afraid ... I shall never change my mind where you are concerned. Sometimes one knows beyond all doubt that a thing is right. I feel like that about our love. I shall never stop loving you, my darling. Our love is not impermanent, neither is the beauty we have found and shall go on finding a delusion. It is real and lasting. Have no fear, my sweetheart.'

Comforted, she stood there, leaning her slender weight against him, her cheek pressed to his.

'What are we going to do, Stephen?' she whispered.

'I don't know, darling,' he said candidly. 'I haven't quite made up my mind what is the best thing to do now that Elizabeth has taken up this attitude. The only thing I have *quite* decided is that I could never marry her now; that it must be you ... or nobody.'

'Then it will be me, my Stephen,' Iris said on the old joyous note. 'For I love you so much that I cannot even visualise an existence which does not include you.'

'Darling,' he said unsteadily, 'darling ... I'm very grateful ... and humble ... and God forgive me if I ever hurt you or your love.'

Once more they kissed ... lingeringly, deeply, conscious of a unity which was of the mind as well as the body ... and Iris in particular, with her strong psychic sense, knew as she stood there in his embrace that they had loved like this a thousand years ago ... in another life ... another form ... but under these same stars ... beside the green, brooding waters of this same Nile.

Suddenly, with one of her queer mental flashes back to the dead yet unforgotten past ... as though she saw it written and illustrated on one of the parchment sheets of papyrus excavated from the Isis Temple ... a vision came to her.

It was a vision of ancient Egypt ... and of her temple as it used to be, before it half crumbled into the dust of time. On such a hot, moonlit night as this she saw it ... rising in all its magnificence of colonnade and courtyard ... of great fluted pillars on lotus-shaped base, painted with the violent colours loved and so often adopted by the people of that epoch.

She could not see into the inner darkness of the great edifice. But outside, in what her father had reproduced as the Court of Lions ... alabaster animals, lying supine on marble pillars, forming an avenue ... she saw two figures, both clad in long linen dresses and headcloths. A man and a young girl.

So strong was the hallucination that Iris could almost smell the odour of musk and amber and incense ... drifting from the inner temple ... a perfume she knew and recognised. For in that other life she had been of royal descent ... and admitted into the mysteries of Isis worship. Now she could see the face of the girl ... *as her own*. Then the man's face, too, became distinct ... and it was Stephen's. He, too, was of noble lineage. She knew that from the type of garment he wore, his headdress and the big jewel ... an emerald ... on the third finger of his left hand. Now the two figures were merged as one in an impassioned embrace. Iris's heart beat quickly ... she wanted to look away ... to break this spell... She did not wish to look upon disaster ... if it was to follow. *But she could not turn away.* The hallucination persisted.

Stephen saw her staring towards the ruined temple with a fixed, terrified expression on her white face. He touched her arm, but she did not move or look at him. It was as though she was in a trance. Only her slim fingers writhed, suddenly, convulsively, locked together.

The premonition of disaster was now an accomplished fact in Iris's vision. For suddenly the Court of Lions was disturbed by a crowd of people ... strongly lighted by slaves bearing torches ... and the young lovers were rudely torn apart. Iris could not at first see who parted them...

The man was held and bound on one side,

the girl on the other. Iris could plainly define the despair and horror *on the face that was her own.*

But the face of Stephen was hidden from her now. Another figure hid him from view. A voice said:

'The woman ... and the man shall die ... for it is forbidden that they should unite ... I, myself, shall put the man to the death...'

The one who spoke turned and Iris saw him – recognised the handsome, malevolent features of *Mikhilo Usref* ... saw the gleam of a knife in his hand. Then the vision was blacked out and faded before her horrified gaze.

She screamed. Miss Morgan up in her room heard that cry and came hurrying to the window. Ayesha and two sleepy *suffragis* ran on to the terrace. Stephen caught Iris in his arms. He saw that her face was ashen, wet with terror.

'Darling!' he exclaimed. *'Darling,* for God's sake what is it?'

She clung to him, shivering violently, unable to speak. She could not tell him what she had just seen. She dared not. Somehow she felt that if she recounted her vision it might come true ... that separation and death might indeed be the end of their love, their loving.

Mikhilo Usref was going to try to kill Stephen. Of that much she was certain.

Half walking, half carried by Stephen, she managed to get up to her suite. But he could not make her tell him what she had seen to terrify her so. And all his kisses, all his assurances of love, could not comfort her.

15

The effect of the extraordinary and terrifying vision which Iris had seen as she looked at the excavated Isis Temple that night was far-reaching. In the morning Stephen waited vainly for her to come down and join him in the cool library where they had talked and studied her father's papers during the last week. Instead, Miss Morgan appeared, her gaunt face still showing signs of her recent fever. She bade the young man 'good morning' with the amiability which she always felt towards him, then said:

'I am sorry ... Iris is not well. She has asked me to send you her dear love and to beg you to excuse her today. I do not think she will come down.'

Stephen's pulses jerked. He looked anxiously at the governess.

'Is she ill? Hasn't she recovered from last night?'

'No, she seems to have had some kind of shock. She has a slight temperature and feels ill, although she has refused to see her doctor and assures me there is nothing radically wrong. So I have left her, as she wishes, to be alone and to sleep if she can.'

'But, Miss Morgan, what is it? What threw her into that state last night?' asked Stephen, pulling a chair forward for the old woman.

She sat down and gave another long sigh.

'It is more difficult for you to understand than I ... I who have looked after her since she was a small child... Her mental processes are not as other girls'. Until the Pasha's death and your entry into this place she was not encouraged, as you know, to think along normal lines. That is one of the great wrongs her poor father did her. He forgot that by secluding her from realities, and concentrating on the development of her mind ... in the cultural sense ... steeping her in the history and mysticism of ancient Egypt ... he was risking her whole life's happiness. And it was a risk which we have now proved to be unjustified. For she is like a delicate, exotic flower which has suddenly been torn from a greenhouse and subjected to the cold and harshness of the weather outside. It is an ordeal for her – a fearful test for her strength. Her mental strength, you understand?'

'I do understand,' said Stephen, his brows knit, his grey eyes clouded. 'My poor little Iris. She is so full of strange fancies and psychic premonitions, and all the trappings of the dead civilisation, that this sudden precipitation into modern life with its mixture of hard commonsense and rather cruel realism is enough to shock her.'

'Although on the whole I am proud to see that she has stood up to it bravely. She has great courage,' added Miss Morgan. 'And her feelings for you if I may say so have been a tremendous help to her... Love is a great thing, Mr Daltry. To her, the greatest ... and it has taken the edge off the pain of losing her father. In time it will, I think, even reconcile her to being uprooted from the "Little Palace".'

'That is a thing which I sometimes debate in my own mind,' said Stephen gloomily. 'In fact I am now very uncertain as to the wisdom of Lowell Pasha's final request. Having seen so much of her here in her own surroundings, I doubt if it *will* be best for her to be forced to lead the life of an ordinary modern girl in a place like London. The idea is beginning to horrify me. And yet ... one has no option but to carry out the Pasha's wishes.'

Miss Morgan bit her lip.

'It would all be so much easier for her ... and I would be so much easier in my mind *about* her if...' She broke off, colouring a little. Stephen finished for her quickly.

'If I could take care of her – as my wife?' he said in a low tone.

'Yes. That would be the perfect solution,' said the old woman with a kindly look at the young man's handsome, sensitive face. 'I believe in my heart that you two were meant for each other. I have watched ... and waited to say this.'

'I am grateful for your belief in me, Miss Morgan. And I can never tell you what *she* means to me.'

'But the way is not yet clear, alas.'

Stephen dug his teeth into his lower lip.

'It must be made clear ... it must be,' he muttered.

'Don't lose heart,' said Miss Morgan with a faint smile. 'I know the situation is a delicate one. But Miss Martyn will most certainly see reason in time and release you. Her present unwillingness to do so is, shall we say, only the obstinacy of the young, coupled with pique. That won't last.'

Stephen gave a short laugh.

'You're very comforting. I hope what you say is true. But Miss Morgan – I still fail to understand what disturbed Iris so greatly last night.'

'She has not told me. But in talking to her I gather she had some premonition of tragedy which may or may not be justified. We need not attach too much importance to it. Iris is and always has been tremendously sensitive. As a child she used to have strange dreams and sometimes frightening ones which kept her awake for hours. Her father used to sit with her and talk or read to her.

She would soon recover. She will recover from this ... if she is left alone.'

Stephen sighed.

'Well, God grant there is to be no more tragedy for her.'

'Amen,' said Miss Morgan fervently. 'Mr Daltry, I assure you she is so intrinsically good and sweet, and has always lived in such peace and beauty, I tremble to think of her being plunged into suffering and distress – even though I realise that she cannot escape either ... no man can escape his share of suffering. But one resents it for those one loves.'

'How right you are!' he said. 'I loathe to think of her being so much as touched by unhappiness.'

'Don't worry,' said Miss Morgan, rising and laying a hand on Stephen's shoulder. 'It will all work out. Ayesha and I will take care of her today and see that she rests. I think quite frankly she is overwrought ... after the strain of last night.'

'I think we all are,' said Stephen with another brief laugh.

Mandulis came in, his slippered feet echoing on the polished floor. He announced that Miss Martyn had called to see Her Excellency.

Stephen and Miss Morgan voluntarily turned to each other.

'Iris must not be disturbed on any

account,' exclaimed the old governess.

'And certainly not subjected to a cross-examination by Elizabeth,' muttered Stephen. 'I will see her. I don't know why she has come. She asked me to call on her this morning, and I had meant to do so later.'

'I'll leave you,' said Miss Morgan.

A few moments later Elizabeth was shown into the library.

Stephen was prepared for fresh obstruction and unpleasantness. To his surprise he saw that Elizabeth was dressed in a grey flannel suit, wearing a big straw hat and looking ready for a journey rather than a day in the sun. She gave him a quick, rather sulky glance, then uttered one of her nervous laughs.

'Oh, so I'm not to be allowed to see Her Highness or whatever she is called.'

'Iris is ill, Elizabeth,' said Stephen.

'Oh!' said Elizabeth.

Stephen, hands in pockets, eyed her dubiously.

'What did you want to say to her?' he asked.

'Oh, I wasn't going to be unpleasant,' said Elizabeth. 'I just thought I'd ask her a few things ... such as whether she really thinks she can make you happy – considering the life she has led – and the one *you* lead.'

Stephen's face coloured.

'That is scarcely the kind of question she could be expected to answer rationally, my dear girl. Naturally she thinks she can make me happy ... as I think and hope I shall be happy with her – strange though that may seem to you. But we do seem to understand each other.'

'I see. Well, I admit *I* don't understand you. You're not at all what I thought ... or what Mummy and Daddy thought.'

'I'm sorry, Liz,' he said gently.

'Oh, it's all right. I'm not sure I ever was in love with you in the way a girl should be in love with the man she marries. We hadn't much in common really. I realised that at the dinner last night.'

Stephen's heart jerked.

'Do you mean that, Elizabeth?'

'Yes,' she said, shrugging her shoulders. 'I thought it over most of the night and came to the conclusion I was making myself jolly cheap by trying to hang on to you. I know Mummy'd think the same. We just weren't meant to marry. So far as I am concerned ... it's over. Here you are.'

She opened her bag, drew out the solitaire diamond he had given her and dropped it into his hand.

He took it for a moment, nonplussed, then gave it back to her.

'My dear Liz, I don't want this. If you don't hate me too much, please keep it as a gift from a friend. And Liz ... if you really mean this ... I thank you very much, my dear, and I do most deeply regret–'

'Oh, you needn't bother to apologise,' she broke in with a short laugh. 'I behaved rather badly yesterday and I admit it.'

'I've behaved badly too, Liz. But I just couldn't help it and that's that...'

She shrugged her shoulders again.

'There you are! I admit she's pretty attractive.'

'It's more than that,' said Stephen. Then, with the feeling that a huge weight was being lifted from his shoulders, he looked at Elizabeth and added: 'What made you change so suddenly, Liz?'

'Oh, what I've just told you.'

'Did Nila Fahmoud say anything?'

'Oh, she's dead keen on me not breaking the engagement. She's all on Prince Usref's side. You seem to have butted in on *his* wicket, Stephen.'

'Not at all. There was never anything between Iris and Usref,' said Stephen angrily.

'Oh, well, I couldn't care less,' said Elizabeth. 'I'm quite impartial this morning. All I want is to get back to Cairo and then home. And as a matter of fact you've no cause to dislike the Prince so much. He was half responsible for me making up my mind to clear out. He suggested it.'

Stephen both looked and felt astounded.

'*Usref* suggested that?'

'Yes. At first he told me to try and get you back, then this morning he changed his mind and said – quite reasonably I thought – that on second thoughts he'd decided all men are perverse idiots and that the more I tried to hold on, the more determined you'd be to get away. So in the long run I shall save a lot of trouble by giving way gracefully now, at once.' She giggled and lowered her eyelids.

Stephen was silent. His brain, the cool, astute brain of the trained diplomat, was at work. Nothing would make him believe that Mikhilo Usref, of all people, would have swung round to this way of thinking and helped to influence Elizabeth to make things easy for him and Iris ... unless there was some base ulterior motive behind it. Stephen knew perfectly well that Usref himself was madly in love with Iris. No ... if he had suggested this breaking of the engagement there was a very good or, rather ... a very bad ... reason for it. At the moment Stephen was puzzled ... he could not make it out. However, he decided that he would be foolish to worry about Usref or his conduct just now. The main thing was that he was free ... Elizabeth had given in and was going home. *He was free to marry Iris as soon as her aunt gave him permission to do so.*

Stephen's eyes shone with sudden exultation. He put out a hand and gripped Elizabeth's.

'Thanks, Liz. You *are* a sportsman,' he said huskily. 'Try not to hold it against me. And Liz, if it'll make things better for you and in Lady M.'s sight, will you say *you* broke it ... not I ... that when you got out here you decided you didn't care for me any more?'

Elizabeth looked rather pleased. After all, that *did* put a better construction on things.

'Okay,' she said. 'If it's all the same to you, I'll say that. And there's one thing I am going to ask you.'

'Anything, Liz.'

'Will you take me back to Cairo? I hate travelling alone in Egypt.'

'Of course,' said Stephen. 'We'll drive to Assuan and fly from there. Leave it to me. I'll fix it.'

Some hours later Iris awoke in her flower-filled bedroom to find that it was afternoon. The green shutters were closed, excluding the hot sunlight. Ayesha sat beside her, watching her beloved mistress. Iris sat up, conscious of fatigue and headache, despite her long slumber. And suddenly more than anything in the world she wanted to see Stephen ... she must get up and go down to him ... she must be held close in this arms ... close ... close ... so that all her dark visions, all the fear and horror of last night, should be finally and absolutely banished.

But before she could even issue the order to the old nurse to run her bath Ayesha handed her an envelope.

'A note to be given to my Lady as soon as she awakened.'

Iris pushed the dark cloud of hair back from her hot young face and opened the envelope. The note was from Stephen. Rapidly she scanned it.

My beautiful darling, our troubles are more or less at an end. Elizabeth came here this morning to give me my freedom. All is well for us and you need worry no more, my sweetest heart. She has asked me to take her to Cairo and I could not deny her this. We are taking the midday plane from Assuan. As soon as possible I will fly back to you. I shall live only to hold you in my arms again. I love you more than ever.

Stephen.

Iris's large dark eyes dilated as she read and re-read these words. At first a sharp thrill of relief and pleasure ran through her. Then she caught her breath. *Stephen had gone to Cairo.* He was flying, even at this moment, all those hundreds of miles away from her. Why had Elizabeth wanted him to go to Cairo with her? Just a caprice ... a last wish to be possessive ... to be with him, poor girl ... or...?

Iris's thoughts carried her no farther. Suddenly she clapped her hands. Her face was paling.

'Ayesha,' she said in Arabic, 'go at once to Mandulis. Bid him bring His Excellency Prince Usref here. I must speak to him at once.'

Ayesha bowed and retired. Iris sprang out of bed and began to dress, a dozen troubled thoughts spoiling her original pleasure in the thought that Stephen was free at last. She was only half dressed when the old nurse returned.

'Well … has Mandulis gone?' demanded Iris.

'No, my Lady. Mandulis bids me tell you that His Excellency is not here. My lady Nila is even now downstairs talking with my lady Morga…' (The old woman used Iris's name for the governess.)

'What do you mean that His Excellency is not here? I wish him sent for.'

Ayesha bowed low.

'Your pardon, my Lady, but His Excellency is no longer in Upper Egypt. At the last moment I believe he decided to fly also to Cairo with the English lady and gentleman.'

Iris stared wildly at the old nurse. Her face was as pale as the white linen gown she had just put on. She felt herself trembling … sick with nameless fears.

Usref had gone to Cairo ... with Stephen.

She saw again the dark, malevolent face of Mikhilo as she had seen it last night in her vision ... the wicked gleam of the blade in his hand ... and Stephen, bound and defenceless.

She gave a despairing cry.

'Send my lady Morga up here at once ... *at once,* Ayesha...'

For she knew, with unswerving instinct, that Mikhilo Usref had not decided to go with Stephen to Cairo just for the fun of the flight. Usref disliked flying. He had often told her so.

Iris made up her mind, wildly, in that moment, that she must come out of her life-long seclusion in the 'Little Palace,' and follow Stephen and Usref to Cairo, taking Morga with her.

16

It did not take Miss Morgan long to realize that she was up against the steel will and indomitable purpose which had always lain hidden under the soft, gentle façade of her beloved pupil.

Iris had made up her mind to follow Stephen to Cairo and nothing would dissuade her. Miss Morgan kept saying:

'But why, why do such an unorthodox thing? It is madness. No good can come of it. Stephen Daltry can take care of himself, and you have no real reason to suppose he is in danger. Stay quietly at home, my child, and I am sure that your tranquility will be restored to you.'

Like this she tried to reason with the girl, but Iris would have none of it. Having at last poured out the story of her vision of disaster and death she tried to make Miss Morgan believe, too, that Stephen was in peril of his life and that she must follow and warn him; or, better still, find Prince Usref and discover for herself what lay in his mind. Nothing would convince her that there was not treachery in the air until she had made sure of it for herself.

Miss Morgan argued ... what could Iris do even if she reached Cairo and saw Stephen and Mikhilo? They would both look upon her hallucinations as childish nonsense. She would be laughed at. Indeed, the old woman tried to stop Iris from going by intimating that she would be lowering herself in Stephen's estimation – making herself look ridiculous.

But Iris remained deaf to such protests. Having once got into her head that Mikhilo was dangerous – a man whose jealousy might lead him to do terrible things – she could not get it out. She had courage. Now she would have to exercise it, for, as she admitted to Miss Morgan, the idea of leaving the security and peace of the 'Little Palace' for Cairo filled her with dread. She had been to the city only once or twice in her life; when she had driven through the streets in a car sitting veiled, secure beside her father.

She knew that she would loathe Cairo and find much in it to frighten and puzzle her. But obsessed with fear for the man whom she loved so desperately, she did not draw back. Her one concern was for the health of her old friend.

'If you are not well enough to come with me, Morga,' she said, 'you must say so. I will take Mandulis with me. He can be my guide.'

219

But here Miss Morgan showed her own spirit. She was English to the backbone and had never been one to give in. True, she was not quite fit after her bad bout of malaria, but she was well enough to go to Cairo with Iris. Nothing would induce her to abandon her precious charge in a crisis like this.

Miss Morgan knew Cairo. But, filled with doubts and misgivings, she surveyed the girl's white, determined young face.

'Goodness only knows what I am going to do with you, Iris,' she groaned. 'It will be like taking a nun out of a convent. You are not prepared for it.'

But this was defeatism which Iris would not accept. She reminded Miss Morgan that both she and Stephen had been pressing her to come out of her shell and face life as it was lived today. Why not begin now?

To this Miss Morgan had no answer. But on the subject of Iris's clothes she was firm.

'You cannot go to Cairo dressed like this, my poor darling child. You would be too conspicuous. What are we going to do about it? And then, what use is it to rush off now when we do not even know what time the next 'plane leaves Assuan? The one which Mr Daltry and Miss Martyn took has already left.'

'And Mikhilo is with them,' said Iris agitatedly. Then she added: 'But fortunately money is no object with us. You shall telephone to the airport and order a special 'plane to take us at once to Cairo. As for my clothes...' she looked a trifle wistfully down at the long, exquisitely embroidered linen gown that swathed her slender body... 'No, I suppose I cannot go to Cairo like this.'

'You have no clothes and mine would be laughable for you,' said Miss Morgan plaintively. 'Oh dear, I wish you would give up this wild-goose chase...'

Iris shook her head.

'We leave as soon as possible, Morga. Tell Ayesha to pack a bag for me. Go, command the 'plane for us and let us waste no more time. It may seem crazy to you, dear Morga, but I know that I am right. Every instinct in me tells me that Mikhilo is a traitor.'

Miss Morgan retired, defeated. This was an echo of the old Iris, issuing royal commands. In this mood she was not to be argued with. And perhaps, after all, there might be something in it, the old woman thought. Iris did have the most uncanny premonitions.

Nila Fahmoud had gone back to her own house without seeing Iris. At one time Iris would have welcomed her little Egyptian friend, just as she had always welcomed Usref. But today she could think of neither of them as her friends.

She busied herself now with the problem of dress. She had no modern clothes of her own, but she knew that in the wing of the 'Little Palace' in which her beautiful mother had once had her rooms everything had been left untouched. Romney Lowell had wished it so when he had returned from London after his wife's tragic death. He had ordered Helena's suite to be left untouched … save that it was to be regularly cleaned and her clothes preserved in drawers and cupboards, filled with spices and perfumes which kept them from the moth.

With a queer, fatalistic feeling in her heart, Iris entered the big bedroom which had belonged to her mother and ordered the *suffragis* to open the shutters.

She had never been here before. Her father used to visit this wing occasionally. To him it had been a shrine wherein lay stored the endless, treasured memories of his love.

The sun poured in … the beautiful, luxurious room came suddenly alive. It was all silver and a soft madonna blue which had been Helena Lowell's favourite colour. The faint perfume of cedarwood, of lemon and eucalyptus, the unguents which were used to keep everything fresh, lingered here. The tall windows, like Iris's, opened on to wide balconies overlooking the Nile and the excavated Temple of Isis.

A feeling of deep awe and sadness gripped the young girl as she stood looking around her. Somehow she felt that the spirit of her mother was near. *She* would understand ... she who had loved so much and whose heart had belonged to Egypt.

'*If only my mother were alive and here today!*' thought Iris in anguish. Never had she needed her advice, support and her knowledge of the world more than now. So complete had been the metamorphosis that had taken place in the soul of Iris since Stephen's coming and her chaotic plunge into a life far removed from the one she used to lead that in this moment – for the first time – she realised the mistake her father had made.

Standing here in this room, haunted by the ghost of Helena Lowell ... Helena's daughter could see how unfit she was to go to Cairo and deal with the sinister problems which had suddenly arisen. She trembled at the mere idea of it. She would like to have flung herself down on her mother's bed in a passion of tears. But, instead, she controlled her emotions and went on with the task she had set herself.

She bade Ayesha open the great cedar-wood cupboards. With a trembling hand she touched the clothes that hung therein; one by one she lifted them out and looked at them.

She knew what girls 'in the world' were wearing today. She was used to Nila's modern style of dress although she did not care for it. Now she saw that many of her mother's things, which had been made for Helena twenty-one years ago, were quite fashionable. By no means would Iris look out of place in them.

She chose a dress of cool grey linen imprinted with a floral design of pale yellow and a grey coat of the same material waisted with a wide yellow belt of soft suède. It was very French and chic. Taking off her long white gown she put on the grey dress and coat. She was amazed to find that they fitted her perfectly. Her mother had been of the same slender build. Ayesha found silk stockings, gossamer thin, and little grey lizard shoes. These, too, fitted Iris.

Amazed and somewhat scared, she looked at herself in one of the long mirrors. She could not recognise herself. It gave her almost a shock. For she had seen a photograph of her mother, amongst the thousands that Romney Lowell had taken, in this same suit. Iris remembered suddenly her father telling her that the ensemble had been made by a Paris *couturier* in Alexandria for Helena to wear when they spent a brief holiday there.

It might have been Helena Lowell looking at herself in that same mirror; only she had been golden-haired and this girl was dark, and Helena had laughed and loved and been happy and fulfilled. But Iris, also in love, was at the same time most unhappy and afraid.

Quickly she chose a *crêpe* silk scarf, daffodil-coloured, to wind around her head; a pair of gloves and a grey lizard bag ... yes, everything to match was there ... all the lovely things her mother had used before she, Iris, was born. Then, feeling almost that she had desecrated the shrine, Iris bade Ayesha lock up the cupboards again and went back to her own wing.

She felt embarrassed and unlike herself in the short skirt and high-heeled shoes – accustomed as she was to sandals and her long robe. But her mind was made up and she was not to be deterred. She even wondered, with the faintest and most normal touch of girlish vanity, what Stephen would think of her dressed like this!

She met Miss Morgan in the corridor. The old woman gave a little scream at the sight of her.

'Mercy on us, what a fright you've given me! I thought it was your dear mother herself come back,' she said in a shaken voice. And she stared at the little grey-clad modern figure hardly able to credit her eyesight. She thought how lovely the child looked – perfect. The cycle of Helena Lowell's fashion had come round again. She looked right, even to the dark braided hair. That style of coiffure was up to date.

'We must hurry, Morga,' said Iris. 'What news of the 'plane?'

Somewhat reluctantly Morga announced that whilst Iris had been dressing she had arranged everything, and a special 'plane was being flown at their expense to take them to Cairo within the next couple of hours.

Later that day Iris and Miss Morgan started out on their journey.

Iris felt no fear as she sat beside the old governess in a deep-cushioned seat of the small aircraft in which they were being piloted across the desert.

It was the first time that she had flown. It was the first time that she appeared in modern dress before the eyes of the world or walked through an airport and been spoken to by officials, treated as an ordinary human being.

Ordinary, except that it had soon been rumoured at the airport that Lowell Pasha's daughter had chartered 'a special' and everybody had had a good look at her. The young pilot flying them had, in fact, given one look at the girl in grey and yellow and decided that she had the most magnificent eyes he had ever seen, and told his friends that he was 'knocked flat.'

It had all seemed strange to Iris, but her fears were for Stephen alone. For herself and her personal safety she had none. As the machine left the ground she had only one burning resolve in her heart ... to follow and find her love and make sure that her terrible vision had indeed been only hallucination and nothing more.

She did not find flying a particularly agreeable sensation, although the speed seemed to her miraculous. And being the girl she was, she looked with deepest interest at the desert and the Nile valley over which they were flying. Finally she was both moved and thrilled when they came within sight of the Pyramids ... the great Tomb of Cheops ... and the immortal shadow of the Sphinx lying there thousands of feet below them.

Now she could see Cairo ... the Citadel, the mosques and minarets, the old Mousky, the tortuous streets and alleys, then the modern buildings, built along the broad ribbon of the Nile, with its many bridges, Cairo in early summer, with that faint haze ... almost like a cloud of dust ... that seems to hang over it like a faintly ominous veil.

Miss Morgan buckled on her safety belt as they began to make a landing at Heliopolis, and glanced dubiously at Iris. But the girl was truly wonderful, she thought, so calm and collected. No nerves.

'Where do you wish to go first of all, my dear?' she asked.

'First of all, how are you feeling, Morga?'

asked Iris in return.

'Quite all right. Would it not be best for us to drive direct to the Heliopolis Palace where your father and mother used to stay and get our rooms there before we go on to Cairo?'

Iris considered this. Yes, she said, they could do that, then take a car and drive straight to the city.

'To the Legation – to find Mr Daltry?' asked Miss Morgan.

'No,' said Iris slowly. 'To Shepheards.'

'Good gracious, why Shepheards?'

Miss Morgan's memory of the famous hotel was that at this time of the year it was a crowded and noisy place, overlooking a dust-laden street teeming with tourists and beggars, and not at all suitable for her unfledged girl.

But Iris said:

'We will go there, Morga. I do not want to see Stephen yet. I want to see Mikhilo. When he is in Cairo he stays at Shepheards. He has told me so.'

'As you wish, my dear,' said the old woman meekly.

17

Mikhilo Usref walked into the crowded vestibule of Shepheards Hotel at six o'clock that evening, wiping the perspiration from his handsome, aquiline features, although he looked cool enough in his smart white suit. But as he took off his sun-glasses his eyes expressed acute dissatisfaction.

This trip to Cairo (which he detested in the summer) had not been at all to his liking and he half regretted having advised that little fool, Elizabeth Martyn, to break with Stephen and persuade him to see her off. But Usref had done this for a variety of reasons. Predominating was the belief that if Elizabeth refused to release her fiancé (which Usref had at first wanted her to do), it would only result in Stephen remaining at the 'Little Palace.' A sort of three-sided battle would ensue between Stephen, Iris and Elizabeth, and it might even end in Stephen and Iris feeling so frustrated that they would decide to run away together.

Mikhilo's passion for Iris had assumed such mad proportions now that he had made up his mind to go to any lengths in order to gain his desire. He had also decided that there was only one way of doing it and that was to make sure that Stephen Daltry was given no further opportunity to get Iris for himself.

No, Mikhilo had decided that the world could no longer hold both the Englishman and himself.

In Iris's well-guarded Palace he could do Stephen no harm. There *her* word was law. He must therefore get Stephen to Cairo, where there were ways and means ... many dark alleys at night ... many prowling figures ... men of mixed blood who would commit a crime for a few *piastres*.

So far, so good. At the last moment he had joined Stephen and Elizabeth at Assuan, telling them that urgent business recalled him to the city. Nila had been surprised, but the other two were neither interested nor concerned. At the airport in Cairo they had parted. And when Stephen drove off in a taxi with Elizabeth he had had no idea that Usref 'shadowed' him.

He had followed them to the B.O.A.C. Booking Centre (presumably Elizabeth was going to get the first possible passage home). Then they had come out again and gone to Zamelek, crossing the famous Kasrel-Nil Bridge to the Wilsons' flat, facing Gezirah Sporting Club. Usref guessed that Stephen would deposit his one-time fiancée with her friends and leave her there.

Usref had had to crouch, unseen, in his own car, hot and cursing, for two hours before Stephen emerged again ... this time alone. Then Usref had presented himself ... on pretence that he had just arrived at this particular block of flats to see friends of his. He had suggested that Stephen should drink with him later on. Stephen had declined coldly. Then when Usref had ventured to ask if he were staying in Cairo the night, Stephen had, with the same coldness, answered in the affirmative and said that Miss Martyn had managed to find a seat which someone had cancelled on tomorrow's flying-boat to England, and that he was waiting at her request to see her off.

'I presume that you will then go back to the "Little Palace"?' Usref had said with a glittering smile.

Without a smile Stephen had answered: 'Yes, that is my intention...'

And then Usref had lost sight of him, which was his reason for returning to Shepheards in an ill-humour. Of course he could easily find out where Daltry was going to spend the night and the rest would be easy ... Mikhilo had one or two useful friends – some of his own starving country-men, for instance – in this city. But Mikhilo was not particularly enjoying himself.

And now, with a considerable shock, he saw the dark-eyed, slender girl in grey and yellow who sat alone at one of the tables in the dim, cool, Moorish lounge of the hotel. At first he thought his sight played tricks with him. They had left his Lady of Moonlight hundreds of miles away in Upper Egypt. *This could not be the same girl.* But it was ... and Mikhilo, quite pale with the shock, heard that well-remembered voice:

'I have been waiting for you,' Iris said.

He came up to her, his eyes staring, the sweat breaking out on his forehead anew.

'You!' he exclaimed.

The dark eyes looked up into his with a profound and piercing scrutiny which seemed to read into the man's very soul. He did not like it. He did not like the fact that she had come here in modern dress like this. He was reduced to stammering.

'My Lady ... what does this mean?... What brings you to Cairo? You should not be here in this place, alone.'

Iris's heart beat rapidly but she retained her composure. She had schooled herself to be very calm; to deal with this thing astutely for Stephen's sake.

'I am not alone,' she said; 'Miss Morgan is with me. We have been sitting here together. When I saw you enter the hotel I asked her to leave us alone. I wish to speak to you.'

He sat down beside her. Half of him was vastly intrigued by the new beauty and attraction of her, dressed like other girls; the

232

other half was afraid. He had an almost superstitious dread at what this strange girl could see written on his face. He knew her extraordinary depths of perception. But he tried to laugh and appear at his ease. He ordered drinks and cigarettes. He bent over her in a caressing way.

'It is divine surprise to find you here,' he murmured. He was enormously flattered that she should wish to see him. 'But you are curiously changed, my Lady,' he ended on a lame note.

She eyed him with that direct and disconcerting scrutiny.

'Yes, I am changed, Mikhilo. And *you*, too, have changed.'

'Why me?'

'Once you were my friend.'

'I am still that and more,' he said eagerly.

'No,' she said in a queer voice, 'you are no longer so. You are my most bitter enemy.'

His olive face coloured and he stiffened.

'What reason has my Lady for saying that?'

'I have seen a vision, Mikhilo,' she said in a low, clear voice. 'A vision of you, Stephen Daltry and myself in the days of the Pharaohs. We loved each other, Stephen and I, but you came between us. There was a knife in your hand. You were going to kill him, Mikhilo. *You have come here to kill him, haven't you, Mikhilo?*'

He was totally unprepared for such a blunt declaration. For an instant he sat beside her dumbly, the beads of sweat pouring down his cheeks, his hands clenched in the pockets of his linen coat. It was as though she had hit him between the eyes. All his superstitious fears returned in full force. There was something more than uncanny about this girl. She literally appalled him by her insight, the grasp of the naked truth which, in its very nakedness, was an ugly thing.

'Well, Mikhilo,' came her inexorable voice, 'am I right?'

He did not answer. It was as though he were stricken dumb. He trembled. But Iris went on:

'I *am* right. You wish to kill the man I love. That is why you came here with him. You are a would-be murderer, Mikhilo. Oh, Mikhilo – are you not afraid of the Hereafter?'

The Serbian strove to find words, to laugh, to deny. But still no words came. Iris went on:

'You *should* be afraid. There can be no peace either in this world or the next for those who stain their hands with crime.' And she added softly. 'But you shall not kill him, Mikhilo – I shall prevent it.'

He said hoarsely:

'My Lady is deranged. There can be no

foundation for what she says. None at all.'

But Iris had seen guilt written on every feature of the man's face and she knew in this instant that she had not come on a fool's errand. She said:

'Nevertheless I shall go to Stephen and warn him of what you mean to do.'

Then Usref recovered his balance. He grew cold and as pitiless as a snake. He had only one desire: to get this girl for himself, and he was not going to allow any of her psychic fancies, her talk of crime and punishment, to deter him. He was in a mood now where he would do anything before he would voluntarily see Iris and Stephen come together.

He stood up and looked down at her through half-shut lids.

'My Lady... You have all my adoration. I will do anything in the world except one thing... I will not see you go to England with Stephen Daltry.'

Now Iris recognised that the challenge had been accepted and the fight was on. With the blood rushing through her veins she also stood up and looked proudly into the man's cruel, handsome face. She wondered why it had been given to her too late to see how cruel that face was in its every contour.

'I love Stephen Daltry and I am going to marry him,' she said steadily.

'No, my Lady,' said Usref softly, 'you are going to marry *me*.'

A look of intense anger and contempt – a look which made him writhe – blazed in her eyes.

'How dare you even suggest such a thing!'

'A man will dare much when he loves, my Lady.'

'You and I have a different idea of the meaning of love,' she said.

'Nevertheless my feeling for you is so strong that nothing and nobody on this earth shall stop me from making you my wife, my Lady of Moonlight,' he said with that smile which showed his white teeth and had nothing of humour or gentleness in it.

She said, 'If I had to choose between you and the grave, Mikhilo, I would choose the grave.'

Then the snake struck.

'But if you had to choose between me, my Lady, and the grave of your Englishman ... what then?'

Iris, brave as she was, with all her tremendous love for Stephen to the fore, felt a little sick and frightened. She sat down again, hurriedly, as though her legs were weak.

'So you *do* mean harm to him,' she whispered.

'It is for you to say.' Mikhilo shrugged his shoulders, then added with one of his flashing smiles: 'I assure you he is not for you, most lovely lady. Neither Stephen Daltry nor an English marriage could make you happy. You were born for me ... for Egypt ... for all that I will be to you if you will give me the chance.'

She was white to the lips now. Her great dark eyes, hunted, looked up at him.

'You mean harm to him,' she repeated.

He shrugged his shoulders.

'Give me that chance which I ask for and Stephen Daltry shall go as free as the air. If he does not interfere with us there will be no need for me to concern myself with him.'

Iris felt herself shivering.

'I shall go to the police ... I shall warn him ... he can be protected.'

Usref smiled again.

'My Lady of Moonlight would be laughed at. She has, after all, nothing to justify her accusation against me save a ... shall we call it ... a mere nightmare? She would be laughed at, and Stephen Daltry would still walk unprotected in Cairo.'

Iris put a hand to her throat. Usref was laying all his cards on the table. All her worst fears were being justified. Sick with horror, she considered what he said.

For an hour they sat there, parrying words. The man cold as steel and ruthless. The girl fighting at first ... fighting for her lover ... and then gradually beaten down, defeated by her very love and fear.

Mikhilo had made it quite clear that if she so much as breathed a word of her fear to Stephen – or the police – or if she allowed Miss Morgan to speak – Stephen would never leave Cairo alive. In turn, Usref threatened and cajoled. Stephen Daltry could never make her happy, he said ... he, Usref, would take her away and teach her what love really meant.

'You will forget the Englishman. You will admit in the end that I have done the best thing for you,' he said, and tried to take her hand.

White and shaking, she drew her hand away.

'Don't touch me; I loathe you,' she said.

His lips curled a little but his veiled eyes drank in the slender beauty that had driven him to such desperate measures.

'All the same, it is to be Stephen Daltry – or me, *and I think you will choose me,* will you not, my Lady?'

She tried to stop herself from trembling. In despair she looked through the lounge, through a crowd of people ... at the figure of Morga faithfully hovering near them. She would not even be able to tell *her* what had passed between Usref and herself. If Stephen was to live she must keep absolute silence. She must say goodbye to him for ever. They would never now live their dream of love together. All their brilliant hopes must die. But anything was better than that *he* should die. It was unthinkable that Stephen, with his lithe body, his fine, sensitive face, his quick mind, should be consigned to the grave by Mikhilo Usref. Oh, God, what a catastrophic end to their love and their desire for each other! Oh, how she hated Cairo, all these people, the noise and clatter and babble of voices ... the curious eyes that peered at her, this ugly, sordid world so different from her home! Oh, if only she could wipe out this obnoxious reptile who sat beside her, daring to speak of love!

But she had come here to save Stephen's life. And she must save it at all costs – even if that cost was to be herself. For she knew that while Stephen and Usref remained together in Egypt Stephen's life would be threatened, and that only she could save him.

After a long, bitter struggle, she surrendered.

'Very well. I must do as you say, even though I loathe and despise you I will do it rather than see Stephen harmed. I will not be responsible for the ending of his beautiful young life.'

Mikhilo gripped her hand. Now it made no resistance, but it was ice-cold in his grasp despite the heat of the evening. His face expressed triumph.

'I swear you will not regret it, my Lady of Moonlight,' he said.

She looked at him with sick scorn.

She wondered how she could bear to pay the price he was demanding from her.

'Very well. But if I am to endure *this* for the rest of my life, you are going to give me one week's grace,' she said slowly. 'My life with you will be death in life, so I demand, first of all, one week's freedom and happiness.'

'What do you mean?'

'I mean that you will go away and stay away and leave me for one week in peace with Stephen and Morga.'

He stared.

'Leave you ... with *him?*'

'Leave me with Morga ... free to see Stephen Daltry when I choose.'

Mikhilo laughed.

'You must think me crazy, my Lady.'

'I think you are the vilest creature on earth – you who were once my friend, and my father's friend,' she said in a low, concentrated voice.

He reddened very slightly, then shrugged.

'There is an English saying, *"Needs must when the devil drives."* I am driven to hard measures ... because I want you for my wife.'

She shuddered.

'I shall always loathe you. But leave Stephen alone and I will keep my share of the bargain. And leave me one week ... leave me these few days to be with him ... to see him ... speak to him.'

'He will guess that something is wrong.'

'He will not guess,' said Iris, her small hands clenched, her breath quickening. 'If it is a question of his safety and well-being, I can act my part.'

Usref eyed her with some doubt and repeated, frowning:

'He will guess.'

'I tell you I can play my part,' she said, and added with sudden passion: 'If you do not allow this ... if you do not let me have one week of peace and happiness, I will risk even *his* precious life! I will go to the police and in my father's name ask them to believe me and give Stephen protection.'

Usref bit his lip. He could see that he was driving this girl to the limit of her endurance. He was even surprised at the force of her feelings for the Englishman. But it did not make him ashamed of his baseness. On the contrary, it roused him to a more burning hatred and jealousy of Stephen Daltry.

He said:

'I assure you that your story would be considered childish and that since you have no proof they would not bother to safeguard

241

Mr Daltry. However ... have your week with the old woman and see your Englishman. But remember – at the end of the week I shall be waiting for you.'

Her small face was colourless. Her great dark eyes held a look which made even Usref, hardened though he was, writhe a little.

'I shall keep my word and shall expect you to keep yours,' she said in a steady voice.

'What will you tell him?'

'I shall say that I wish to see a little of the world before I go to England,' she said after a painful silence. 'I shall say that at the end of the week I will prepare for my journey with him to London. And then ... I will send him a note to say that I have changed my mind and never wish to see him again. To Miss Morgan I shall tell the same story. Neither of them will guess the truth, and I will then disappear from his life.'

Usref regarded her, a certain admiration mingling with his soul-destroying passion for her. She was brave, this young girl. And she was infinitely superior in intellect, in character, to himself. But he had no pity and no remorse.

'Very well,' he said after a pause, 'but I warn you, sweet lady, that one hint to Stephen Daltry of the truth and–'

Iris suddenly interrupted on a note of hysteria foreign to her.

'Oh, go ... get out of my sight!' she said between her teeth. 'Do you not think that I meant it when I told you that I love this man, and that rather than you should hurt a hair of his head I would throw myself into the Nile?'

'But that is not what I wish,' said Mikhilo with a bow. 'I only ask that you should throw yourself into my arms, most Beautiful.'

She picked up her bag which was lying on the table, turned and began to walk away. He thought that even in that modern dress she walked like a queen. Then she turned and gave him a quick look over her shoulder. She said:

'One week from today Mikhilo, I will return here with Morga. You will find us here.'

He bowed again. With that he had to be satisfied. But he knew that Iris Lowell would keep her word. He wondered a little uneasily how the Englishman would accept his *congé*.

Much later that night Stephen Daltry came out of the Wilsons' flat and paused a moment to light a cigarette before walking (as was his intention) back to the Continental Savoy, where he was staying the night.

It was one of those warm, still, starlit

nights of early summer when Cairo is at its best, the dust and heat of the day seem to give place to a tender starlight, an air of mystery and glamour, of moonlight on the Nile, brilliantly lighted bridges, and neon lights flashing from the heart of the metropolis.

Stephen liked walking through Cairo at night. He detested it during the day. At the moment he disliked it altogether. He had but one longing – to return to Upper Egypt where Iris waited for him; Iris and the most exquisite happiness he had ever known.

He had a feeling of inestimable relief tonight. Things seemed to be going right at last. He was able to think of Elizabeth and his engagement without guilt – indeed, Elizabeth had been her old sporting self since they left Upper Egypt; she had even told him that she now shared his opinion that their marriage would never have been a success.

At her request he had spent the evening at the Wilsons'. It had been a friendly dinner party. Sam, in his jovial fashion, introduced a happy note, slapped Stephen on the back, and assured him that a broken engagement was all in the day's work. Mrs Wilson cunningly introduced into the circle a certain Captain Mitchell, a good-looking and charming young officer who had recently come out to the Middle East, and he speedily attached himself to Elizabeth, who was not unmoved by his attentions.

Indeed, so well had the evening gone that Stephen believed it was quite on the cards that Elizabeth would in the future want to see more of her attractive soldier. And the sudden romance developed so far that Elizabeth suggested that Captain Mitchell might see her off tomorrow, and that Stephen could go his own way.

Well, thought Stephen, as he lit his cigarette and flung away the burnt match, it was more than satisfactory, and his heart was lighter than it had been since realising and admitting his love for Iris Lowell.

Suddenly a shape loomed out of the darkness. An Egyptian, wearing a *tarbusch* and with an English tweed coat, incongruously, over his long striped gown, padded up to him.

'Plees, sir ... you, Mr Daltry?'

Stephen stared at the man.

'Yes. Who the devil are you? What do you want?'

The man grinned, and in a jumble of English and Arabic intimated that he had a friend who drove a taxi; that he had just come from Heliopolis to Zamelek with this friend. They were waiting round the corner for Mr Daltry.

Stephen smiled faintly. He knew the strange and wonderful propensities these

245

people had for getting customers. But he did not want to drive. He wished to walk and told the man so.

The Egyptian grinned again.

'Lady wait for you in taxi – very special.'

Stephen blinked at that. Now what the devil was all this about?

'Lady wait in taxi. Told me to fetch you,' repeated the Egyptian.

Stephen put his tongue in his cheek. A few months ago a boyish love of adventure might have led him to investigate this with interest. But so full was his mind and heart of Iris there seemed no room left for any other woman in the world.

'*Impshi* ... *yaller*,' he said good-humouredly, and started to walk away.

But the man ran after him and tugged at his arm.

'Come plees, lady wait long time. Plees, sar–'

Stephen paused, eyed the man dubiously and then said: 'Oh, all right, where is she? What does she want?'

The man piloted him to the corner of the street. A smart new Cairo taxi waited there. Stephen, who was feeling tired now, and anxious to get back to his hotel, opened the door somewhat impatiently and peered inside. The next moment his whole face and demeanour changed. He gave an exclamation.

246

'Good heavens!... Iris!... *You!*'

The girl sitting in the taxi did not speak but held out both hands. Stephen, his heart hammering, his whole body singing with the joy of this totally unexpected meeting, did not pause then to wonder how or why his adored Iris was here. He tossed a ten-*piastre* note to the man who had brought him to her, sprang into the car and slammed the door.

'Iris my *darling*, what a wonderful surprise! I don't think I have been so thrilled in all my life. Where shall I tell the fellow to drive? Where do you want to go?'

He felt her slender fingers twine feverishly about his own, caught the well-remembered, subtle perfume that drifted from her hair ... saw vaguely, and with astonishment, that his beloved wore modern attire and a scarf over her head ... then heard her low, murmured voice:

'Just let me drive with you for a little while. I am staying at the Heliopolis Palace. Morga is there. Let us go out in that direction. But tell the man to drive slowly.'

Without releasing her hands Stephen gave the driver his orders. The fellow grinned, touched his forehead, and they moved smoothly down the Sharia el Gezirah, past the Club, and out towards the Kasr-el-Nil Bridge.

Stephen sat back. With a quick, eager

movement, he drew Iris into his arms. He held her passionately, rapturously close.

'My adorable darling ... this really is the most stupendous surprise. Tell me how you came... *You*, leaving the "Little Palace" ... to come to Cairo ... I can hardly believe it! Tell me everything, my darling.'

But she did not speak. Her heart was too full. He could not know the appalling burden of her thoughts. He must never guess it, she thought in agony of mind. Ever since Usref had struck that vile bargain with her she had been in a state of suppressed emotion. After he had gone she had played her part well, even to the pitch of convincing Miss Morgan that her meeting with Usref had set her mind at ease, and that she was no longer worried about her 'vision.' And all the time, deep down within her, there raged a veritable torrent of longing to see Stephen, to make sure that he was indeed alive ... to find him ready and waiting to hold her in his arms again.

Feverishly she had set to work to trace him ... first of all discovered that he had booked a room at the Continental Savoy ... guessed that he was spending the evening with Elizabeth and her friends ... found the Wilsons' address through the Legation ... and then, after dinner, driven here alone. She had paid the man handsomely to wait, and his friend to watch until Stephen came out of

248

that block of flats. See Stephen tonight she *must* ... see him ... hear him ... be close to him, if only for an hour before this terrible long day ended.

He felt her arms about his neck ... she seemed to melt into his embrace ... her lips clung to his with an almost desperate passion. He was deeply touched and a little astonished to feel how she trembled ... and that her lashes were wet with tears.

18

Again and again Stephen's lips burned against Iris's mouth with those long, deep kisses which were so infinitely satisfying to them both. Again and again he smoothed the dark, silken hair back from her tear-wet cheeks and murmured his passionate love and longing.

'I adore you, Iris, my darling, adorable Love, I love you. What made you come all this way to me? And why the tears? Oh, my precious one, don't cry, I can't bear you to cry,' he whispered against her ear.

She rested a moment in his arms, breathless, arms clinging, eyes shut. The taxi was moving slowly now along the crowded thoroughfare that led from the bright lights of central Cairo into the long road that leads to Heliopolis.

But Iris did not see the lights, or the traffic. Going to Zamelek from her hotel, earlier this evening, she had shrunk back in the car, hating the crowds ... the faces that peered at her curiously from other cars whenever they stopped in a traffic jam or waited for the green lights. She hated the noise, the continual blaring of horns and shouting of native voices. If this was city life, then all she prayed for was to be allowed to return to the serene, gracious atmosphere of her Nile home. For that was the *real* Egypt ... the *fellahin* working there, tilling the soil, drawing water, reaping and sowing, were the real Egyptians whom she loved and understood. She found this Westernised city both vulgar and terrifying. She knew that it would be a long time before she would ever be able to accustom herself to publicity, to modern clothes ... to other cities like London and Paris. More than ever, she felt a heart-breaking longing to escape from the present, awful burden Fate had put on her shoulders ... take Stephen's hand and vanish with him into the mists of the Past ... back to the age-old days of her temple ... there to live and love in splendid perfection and peace.

Only during these last twenty-four hours had Iris Lowell really forced herself to abandon her dreams and to face cold, hard facts. The metamorphosis was both difficult and agonising for her. It seemed that there was no turning back. She must go forward. And now that she had been forced to strike that terrible bargain with Mikhilo Usref ... it was as though her very spirit was being crushed within her, slowly and remorselessly.

But in Stephen's arms she felt almost

happy again. She did not want to open her eyes ... or speak ... and utter the inevitable lies which must be told if she were to guard his very life.

But soon Stephen's anxious voice dragged her back to action. She stirred in his embrace, gave a long and bitter sigh, and tried to satisfy his natural curiosity.

'It was like this ... I ... missed you so much ... I *had* to come to Cairo...' she said, looking at him through the dark veil of her lashes, whilst with one slender finger she traced the outline of his profile... 'I could not rest while you had gone. I commanded a special 'plane ... and Morga and I arrived here not many hours after you yourself.'

He held her a little apart from him now, unbelievedly stirred by her sweetness and the magic quality of her kisses. Now, in the dimness of the taxi, he saw her short grey dress, the exquisite ankles and small shoes. He uttered an exclamation.

'You are my Iris ... and yet quite changed. I don't really know you like this,' he said with a short, happy laugh.

'You like the new Iris?'

He did not notice the underlying sadness in her voice.

'I love her. All the Irises ... they are all marvellous.' He laughed again. 'And you always will be marvellous, my darling. For you, those famous words might have been written, *"Age cannot wither her nor custom stale her infinite variety."'*

She leaned her cheek against his shoulder, once more closing her eyes.

'Oh, Stephen ... Stephen!' she sighed.

'I was so amazed to see you in this taxi,' he went on. 'It just knocked me flat. But, darling, it was a wonderful thought of yours. It just makes all the difference. Cairo is not my favourite city, but now it is touched with your magic.'

'You say such lovely things to me, Stephen.'

'Nothing lovely enough, Iris, my own.'

His own! she thought bitterly. If only that were true! If only this meeting could have been as ecstatic, as joyous, for her as well as for him! In his arms, under his kisses, his caresses, she was like one intoxicated ... almost able to forget. But always in the background hovered the memory of Usref ... and the dreadful way in which her vision had materialised.

'Tell me about your flight,' he added.

Briefly she described it. He kept her close in the circle of one arm, watching her, as though his delighted eye could not bear to look anywhere else.

'How brave and sweet of you ... to take that journey ... and old Miss Morgan, too. How did she stand it?'

'Quite well. I left her in bed in the hotel,

tired but quite pleased to be here. She liked to see the shops...' Iris tried to introduce a cheerful, ordinary note into her conversation... 'We need not worry about Morga.'

Stephen glanced at his wrist-watch.

'It's quite late, my darling. What do you want to do ... go straight back to your hotel?'

She shuddered and clung to him again.

'No ... please ... let me be with you for a little.'

He bent and kissed her lips, his heart beating fast.

'Darling, you don't have to ask ... it is my one wish ... to be with *you*. Shall we ask the driver to turn back and drive along the Mena Road ... out to the Pyramids?'

'Yes,' she whispered.

It was wonderful out there by the Great Pyramid of Cheops which Iris had seen this afternoon when they flew over the desert. The car waited for them at the furthermost end of the road.

They got out and walked, hand in hand, over the soft sand, under a white blaze of moonlight and a glitter of stars. The sky was deep indigo. The gigantic Pyramid and the smaller ones behind it ... were splendid, dignified shapes silhouetted against that luminous sky. Farther along they came to the immortal Sphinx ... that ageless, solemn effigy ... with its queer, flat, human face, and great blind eyes staring into Time ... yet regardless of time... The Sphinx waiting, watching a long endless procession of men and women pass by ... return to dust ... and pass again.

What had those blind eyes not seen? What had those deaf ears not heard? The riddle of the Sphinx is yet unsolved. The sun, the stars, the moon shine on ... the great sandstorms blow ... the soft-footed camels pad to and fro ... the hot, bronzed faces of Egypt's sons, and the pale ones of the European visitors, turn to that strange, fascinating monument ... ever seeking the answer ... and receiving none.

And tonight Iris and Stephen, gripping each other's hands, stood there, small, insignificant figures silently asking their questions of that same Sphinx ... and they, too, were left unanswered.

A great sorrow enveloped the girl like a heavy cloak.

It was the first time she had come here ... and stood before the Sphinx ... or seen so close the vast Pyramids. They did not frighten her. But she was filled with nameless grief. For in her psychic fancy she knew that she had stood here with Stephen before ... and here they had loved and suffered. Love was inevitable for them. But sorrow, too, was unavoidable. Now, in the brilliant glamour of the moon ... in the silence of the night ... she and Stephen were inseparable, mentally and physically one. They loved greatly, and Cairo was the city it once had been. But tomorrow ... in the glare of the sun ... would come the sight-seeing crowds, the vendors, with their sordid, ugly efforts to beguile the tourists. There would be cries for *baksheesh;* quarrels over a *piastre* ... life as it was today ... full of greed and disillusionment. This lovely, lonely moment, standing here with Stephen, with the desert wind blowing her hair ... this moment would go. With all other moments. And the Sphinx, immune to petty griefs, to everything mortal, would stare blindly on ... towards eternity.

Stephen felt the slim fingers trembling in his own. He turned to her. He, too, felt the tremendous importance and solemnity of this nocturnal visit to the Sphinx with his beloved Iris. He was less psychic, less highly tuned, than she ... but nevertheless acutely aware of things far removed from the ordinary ... and infinitely conscious of the link between this girl and himself ... of a love that was being reincarnated ... relived between them.

Gravely he looked at her ... at the dark fronds of hair ... blown by the wind, escaping from her yellow scarf ... at the pale oval of her face ... her great sad eyes ... at the poetry and grace of every line of her slender figure.

'Iris,' he said, 'my dear one ... I am so

thankful you came to Cairo. Being here with you tonight, like this, has shown me yet again how dear you are to me ... and how united we are. I have seen the Sphinx ... these surroundings ... so many times. But never feeling as I do tonight.'

She looked up at him with tremendous yearning.

'I am glad, too, that I came to Cairo ... and that we are able to see these immortal shapes together,' she said in a low voice.

He put an arm about her shoulders and drew her close. In silence for a moment they stood looking around them. After a moment she said:

'And Elizabeth has gone?'

'She is going tomorrow. We have reached an understanding. There is no further need to feel worried or depressed about her, darling. I think she realises that we were not suited.'

Iris nodded. But it was as though a knife went through her heart. Elizabeth gone ... Stephen free ... under ordinary circumstances free to marry her. Oh, heavens, why should such people as Usref be allowed to *live?*

He felt the shudder that passed through her. He drew her closer.

'What is it, my darling? Sometimes I feel you tremble and you look ... tragic. You must not look like that. Dearest, I love you so much. We are free to love now, Iris. We must go to England as soon as we can … and get your aunt's permission for our immediate marriage.'

He felt her lean closer to him, but she did not speak. Anxiously he looked at her.

'Is that not agreeable to you, darling?'

She forced herself to dissemble. She *must* … she must play the part she had set herself … if she were to safeguard him from Usref's abominable hatred and jealousy. She said:

'Yes, yes. Of course. But I don't want to go to London for … another week. I want to … stay here … with you and Morga.'

'Here – in Cairo?' he asked, surprised.

'Yes…' the lie came with difficulty from Iris – she, who longed so ardently to return to the 'Little Palace' with him. 'I … thought that now I am here … I would stay … buy some suitable clothes … get my passport … prepare for our journey, Stephen. Do you not think so?'

His brow cleared.

'Yes … it might be a very sensible plan … if you think you can stand Cairo life for a week,' he said with a laugh. 'It is so difficult for me to get used to seeing you dressed like this … in any surroundings but your own.'

'It is difficult for me, too, Stephen,' she said with a bitterness he did not detect.

'We shall both have to get used to it, sweet.'

She nodded her head. He added:

'Shall I have to let you go shopping with Morga ... and see nothing of you ... for a whole week?'

Her face coloured swiftly, sensitively.

'No, heavens, no! I shall be with you every hour that is possible. You shall take me with you everywhere. We will go for long drives ... into the desert ... to see the other Pyramids ... the old Cairo ... the Egypt I love ... as far from shops and hotels as possible.'

She might have added, *'As far from Mikhilo Usref as possible'* ... but dared not. Nor for one moment must Stephen be allowed to guess what lay in her mind. And now, carried away by the force of her feelings, she turned her pale, lovely face up to his.

'Every moment must be ours ... only ours, my beloved Stephen,' she whispered. 'You ... and your love ... are all that my heart desires.'

Passionately he held and kissed her. He felt that life could offer him little more than the love of this bewitching woman. Not dreaming of the fact that she was facing a terrible sacrifice in order to save him from a madman's jealousy ... he thought rapturously of the future ... of the wonderful years ahead, when Iris was his wife. He spoke to her of his love, his hopes ... and of their life together, and she listened, biting hard the lips he had just kissed to keep herself from telling him the truth. For she knew, if she so much as dropped a hint of what Usref had done, he would forbid the sacrifice and defend himself. And that ... she believed ... would mean his death. Usref would never spare him.

So in silence, adoring him, she stood there in the shadow of the Sphinx, held close to his heart ... and prayed to all the ancient gods of Egypt to give her the strength and courage to go through with this thing.

19

There followed five or six memorable days for Iris and Stephen. They were seldom apart. Every morning he came to the Heliopolis Palace Hotel in his car to fetch her. They spent the golden, sunny hours of the morning together. After lunch Iris rested with the faithful Morga, then, later, Stephen fetched her again and they had tea and drove on to the fringes of the desert, or out to the famous Barrage gardens, or sat together in long chairs in the hotel gardens, hands linked, wrapped in each other. When the swift darkness fell they parted for an hour or two, only to meet again, dressed for the evening's entertainment – at the famous Grill Room of Shepheards; or on the roof-garden of the Continental Savoy Hotel, where one could dine and dance; or out towards Mena House at the *Auberge des Pyramides,* there to dine and dance under the stars.

It was a new world for Iris. Strange, fearful in many ways because she was so unused to publicity and the prying gaze of the men who were attracted by her unusual beauty.

In some ways she found it exciting and

pleasurable, as it was her first introduction to this new world ... to modern life. But the main lay in the fact that she was with Stephen – that she was sharing with *him* all these interests and amusements. And with resentment against Usref, against fate, burning in her breast she was determined that Stephen and not Mikhilo should be the first to show her the life that lay far beyond the walls of the 'Little Palace.'

In order to keep her dark, bitter secret away from Stephen and play her part properly she agreed to go to the shops with Morga and buy a suitable 'trousseau' of modern clothes. It would be the commencement of the English summer when they got to London, Stephen told her gaily; but it might be cold. It often was. She must expect cool, damp weather, with none of the shimmering heat of Egypt. She should buy furs and warm coats, he advised her, as well as light clothes, and be well prepared.

Money was no object with Lowell Pasha's daughter. A visit to the bank of the late Pasha, and a fawning manager assured Miss Lowell that she could draw as many thousands of *piastres* as she required. Iris was not interested in money. She knew nothing of the word 'economy.' All her life she had been surrounded by wealth and magnificence. So she spent freely. And if things had been different ... if only this had really been the prelude to her life with Stephen, she thought, how wonderful, how thrilling it would all have been. But her dread secret weighed heavily on her. She smiled with her lips ... but her great eyes held dark tragedy. She was forced to dissemble, to lie, to make Stephen and Morga believe that she was content. But her cheeks grew thinner, and all the shopping, the restaurants, the gay music, the opera and dancing to which Stephen escorted her seemed a hollow mockery.

She was haunted by the thought of Usref ... and the end of this week. Every time Stephen asked, 'Are you happy, my Iris, my Lovely One?'... she answered, 'Yes, my beloved' ... but she remembered with a sinking heart that it was a happiness hovering on the brink of disaster ... that it must end all too speedily... Every time Stephen spoke of their journey to London and their subsequent marriage she stayed mute, her great eyes staring mournfully into the distance. For she knew it could never be. Usref had given her only this one week ... after that she must disappear out of Stephen's life. She must make him believe that she was fickle and faithless, and had changed her mind, and that she intended to remain in Upper Egypt ... married to Mikhilo. (That idea filled her with horror.)

So thin and pale did she become that Miss

Morgan regarded her anxiously.

'Cairo and modern life do not suit you, my darling child,' she said. 'It is high time we went home...'

Iris essayed a laugh.

'I am quite all right, Morga. It is only the heat and the unaccustomed excitements.'

Miss Morgan hummed and hawed. She was not satisfied. There was something so strange and withdrawn about Iris these days. She ought on the face of things to be sublimely happy. She was with Stephen Daltry. Elizabeth had gone back to London. He was free now to marry Iris. All the plans were being made: the passports had been obtained and seats booked for all three of them on a flying-boat, for the end of the month, which would take them to Sicily and thence to England.

First of all Iris wished to fly back to Upper Egypt. Stephen was to await her return to Cairo. She and Morga must settle affairs at the 'Little Palace,' she said ... put Mandulis and old Ayesha in charge ... and pack various papers and books which she wished to take to London.

Thus, on the surface, Iris made her plans and Stephen cheerfully accepted them. He had no cause to believe that anything was wrong. Morga was worried about her; she knew Iris so well. But Stephen – man-like, he was deceived into thinking her entirely happy. She was always sweet, tender and content in his company, and if those wonderful eyes looked sad he put it down to her acutely sensitive nature, her serious mentality, she was not by temperament casually gay. But he never for an instant guessed her true state of mental torment.

He found it entrancing to introduce her to the kind of existence which was so ordinary to him and so extraordinary to her. He liked to watch her startled expression ... her wondering gaze ... the sensitive colour flooding her cheeks ... her surprise and delight when she saw something she particularly liked. Her taste was unerring. She chose the loveliest clothes. The little grey dress that had once been worn by lovely Helena Lowell was put between folds of tissue paper in a case. Now her lovely daughter appeared in Cairo as one of the most fashionable of modern women. French tailors and modistes in Cairo put aside all other work to fashion in a few days perfect suits and dresses for the fabulously rich Miss Lowell. Sheer linens, Damascus silks and brocades, rich smooth satin, delicious *crêpes* and filmy, gossamer lingerie. And, to please Stephen (although she knew in anguish that she would never need them), warm coats, soft angoras, expensive furs – even to a mink coat, and a soft sable cape for the evening. All these, added to beautiful hand-made shoes, which are a speciality in Cairo ... and the last word in Paris hats, completed a new and amazing wardrobe for Lowell Pasha's 'goddess.'

Wherever she went Iris was stared at with an obvious intensity which delighted Stephen. Sometimes he stole a glance at the chic, exquisite young woman at his side and wondered humbly why it had been given to him to be loved by such a peerless creature. Heavens! he thought, what a sensation she would make in London society. Her aunt ... his own relatives ... and friends would surely be enthralled. But although he found the physical side of her a never-failing source of wonder and joy, he was even more deeply in love with her intellectual qualities and the ineffable sweetness of her disposition. Her little acts of generosity, of tenderness, of unselfish thought for himself and for her old governess, asserted themselves many times a day. She embarrassed them both by buying expensive presents for them. The old autocrat of the 'Little Palace' had disappeared for ever, he thought ... the 'goddess' was still, in his estimation, a goddess to be worshipped. But she had also become a simple and lovable woman ... adorably unspoiled.

He taught her to dance. Iris, who never before had been held in the circle of a man's arm, before other men's gaze ... was shy at first of this modern dancing. But Stephen was an excellent dancer, and she was so naturally graceful, and moved so exquisitely, and was so responsive to music, that she soon learned to follow his steps. Night after night they danced together, and were always the cynosure of all eyes ... the tall, slim, well-bred young man in his white dinner-jacket ... face lean and brown against the collar ... and the slender, startlingly beautiful girl in one of her new evening dresses ... sometimes a pencil-slim, tailored black ... sometimes a full, Victorian, billowing gown ... or midnight blue, glittering with sequins ... or white *crêpe* severely tailored, shoulders and sleeves embroidered with seed pearls ... and jewels that had belonged to some buried Egyptian queen flashing around the slender throat ... on the slim fingers ... in the tiny ears.

Iris Lowell became a sensation in Cairo ... eagerly followed and watched wherever she went, even in that short week.

But the heart of the girl was breaking. Sometimes, dancing with Stephen, feeling his heart beat against her own, seeing him smiling deeply into her eyes, she wondered how she could endure another moment of it without pouring out the truth. Time and time again her hunted gaze looked around, watching for Mikhilo Usref. She had not seen him since their momentous meeting in

Shepheards. *But she knew he was here ...* waiting ... waiting like a panther, to spring ... to devour her happiness ... to claim her.

It was a fearful strain. And there were moments when she felt ill ... weak ... powerless to carry on. Yet those were the very moments when she had to summon most strength ... to smile and laugh and reassure Stephen that nothing was wrong ... and that, like himself, she was blissfully content.

She never really cared for the amusements of Cairo. She was happiest when she and Stephen drove together into the solitude of the sunlit desert ... or sometimes drove by moonlight to the Pyramids, back to the Sphinx ... for there in the silence, the vast splendour, she felt more at home ... more closely knit to her beloved Stephen. There, away from prying eyes, she was able to cling close to him, surrender her lips in endless hungry kisses ... respond to the rapturous passion of his lips, his caresses. Then and only then could she forget...

There were moments when a wild desire seized her to defy Usref ... to tell Stephen everything, go to the police ... *anything* rather than go through with this awful ordeal and send Stephen from her for ever.

But she had always to crush these longings ... telling herself in fear and trembling that Usref would only seek Stephen out and kill him. It must not be. The more she saw of him ... her wonderful, charming lover ... the more horror-stricken she was at the idea of him dying a violent death at the hands of an assassin.

So the days slipped by...

Iris ... whom Romney Lowell had dreamed of as the incarnation of the goddess Isis ... ceased to be a stranger to Cairo and modern methods. But Iris's heart remained buried in her old home ... with her old life. She knew that she would never really be happy outside the gates of her beloved palace. Sometimes at night her pillow was drenched with tears ... she gave herself up to wild fits of sobbing ... heart-broken at the thought of losing Stephen in so short a while. She prayed to be allowed to slip back to the past ... to see again the tranquil beauty of the Palace garden and terrace beside the green Nile; to smell the perfume of roses; of the hot earth sprayed by the gardeners; to see the candles gleaming in their lovely sconces, lit by Mandulis, at dinnertime. To hear the plaintive cry of her white peacocks ... to wear again her long linen robes, her turquoise necklace which had been a Pharaoh's gift ... her sandals ... to sit in her beloved temple ... the Courtyard of the Lions ... the great pillars of the Hall ... the inner sanctuary.

'If only I could go back...' she moaned

into her pillow. 'If only I could be lost in the mists of time with *him* ... out of Mikhilo's reach. *Oh, Stephen, my beloved!'*

On the last day of that week, before she was due to return to Upper Egypt ... Stephen took her to a *soirée*, held at the Legation, and introduced her as his fiancée to some of his friends. There were men of every nationality there. Tall, proud, dark Egyptians, wearing their scarlet *tarbusch* ... who spoke to and were answered by Iris in their own language, and bowed low before Lowell Pasha's daughter. French, English, Greek, Americans, Turks, Arab sheiks in their picturesque attire. And all in turn kissed the hand of the wonderfully beautiful girl with the dark eyes and braided hair, who had an air of ageless dignity and a proud bearing such as they had never seen before.

An old friend, who was at Oxford with Stephen, whispered his congratulations.

'I say, old boy, you've chosen an absolute dream ... I envy you. I'm very glad, too. I never thought that Elizabeth Martyn was your cup of tea. We all said that Lady M. noosed you. But this is *it.'*

Stephen smiled and looked proudly at Iris. She was talking, in her grave, intelligent fashion, to a bearded French diplomat. She held an untasted glass of champagne in one hand (she did not care for drink). She wore white ... a tailored dress, with a small cape of black-and-green glistening coq-feathers, and a large white hat with a turned-back brim, trimmed with the same sheen of feathers, sweeping down to the nape of her neck. She was, as usual, exquisitely made-up.

The Oxford friend, George Pollendine, also looked at Iris, and added:

'Straight out of *Vogue,* my dear chap. Perfect!'

'That doesn't really describe her,' said Stephen, with a laugh. 'Iris's looks are a façade for a very wonderful mind. She is straight out of a dream, my dear Pollendine.'

'Damned lucky chap,' said Pollendine again, and went off reluctantly to pay his respects to the stout, perspiring wife of their host. He had brought a pretty blonde girl friend to the *soirée* ... but this new fiancée of old Stephen Daltry's made all the other girls look ... what was it? ... ordinary and second-rate, Pollendine ruefully decided.

As they left the big apartment in which the party had taken place, and emerged into the breathless heat and glitter of the Egyptian night, Stephen took Iris by the arm and stood waiting with her for the car to pick them up. He felt happy and successful, and boyishly proud of his lovely future wife. He told her in glowing terms how much she had been admired.

'I'm terrified of taking you to London,' he added. 'All the chaps will be at your feet. I shall lose you...'

She looked up at him with her melting gaze.

'Never, *never*,' she said passionately.

He pressed her arm against his side.

'It's good to hear you say that, my darling.'

She put a delicately gloved hand against her lips. Almost she cried out, *'Oh, my love, my love .. it is not true ... you will have to lose me ... or lose your life.'*

While Mikhilo Usref persisted in his cruelty and covetousness ... there was no escape for either Stephen or herself. One way or another they must suffer. But she did not hesitate to make the choice. She was willing to sacrifice herself ... she was not vain enough to believe that Stephen would find life intolerable without her.

Stephen was in high spirits. Driving with her back to Heliopolis, he told her that he had seen his immediate Chief and told him that he wanted an extension of leave in order to take her back to England and that in all probability they would be getting married in London at once. The Chief had immediately offered him another month's leave. He need not commence his new job at the Legation until the end of July.

'That means we shall have the best summer month together in England,' he said. 'I shall take you to see my favourite aunt in Devonshire. You will love Devonshire, with its fine moors and red soil, and soft, pastel colouring. It will be a complete change for you, my Iris, after the exotic brilliance out here. You shall learn to ride with me. You will look superb on a horse, my darling. I shall drive you down to Cornwall, too, where I lived when my parents were alive ... I only wish they were still alive to see the glorious creature I have found for a wife...'

She did not answer, but let him talk on, freely and happily. With her hand locked in his she stared blindly at the passing traffic. She felt like a person who has been wounded ... and is slowly dying. She could only think:

'Tomorrow I shall shatter his illusions and destroy his hopes, and he will not understand. He will think when he reads my letter that I have gone back to the "Little Palace" in order to be with Mikhilo ... he will think me despicable and hate me. If only it were possible for me to die ... instead of *him* ... die and be buried in Egypt ... and forgotten by all men...'

But Stephen, blissfully ignorant of her tortured thoughts, lifted her hand to his lips repeatedly and kissed it.

'Life seems too good, my darling. Iris ... why can't I fly back to the "Little Palace" with you tomorrow? Why do you condemn me to wait here alone while you and Morga get ready? Let me come with you, my sweet.'

She shook her head dumbly. He laughed at her.

'You think I'll interfere with all the packing and plans for shutting up the place. But I won't ... I'll help, darling. I just can't bear you out of my sight.'

Suddenly she drew her slim figure erect. She looked at him with her deep, shadowed eyes.

'Stephen ... what would you do ... if you lost me?'

The good humour left his face.

'Don't even joke about it, darling.'

'But I might ... I might ... die,' she stammered.

He kept one fragrant palm against his lips.

'Don't, please ... I don't want you even to suggest such a thing. You are the whole of my life now, Iris.'

'The ... whole of it, Stephen? Could you have no life apart from me?' she asked almost piteously.

'None,' he said without hesitation.

'Oh, God!'

The cry was wrung from her. She dragged her hand away and covered her tormented eyes. Stephen stared at her in sudden alarm.

'Iris, for heaven's sake, what is it?'

She was shivering violently, and her face

was ashen under the delicate powder and rouge. She had reached, she thought, almost the limit of her powers of endurance. But still she tried to dissemble.

'I am just ... tired ... nervy,' she stammered.

'We're nearly home, darling,' he said, putting an arm about her. 'You must rest. It's been far too hectic a week for you. Morga was right. She said you were doing too much. You've always led such a calm, solitary sort of life, my poor darling... I feel to blame...'

He went on talking to her with that tenderness which always disarmed her and was as necessary to her now as his passion. She sat still, mute, the hot tears forcing a way under the silken lids ... her heart almost bursting with grief.

'If it is true ... if it is true that I am necessary to his life, then what use is his life apart from me?' she began to argue with herself. 'Why should I submit to Usref's monstrous bargain? Why not make one frantic bid for freedom ... freedom for both of us ... for Stephen and myself!'

Once alone in her bedroom, where she had gone presumably to change her dress, she sat on the edge of her bed, thinking with desperate intensity ... cheeks burning red ... eyes glittering as though with fever. Stephen had gone back to his own hotel, also to bath and change. Morga was in her own room. Iris was alone … alone with her chaotic thoughts and emotions. And with the awful prospect of tomorrow … the end of the week Usref had granted her … the prospect of going to her promised meeting with him at Shepheards … and then of the total separation from Stephen. And she felt that somehow she must circumvent it. *Somehow.*

Where was Mikhilo? She had not seen him all this week. But of course he was here … biding his time … ready to pounce on Stephen if she failed.

But supposing she could get Stephen out of Cairo without Mikhilo knowing … get him back to Upper Egypt, and into the 'Little Palace' … then place her guards at the gate … forbid entry to Usref … and refuse to allow Stephen to leave. Yes, out of her love and fear for him she would resume her autocracy … her rights as a goddess who must be obeyed… She would not allow him to go into danger. She would keep him at the Palace … and they would forget her father's will; marry and live in love, in happiness always in her beautiful home. Mikhilo would never be able to get at them. The place was and always had been impregnable to those to whom she denied admittance.

She did not pause to wonder how Stephen would react to such a scheme. She was ready now to gamble ... stake all ... on one throw of the dice ... anything rather than submit to Usref's tyranny tomorrow.

She had worked herself up into this fever of action, of defiance which was part of Iris's make-up ... and changed her so completely. She wanted to act *now*, or never.

She put a telephone call through to Stephen's hotel.

For a moment she spoke to him rapidly. He listened, half astonished and wholly thrilled. She had decided on an impulse to return to Upper Egypt tonight. Yes, on this brilliant moonlit night ... and by special 'plane. She had a reason for wanting to go now, at once, she said. He was not to ask questions. Once there, she might tell him. But now, if he loved her, he must do as she asked. Morga was used to her whims, she said ... she would meekly pack and follow. Stephen was to arrange all at the airport immediately ... even if it cost a small fortune. They would do anything for money. But she must be back in her home before the dawn.

'Darling, are you sure you wouldn't rather wait ... as your seats are booked for tomorrow?' began Stephen, who was half-dressed and just about to shave when the bell had rung.

But this was where Lowell Pasha's daughter asserted herself. On a note of excitement, of insistence, she said:

'No, no, Stephen – don't try to make me change my mind. We must go tonight ... together ... as soon after dinner as possible ... you and I. I want you with me, Stephen.'

'Sweet, I always wanted to go with you. Why have *you* changed our mind so suddenly?'

'Don't ask me now,' came her pleading voice. 'Just do this ... for me.'

'Your wish is my command,' he said.

And finishing his dressing rapidly, he thought how irrational and incomprehensible women were ... and Iris was no exception ... but he adored her ... and he really rather liked this idea of hers ... he was always ready for an adventure. And it was an adventure ... to take a sudden precipitous moonlit flight out of Cairo, back to the 'Little Palace,' with *her.*

Iris was right. Money could achieve anything in Cairo. And by midnight a private 'plane was ready, the engines tuned up, the propeller whirring ... and three people stepped into it. Iris, wrapped in one of her new coats, her head veiled, her hand clasped in Stephen's ... and Miss Morgan, shaking her head and muttering. There were times when her young pupil's vagaries and idiosyncrasies were too much for even her patience. But Stephen Daltry seemed quite pleased. He smiled as he took the seat beside Iris.

'I've "had" Cairo, Morga, and I'm sure you have. Now don't look glum. Think how fresh and beautiful it will be on the terrace at the Palace. Tomorrow morning we will breakfast there!'

'Oh well!' said Miss Morgan in a resigned tone.

But Iris laughed. Stephen's heart warmed as he heard that low, contented sound. Iris had not laughed like that since Elizabeth's abrupt entry into their paradise. She looked glowing tonight, he thought. And as the aeroplane taxied across the landing-field and they soared smoothly into the moonlight, leaving Heliopolis' lights glittering far beneath them. Iris did, indeed, feel more herself. All the way in the car to the airport, and while they waited for the necessary formalities ... she had been nervous and ill at ease ... had kept glancing around her in secret fear that Usref would appear ... that a shot might ring out ... and Stephen fall dead at her feet. She was in an agony of anxiety until they were actually in the air. Now she felt much better. She even began to wonder why she had not thought of doing this before ... and if she had exaggerated the importance of Mikhilo's dire threats. He had not followed or appeared to prevent their escape. All was well. And once within the precincts of her home Stephen would be safe. She would not worry too much as to how she would keep him there. That lay on the knees of the gods. The main thing was to get him away from Cairo and Mikhilo.

She looked at him with shining eyes. Her lips quivered. She stretched out a hand to him.

'Oh, darling...' she said.

He found the endearment entrancing, coming from her. He pressed her hand tightly. Miss Morgan was lying back on her seat with closed eyes, determined not to lose all her night's sleep. But Stephen and Iris were wide awake; as the aircraft rose bravely higher ... they looked down at the Pyramids and the Sphinx fast disappearing beneath them. Stephen leaned across and whispered against Iris's ear:

'I think this was a marvellous scheme ... just as thrilling and unexpected as your arrival in Cairo. You are altogether a thrilling and unexpected person, my darling.'

She clung to his hand and her lips brushed his brown cheek.

'I love you,' she whispered. 'I love you, my beloved.'

But as they flew onwards, following the silver course of the Nile ... towards Upper Egypt ... anxiety remained to torture her a little. For Mikhilo Usref was a dangerous man ... and the shadow of his menacing words still pursued her. She had given her word that she would hand herself over to him tomorrow. She had broken her word. Would she be forgiven by the gods who loved mortal lovers? Would they pardon her ... knowing that her promise had been forced from her by base means?

With passionate yearning she looked at Stephen and repeated:

'I love you...'

In the dimness of the aircraft ... unseen by Miss Morgan, who was dozing ... or by the pilot who was intent on his job ... Stephen drew Iris into his arms. She lay like a broken lily against his heart ... arms about his neck. And he kissed her red, sad mouth and the black, curving lashes ... and threaded his fingers slowly, caressingly through the black veil of her hair. He had never loved her more. Never felt so close to her ... his beautiful, wayward, enchanting love.

He felt glad that she was going back to the Palace wherein she belonged. He wished she did not have to leave it again. She was so much better and happier there ... for all her success in the modern world, the new Egypt, she *belonged* to old Egypt ... and to her former life.

After a while, soothed by his caresses, safe against his heart, the exhausted girl slept ... soundlessly, dreamlessly in his arms until they came down at the airfield at Assuan in the golden light of the dawn.

She woke refreshed. She was gay, as

delighted as a child in the car, as they drove along the river-road and she sighted her home. From some way off they saw the marvellous blue-glass dome flashing in the sun. And as the gates opened to receive Iris, and she caught a glimpse of the brown, happy faces of her Sudanese gardeners, their arms full of roses which they had picked before the heat could spoil them ... she nodded and they saluted her... She talked excitedly to Stephen:

'We will have a celebration tonight ... a banquet ... but we will ask nobody. It shall be a banquet just for ourselves. And I shall put on my special dress of silver tissue which belonged to a temple dancing girl in Tutankhamen's time ... and I will wear my white egret headdress and my silver anklets, inlaid with red cornelians. Then I shall dance for you by moonlight in the temple, Stephen, my beloved.'

He felt his heart leap as he looked into her dewy eyes. His imagination was stirred by her words.

'That will truly be a celebration, Iris. Oh, darling, I love to see you like this! Radiant, like one of the lotus lilies in your fountain, with the sun sparkling upon it,' he said.

She laughed and her fingers curled about his.

'You are becoming quite a poet, my Stephen.'

'A man could become anything ... with you ... for you,' he said. The blood ran hotly under his tan, as he felt an irresistible desire to snatch her in his arms and kiss her full, pouting lips; a desire which always seized him when she used the full powers of her witchery upon him.

At the great doors of the Palace she stepped out of the car, flung her coat and scarf on the ground and stretched her arms above her head.

'I'm going to rush up to my rooms and get out of my Cairo clothes. I want to become my real self again!' she exclaimed.

Miss Morgan followed her, yawning... Ayesha came running towards them, her wrinkled walnut of a face creased with smiles. Mandulis and Pilak appeared from the servants' quarters mysteriously ... they too were smiling, delighted to see their adored mistress again.

'I'll walk round the garden and wait for you on the terrace, sweet. Be quick and have breakfast with me,' said Stephen.

She hurried into the cool solemnity of the hall. She was utterly happy and refreshed in body and mind. She had forgotten all the horrors and apprehensions of the last seven days.

Then suddenly she stopped dead. It was as though her blood turned to ice in her veins, and her very heart seemed to fail. For a figure arose from one of the high-backed chairs, half hidden by a pillar. The tall, familiar figure of Mikhilo Usref ... as evilly handsome as ever in his spruce white linen suit.

Iris, hands to lips, smothered a cry.

'You, *here?*'

He advanced towards her, smiling. It was a cruel, sensuous smile.

He said:

'Welcome home, my Lady of Moonlight.'

Her teeth began to chatter.

'What are you doing here ... *what* ... how did you *dare?*'

He answered:

'My Lady must forgive me if I have come uninvited. But I had an idea that she might endeavour to forget her rendezvous with me. And I had a similar idea that she might eventually think of bringing Mr Daltry here with her. It was just a matter of time. I have been back in this vicinity several days. I told Mandulis and that old fool Ayesha that you had sent me here to the Palace to await you. They believed me, I have always been *persona grata* here, have I not? And now ... once again permit me to welcome you. You and I will be remaining, of course. But Mr Daltry ... how long does he intend to stay? I am not fond of trios ... so I trust you will advise him to go back to Cairo as soon as possible!'

20

Like an image, hardly daring to move or breathe, Iris stood staring at Mikhilo. Her heart beat so fast that it was a physical pain. Her face was milk-white under its delicate golden tan. But now her mind, steeped in sick despair, began to work again. She thought dully:

'I might have known ... I might have guessed that he would do a thing like this. A man so vile is capable of ... any vileness!'

Usref drew nearer her. His agate-dark eyes narrowed as he caught the expression on the girl's face. So might she have looked at a reptile, at some crawling insect. His mouth took an ugly twist. But when he spoke again his voice was as smooth, as oily, as before:

'Is my Lady of Moonlight then so astonished to see me? Did she expect me to let her escape so easily, and come here with her lover ... forgetting her appointment at Shepheards with poor Mikhilo?'

She tried to answer, but at this juncture Miss Morgan appeared in her wake. And Miss Morgan's face assumed a look of undisguised disapproval as she saw the white-clad Serbian.

'We don't want you here, young man; you just disappear and be quick about it...' was what she would have liked to have said. But Iris acted swiftly now. Her old terror for Stephen was sweeping across her in full force. She was completely unnerved by Mikhilo's presence at the 'Little Palace' ... this truly awful ironic anti-climax to all her joy in bringing Stephen here without – so she had thought – incident – without interference from Usref. But she could not let Morga annoy Mikhilo ... and herself she dared not annoy him. He might have a revolver in his hip pocket ... or a knife ... or some paid assassin out there, lurking in the green, tree-filled garden. It was for Stephen she was afraid.

She said with assumed nonchalance:

'Isn't this a surprise, Morga? Mikhilo has come to welcome us home.'

Miss Morgan blinked mistrustfully through her strong glasses at the Serbian prince whom she had always disliked.

'Humph ... very nice. How did he know we were coming?'

Iris's great dark eyes grew agonised. Mikhilo smiled and bowed.

'A lucky guess, mademoiselle...' he murmured.

'Well, I'm off upstairs to unpack,' said Miss Morgan, sniffing.

'No ... don't go, Morga...' said Iris

quickly ... her throat dry ... her heart still pounding, pounding ... with fear and bitter disappointment.

The old governess turned back.

'Do you want me, my dear?'

Iris took a grip of herself and managed, somehow, to shake her head and smile.

'No ... on second thoughts ... no ... go along, Morga...'

Miss Morgan gave another disapproving glance at Usref and went her way. Alone with the man, Iris said in a low, urgent voice:

'Why did you want to do this? Why persecute me? How can you reconcile such behaviour with the love you say that you have for me?'

He drew a thin gold case from his pocket, took a cigarette from it, tapped it on the case and looked at her in a ruminating way.

'My Lady forgets ... that love can drive a man to do curious things. She *should* know. Has she not been driven to strange lengths for the undeserving object of her affections?'

Quickly she flashed:

'You have no right to call Stephen undeserving!'

He was irritated by her quick, hot championship of the Englishman.

'Was one week not enough, my Lady?'

The colour rushed to her face. She drew

287

herself up proudly.

'A lifetime with *him* would not be enough.'

'So!' said Mikhilo in his purring voice, but his eyes were cat-like slits now. 'And for me it would not be enough to see him lying dead before my eyes this moment instead of walking on your terrace.'

All the colour left her cheeks again.

'You have sworn...'

'And I will keep my word,' he cut in. 'I will not touch him ... providing you keep to *your* share of the bargain.'

'It is a monstrous bargain, Mikhilo.'

'But it was made,' he reminded her.

She beat one small hand on the other in impotent rage.

'You should be afraid of *your* life, Mikhilo. I have loyal servants,' she choked.

Smoking his long, Egyptian cigarette, he smiled lazily.

'But my Lady of Moonlight is too fair, too gentle, to take a life,' he said, in that smooth voice which she had grown to loathe and fear.

'You are right,' she said under her breath. 'But it is not because of fairness or gentleness that I do not order Mandulis and Pilak to throw you into the Nile, Mikhilo. It is because I would not stain my soul with the crime even of ridding the world of a base creature like yourself.'

Usref changed colour now. He flung his

cigarette through an open window.

'You will gain nothing, my Lady, by abusing me. Get Daltry out of the Palace. And before he goes tell him that you have changed your mind in my favour. Otherwise I shall not remain as patient as I have been this week in Cairo.'

She drew a long breath. She felt defeated. The warmth of the exquisite morning which had been so lovely an hour ago seemed now oppressive and filled with menace. She felt all the bitterness of having to give in to this man whom she had once counted as her friend and whose homage and adulation she had accepted with cool indifference. Now he was like a monstrous shadow blotting out the light of her life ... standing relentlessly between Stephen her beloved ... and herself. She had no course but to surrender ... for the second time. For *his* sake!

She looked through the windows and saw the slim, upright figure of Stephen, standing with his back to her. He was gazing at the Nile. She could imagine how he looked. Pleased ... happy ... in anticipation of her joining him ... and of the hours he believed they were about to spend together now that they were back in these much-loved surroundings.

One cry would have brought him running to her side. She had never felt more helpless ... more powerless to act. The dark, proud head sank. She said:

'Very well...'

'You may not think so now, but I swear I will make you the happiest woman in Egypt,' said Usref in a low voice.

She made a gesture of supreme scorn, but held her peace. Mikhilo set his teeth and stared not at her but at the point of his too-pointed, immaculate, white suède shoes. Iris's continued and obvious distaste of him, her equally obvious love for Stephen Daltry, might have reduced some men to a state of indifference, of feeling that the game was not worth while. There was so little response ... so little hope of reward. But Usref was not built like other men.

From his childhood he had been brought up by foolish, doting parents who made a demi-god of him; he had been hideously spoilt; grown to adolescence amongst women who had thrown themselves at him because of his handsome face and winning manners. He had lived a life of indulgence and extravagance. When Europe bowed its head under a long and bloody war the Usref family, through money and influence, escaped to America, and there Mikhilo was able to continue his extravagant, aimless manner of living. He won people, at first, by his looks, his façade of charm, then disappointed them once they discovered that he was totally lacking in moral fibre, a stranger to truth or integrity and a danger to society. In company with his inherent weakness was all the ruthlessness of the complete egoist, the megalomaniac. So long as Mikhilo Usref could get what he wanted, whether a new expensive motor-car or a pretty woman, he was content. He was even a generous and delightful friend to people like the Fahmouds, who were useful to him. They were still deceived by him. It was Nila who introduced him to Egyptian society, to a country which, with its burning heat, its passionate langours, its sensuous beauty, appealed vastly to the sensualist in him.

Now his parents were dead. He had escaped the rigours of war. He had all the money he wanted. He felt a growing conviction that he was omnipotent ... and could always get what he wanted out of life. *Until he met Lowell Pasha's daughter.*

From that time on Mikhilo Usref fell as desperately in love as he was capable of doing. From the first hour he set eyes on Iris's remote, slender loveliness, and all the glamour of the goddess which surrounded her ... he wanted her.

That desire had become a raging torment ... and her rejections of his love had increased rather than diminished it. Just as her preference for the Englishman roused him to an even greater determination to triumph over Stephen Daltry ... to get Iris despite him ... despite Iris *herself*.

Such was the present abnormal state of mind of this young Serbian prince ... a state which was driving him to criminal lengths.

With a long, almost menacing look at Iris he spoke again.

'Get Daltry out of the Palace ... or I, myself, will deal with him.'

It struck her then that Usref was a little mad. That she had, in truth, a madman to deal with. But, mad or sane, the result was the same. While the threat to Stephen's dear life was maintained, she was cornered.

She said wildly:

'You forget that Stephen is my ... my guardian. That I have an aunt in England who is also a guardian ... and that I am under age in the eyes of the English law. They will not permit me to marry you, Mikhilo.'

That made him laugh.

'Come, come, my Lady ... you were prepared to ask permission to marry Mr Daltry at once, were you not?'

She saw the futility of argument and drew a bitter sigh. She turned from him. Her heart seemed full to bursting. Out there on the beautiful terrace Stephen waited ... his back still towards her ... all unknowing of the evil that was being perpetrated here in the house. Then suddenly she swung round and faced her enemy again.

'Listen, Mikhilo ... this time ... I will not fail you.' She spoke with difficulty, her lips were quivering so and her whole body shaking from head to foot. 'I will ask Stephen to leave ... tomorrow.'

Usref frowned.

'Why not today?'

She made a gesture of one slender hand.

'Because it would not be rational behaviour on my part ... to bring him here only to tell him within an hour to go again. I ... can force the issue ... but only if given time. Tonight I will ... try to explain that I ... have seen you again ... and made my final decision in *your* favour. Then he will go ... tomorrow of his own free will. It is better that way than to create a situation which would make him suspicious that all was not right ... in which case he might refuse to leave me.'

Usref stared at her. How white she was ... white and quivering like a pale flower that bends suddenly against the first hot onslaught of the *khamsin* ... that cruel hot wind that blows from the desert ... breaking, destroying any delicate living thing that stands in its way. He could see what an effort those words had cost her ... how near she was, indeed, to being broken. He thought it best not to drive her too far. He said in a reluctant voice:

'Yes, what you say is reasonable. So I will

give you one more day. But *one more only,* my Lady. Prepare him for the parting tomorrow ... you must make certain that he goes.'

'Very well,' she said, and her eyes looked blindly out at the sunlight ... and at Stephen.

Usref took her hand and kissed it. Then he dropped it. He said in a strangled voice:

'You shall not always shudder so when I touch you. *You shall not!*'

Iris turned and ran ... ran away from the fiend that Usref had become, up the wide, beautiful marble staircase with the Spanish wrought-iron banisters which Romney Pasha had had sent from Madrid when he first built this exquisite home for his adored Helena. The whole Palace was full of such treasures. And here in beauty, in peace, blissfully ignorant of the world outside, the child Iris had grown up, been taught, erroneously, to believe herself invulnerable, safe from the evils and miseries which she had read about but which seemed to be merely legendary. Dear heaven, she thought, as she sped to her lovely rooms, why had she been fated to awaken to such hideousness as this ... Mikhilo Usref's mad passion? The pain of knowing that she must send Stephen away, shake all his beautiful faith in her, shatter the perfection of their love and happiness ... was almost too great to bear.

When at last she had dismissed Ayesha, who hovered faithfully in her room, waiting to serve her, Iris locked the door and lay face downwards on her bed, struggling against the scalding tears that poured down her face.

She must not cry. *She must not.* Stephen would notice and question her. Now that this ghastly *débâcle* had occurred ... now that Usref had forestalled them ... come here to threaten afresh ... there was no way out ... she must play her agonising part to the bitter end and send Stephen from her. But she must do it cleverly ... and well ... or he would guess that something was wrong ... and he would not go. She dared not tell him the truth, nor drop even a hint of what was taking place to old Morga or her faithful *suffragis*. Mikhilo was crafty; if questioned, he would deny everything ... he might even wait until Stephen left the 'Little Palace' for Cairo again ... and then he would strike, like the snake ... pitilessly ... and without warning.

Her mind revolved in circles ... formulating ideas ... then dismissing them in despair ... always afraid for *him*. Finally she accepted her fate and, having accepted it, grew calmer ... seeking for strength from some of the age-old philosophies she used to study. In Egypt fatalism is the keynote of all philosophies. *Malêsh,* they say when a thing is inevitable. *Malêsh! Kismet!* is Fate. Cease to struggle, to beat your head against a stone wall.

Iris was herself again when at length she joined Stephen on the terrace for breakfast. It all looked so dear and familiar ... so beautiful, she thought sadly. A delicate Nankin china bowl full of pink and golden roses stood in the centre of the table which was spread with a snowy, lace-edged cloth. Helena Lowell had loved old, beautiful things, and it was a tribute to the careful brown hands of the Sudanese servants that so much of the china and glass used in her day was still unbroken. This morning, in honour of his Lady's return, Mandulis had put out the loveliest cups and plates, a hand-painted service which was said to have belonged to Marie Antoinette and been used by her in Versailles. Strong French coffee, golden-brown crisp rolls and creamy butter and honey were on the menu. Thin-sliced ham and an omelette, made as only Iris's cook could make it, curled, rich, waited on a silver dish for Stephen.

Stephen's eyes grew grave as he regarded his love. He had been looking forward to this moment ... to the first meal of their return to the 'Little Palace'; and to seeing her dressed again in her long, embroidered, linen gown and wearing the embroidered sandals through which her lovely slender feet and glistening red nails were visible. Iris ... the goddess ... back in her own *milieu* ... whilst across the river, waiting for her, stood the sculptured ageless beauty of the Isis Temple which she loved so well.

But the moment had been spoiled for him ... and despite the fact that her lips mechanically smiled a greeting, he knew that it had been spoiled for her too. *But he did not know why.* For that much she was thankful when she heard his first words:

'I saw Usref walking towards the gates just now. Why is he here? I thought he was in Cairo. How wretched for you to be bothered with him today of all days, my darling.'

She said nothing for a moment. She thought:

'He is jealous of Mikhilo. My poor Stephen ... how easy it will be to make him suffer through his love and jealousy...'

Stephen took one of Iris's hands and led her to a chair at the table.

'You must be tired and thirsty, my sweet. Sit down,' he added.

She took the seat, then looked up at him. Her eyes were sad and inscrutable. He thought that she looked tired ... those velvety eyes were circled with violet shadows. But he did not detect that she had been weeping. She said with difficulty:

'Mikhilo ... came to welcome me back.'

Stephen, sitting opposite her, frowned a

little. Mandulis began to serve the breakfast. Stephen said ... as Miss Morgan had
said before him:

'How did he know we were coming?'

Mechanically Iris quoted Usref's explanation.

'He guessed...'

'Very psychic,' said Stephen; then, feeling
ungracious, gave Iris a quick look of
remorse from his grey, smiling eyes. 'Sorry,
my darling, but I must admit I'm not particularly fond of your Serbian prince.'

She wanted to cry:

'*Do not call him mine. He is the devil
incarnate and I loathe and fear him!*' Instead
she said. 'He is very devoted to me.'

Stephen, feeling suddenly gay and
cheerful again, laughed.

'Well, I can't blame him for that, sweet. I
thought he had every intention of staying in
Cairo. He was in that 'plane with you, you
and old Morga, wasn't he ... the day you
came to Cairo? You said so. In fact, you said
you thought he was staying there.'

She bent over her coffee-cup.

'I ... thought so...'

He was beginning now to notice that the
delicious sparkle, the joyous, childlike gaiety
that had marked her during their flight to
Assuan, had completely vanished. He re-
marked on the fact.

'You are so quiet all of a sudden; are you

298

not well, my darling?' he asked anxiously.

She stirred herself to action. She put down the cup she had raised to her lips and began to laugh ... shook with helpless, hysterical laughter, covering her eyes with her hand. When in astonishment he asked her what she found so amusing, she gasped:

'Just ... Mikhilo being here to welcome me ... it was funny. Oh, Stephen, don't you think it was funny?'

He stared. He saw no particular amusement attached to Usref's coming here and he was bewildered by this sudden strange exhibition of humour. But he was relieved to hear her laughter. How he loved her to laugh ... to be gay and carefree ... his darling, unique love. He began to laugh with her as though he saw the joke.

'Well, he is a bit of a farce, that fellow, I agree. Ye gods, what a conceited bounder, too ... enough to make anyone laugh ... all that bowing and scraping and showing his teeth, that unctuous way of talking. No wonder you laugh...'

She kept her eyes hidden from him and let him talk ... and it was as though a knife were being turned slowly in her heart.

She had the whole of this day left with Stephen, she thought ... this day and this night ... and then ... no more. And she thought of some lines she had read once in a book of Swinburne's poems, taken from her father's library. Lines that seemed to fit this bitter moment:

'Love me no more ... but love my love of
 thee,
Love where thou wilt and live thy life...
Keep other hours for others ... save me
 this...'

So easily could she have quoted those words to him. For after tonight he must not love her ... he must leave her ... and thinking her fickle and unbelievably false, in time he would turn his thoughts to another love... She wanted to beg him to keep this hour for her. Keep it ... and love the memory of her love for him. But she must not, dared not, speak of these things.

Suffering acutely, she sat there in the golden warmth of the morning, her eyes blind with pain. Then, to keep him from guessing that something ailed her, she continued to talk and smile with a wild, despairing gaiety.

21

All was tranquil at the 'Little Palace' during the early part of the hot, still afternoon. All living things drowsed under the fierce rays of the summer sun. The tamarisks quivered in the heat. The glossy green fans of the tall doum-palms stretched upwards to a sky of aching blue. The beautiful yellow flowers of the prickly-pear trees drooped slowly under that languorous warmth. Around the spraying fountain in the courtyards of Romney Lowell's palace the blue lotus flower opened wide its dreaming heart.

Nothing moved save an occasional chameleon ... or a lizard slipping over the dry stones. Once, a solitary white egret skimmed soundlessly across the oily gleaming waters of the Nile.

In the distance, on the same broad river, a felucca lay motionless, its tall, curved mast outlined like a proud sentinel against the undulating, sun-baked desert.

Miss Morgan slept serenely in her darkened room. Stephen, too, slept behind the rush blinds on the verandah outside the late Pasha's study, lying on a silk-cushioned, long-caned chair.

But Iris found no sleep, no peace, in her own cool, shuttered room. Exhausted, utterly miserable, she lay fanning her hot face, striving for the courage to go through with her ordeal.

Already trouble was brewing in this glorious palace. Since breakfast a note of dissension had crept in between them ... disturbing Stephen ... bewildering him, although Iris understood only too well. Was she not deliberately introducing that hateful note ... she, who longed to creep into his arms and find peace?

Alone now, while the household slept, Iris looked back on some of the morning's events, tortured by the mere memory.

Everything that Stephen had wanted to do she had refused ... at first with a touch of coyness, acting the spoiled child ... later the irritable woman. He wanted her to prepare seriously for her trip to England. To go through all her father's papers for the last time. She had refused. It was too hot, she said, too boring an occupation. He had tried to talk to her of their future. They must not stay here – much as he longed to – he had said. He had been granted leave, but he must make good use of it. They ought to plan definitely to arrive in England next week. But she had waved it all aside.

'I'm not at all sure now that I want to go to England,' she had said petulantly. 'I hate the idea. Besides, we have not heard from my aunt yet. She may not want me.'

'But, darling, she *must* have you ... or at least see you and get the legal side of things settled,' Stephen had argued. 'And you must try to accustom your darling self to taking this trip. Surely with me ... you won't mind so much...?'

How gentle he had been... How patient, she thought, as she remembered in anguish of spirit all their discussions. She must have appeared in his eyes a thoroughly difficult, inconsistent creature. In Cairo she had agreed to all his plans. On the face of things ... if she loved him so much she would not mind going to London, there to arrange their marriage. To the baffled Stephen this new Iris must seem so hard to understand.

Then when she had started to discuss, in a hard, bright voice, the party she wished to arrange for tonight, Stephen had at last grown nettled. He had said:

'Look here, darling – this is too much! I thought you wanted to be alone with me...'

She had shrugged her shoulders. Her answer implied that she had changed her mind. Then at last he had been goaded to annoyance and snapped:

'Well, I hope we don't have to ask the Prince, or that frightful Persian poet friend of his. I dislike the pair of them.' Setting her teeth, she had replied that Mikhilo and

Omar were her friends. And then suddenly she had seen Stephen's lips draw together in a tight line and his whole expression change. He became the dry, cynical, flint-like Stephen who had first entered this place and told her that she must leave Egypt and go to England ... the Stephen whom she had feared a little – and even disliked because he had disturbed her peace.

But now ... oh, God, she thought in utter wretchedness, how intolerable to be forced to hurt and disappoint him ... to bring *that* look to his face!

In a sudden access of remorse, allowing her real feelings full sway, she had flung herself into his arms.

'I will not ask them tonight,' she had said in a strangled voice. 'I will not. I want to be alone with you.'

He had held and kissed her passionately, obviously relieved that she was herself again, eager to forget their passage of arms. She had weakened so far as to go with him to her father's study and put some of the many scattered manuscripts in order.

But now ... now she faced the fact that she must not weaken again. Before this night ended Stephen must be made to realise that all their loving ... their hopes of marriage ... were over. That tomorrow he must leave the 'Little Palace' ... alone, and never return.

Once more she built around her an

armour of courage ... the bravery of despair ... and when she joined Stephen down on the terrace again, later that afternoon, she was quite controlled.

Stephen, after a refreshing sleep, was in the best of humours. He had forgotten Iris's surprising display of contrariness this morning. He walked up to her ... took both her rounded dimpled arms and kissed the cool, satin smoothness of one bare shoulder. How he loved her in her straight, virginal linen gowns ... worshipped her white slenderness!

'Loveliest of all women in the world,' he murmured. 'Do you still love me?' And his grey eyes smiled, confidently waiting for her reply.

She stood silent, her red, pouting lips curved in an enigmatic expression which was lost upon him in this precise moment. He shook her gently, still smiling.

'Well ... *do* you love me?'

She drew away from him and turned her head so that he could not look into her eyes.

'I dislike being cross-examined,' she said coolly.

He stared, rebuffed. The smile faded from his eyes. And now he was uncomfortably reminded of this morning ... when she had behaved in this way. What had happened? What was the matter with his beloved? He had a momentary sensation of fear ... the dread that some shadow, some invisible barrier, was fast coming between them.

Any form of rebuff had the effect of making Stephen retire rapidly into a shell. He retired now. With none of the former bantering tenderness in his voice he said:

'Perhaps you would like to arrange that party for tonight. You have been rather too much alone with me. I'm afraid you find it boring. Shall I ask Mandulis to send a message to Nila Fahmoud?'

Her sad, veiled eyes betrayed none of the misery that inwardly choked her. She said:

'No thank you, I do not want a party.'

'What *do* you want, Iris?' He put his hands in his pockets and stood frowning, looking at her with the growing conviction that all was not well between them. How stiff, how unresponsive she had been just now to his eager touch. Perhaps he was over-eager, he told himself cynically. Unwise to show how much he loved her. Perhaps any man is a fool to let any woman know that she is adored. But he had thought that Iris was different ... unspoiled ... above perverse, petty reactions of that kind. And he had been convinced of her own love for him. Good heavens, had she not flown all the way to Cairo to join him? And she had been so exquisitely tender and demonstrative to him all this last week. What had occurred to bring about this strange metamorphosis?

She was moving towards the gardens in that light, graceful fashion which he always admired. Her voice, still cool and distant, floated to him:

'I shall find something to do. And you ... amuse yourself, Stephen. Send for Nila ... if that is your wish.'

Now a look of anger shot into Stephen's eyes. He followed Iris, caught up with her, seized her wrist and swung her round to face him.

'Look here, my child, that is a lot of nonsense. You know perfectly well that Nila Fahmoud does not amuse me. I'm a tolerant chap up to a point ... but beyond that point ... well, I rather think I can be as difficult as you. Two people who love each other must have understanding. I thought we had it ... completely. I was wrong. But if we are going to London together to arrange our marriage ... we must be absolutely sure of each other. Is that clear?'

She dragged her wrist away and turned her head, keeping her face averted so that he should not see it. She was aghast that he should have been forced to speak to her like that. Stephen ... her *beloved*. And she had asked for it ... goaded him into it... Her heart began to beat swiftly, agonizingly. Her very breathing seemed to hurt her. She muttered:

'Oh, leave me alone ... do not worry me,

307

Stephen. You should see that I want to be alone.'

The man, too, was aghast. At her ... at himself ... at this wholly unexpected and unattractive turn of events. He said:

'Very well. If that is really how you feel, Iris. But I think some explanation is due to me. Why have you changed so completely since we got back to the Palace? Have I said or done anything to offend you?'

She clenched her hands. Her eyes closed. She felt blind with mental pain ... with the effort it cost her not to turn and say: *'Stephen ... Stephen ... you are more than my life ... I am giving my very life ... to save yours...'*

Instead the answer was wrung from her:

'Yes. I ... object to your dislike of ... my friends.'

His brown face reddened. He stared at her, then gave a curt laugh.

'Do you mean ... your Serbian Prince?'

'Yes,' she said, under her breath.

Stephen could scarcely credit his hearing.

'You are letting that fellow ... Usref ... come between *us?*'

She could bear no more. She said wildly:

'Oh, leave me alone! ... leave me *alone*, I say...!'

And before he could speak again she turned and walked swiftly through the gardens, down towards the river. He stood rigid, watching the white, slender figure vanish. A feeling almost of horror engulfed him. She, who had become his whole world … to recoil from his touch as though she hated him … to run from him … to let childish, petty resentment, because he had shown dislike of Usref … come between them. It was almost unbelievable. Yet it had happened.

Stephen felt in that moment that his world was crumbling in front of his very sight. He took a handkerchief from his pocket and wiped his face. The sweat was pouring down it. He felt himself trembling.

'Iris…' he said her name once or twice. 'Iris…!'

Something evil had entered this place … something connected, perhaps, with Mikhilo Usref. And Iris was bewitched … yes, it was though an evil spell had been put upon *her*. Her behaviour was so extraordinary, her attitude so unrecognisable from that of the sweet, responsive woman who had joined him in Cairo and who had disliked being separated from him for even an hour.

He thought:

'I can't let this happen. I'm damned if I'll let it happen. She loves me. I know she does. Something's wrong. I'll damned well find out… I won't take this lying down…'

Even as he reached the river's edge he saw that Iris had rowed herself across to her beloved temple. It was her refuge in times of stress. She herself had told him so. Old Morga, too. He remembered how he had followed and found her there on his first night at the Palace ... how there, in the dimness of the inner temple, for the first time he had seen her with the glory of her hair unloosened and known that he had fallen in love with her, fiercely and with finality. He loved her like that still. She was to be his wife. He could not tolerate a strained relationship between them.

And now, as on that first exciting, remembered night, he followed. He rowed one of the small white boats which belonged to the Palace household over to the other side of the river, and walked quickly across the hot sand to the excavated temple.

An old, brown-faced, bearded Arab, in a white gown, wearing the purple sash which marked him as one of the Palace servants, sat on one of the great stones at the entrance to the Court of Lions. Gently he waved a fly-whisk across his face. Stephen knew him. It was old Siroo, one of the custodians of the temple, who had been here when Romney Lowell first began his great work of restoration. He greeted Stephen respectfully.

'*Saiida ... Effendi.*'

'*Saiida,*' Stephen answered abruptly. And then:

'Have you seen Her Excellency?'

The Arab nodded.

'She is within, *Effendi*.'

Stephen walked quickly into the courtyard. He called Iris's name.

'Iris ... Iris ... darling ... where are you?'

His voice echoed through the giant halls of the building. But no answer came. She was not going to meet him halfway, Stephen thought ruefully, and his heart was sore as he began to search for her. How could she treat him like this? How was it possible ... after all the vows of passionate love and fidelity they had so often exchanged?

But he continued to call her name. Outside in the desert the late afternoon sun still beat fiercely down upon the sand. But in the Isis Temple it was dark and chill. Gradually Stephen's eyes grew accustomed to the dimness. He walked carefully through the twilight hall of great columns ... the many inner sanctuaries which he knew so well now. He had been here with Iris so many times. They had wandered hand in hand while she recounted to him the ancient history with which she was so familiar.

Those had been gloriously happy hours. But now as Stephen searched through the ruined buildings he was a most miserable man. For it seemed that he had misjudged both Iris and her feelings towards him ... that nothing was as he had believed it to be.

311

'Iris!' his voice echoed anxiously through the temple. 'Darling ... where are you? Don't hide from me, I beg of you ... Iris ... please!'

Only silence ... and his own echoed words, in reply.

He passed from one shrine to another ... the great black marble images of Isis and Osiris ... of the sun-god Ra ... of Isis, the queen-mother, with a child on her arm, carved in black sacrificial stone, crowned with her double crown ... for ever gravely brooding in the utter silence.

Across Stephen there fell a sudden sensation of coldness ... almost horror. He disliked this temple ... with its history of blood-sacrifice ... of pagan worship ... the cruel, remorseless gods of ancient Egypt. He hated Iris to come here alone. He wanted desperately to find her and take her out quickly into the sunshine and fresh air again. Before, hand in hand with *her*, these giant columns and exquisitely carved recesses containing half-broken images had seemed to hold a classic and romantic beauty. Without her ... separated from her like this by so much misunderstanding ... the whole place to Stephen had become evil.

He called again, roughly, his voice a harsh echo:

'Iris ... for heaven's sake ... where are you?'

Now he came to a roofless portion of the building into which a cascade of golden sunshine poured and relieved the stygian gloom. Here amidst the broken stones little palm trees grew and flourished ... and small, multi-coloured birds nested and circled, wheeled in and out of the splendid stone columns, like charming, iridescent sprites. Here once more was a feeling of warmth, of romance, of all the beauty and delight that Stephen had always associated with his 'goddess.'

He paused to wipe his hot face ... to wonder wretchedly how long Iris would take before she surrendered ... if indeed she meant to do so!

Again leaving the sunshine for the sinister twilight of the inner temple, he continued his search.

Then suddenly he came upon her ... in her hiding-place, to which, so far as he could remember, she had never taken him. The only access to it was down some curved stone steps. Stephen had almost stumbled down the first one, and lit a match before he could plainly see where he was going. He went down these steps only half believing that he would find Iris here. Then he became aware of a light coming from an oil-lamp which illuminated the red-and-blue frescoes on the wall. This in all probability, he thought, was the entrance to some

Pharaoh's tomb.

'Iris!' Stephen called.

And now her voice, husky and almost unrecognisable, answered him.

'You have no right to come here ... no one but I ... ever comes here. Please go away!'

But he moved down the last step and came into the stone, lamp-lit chamber and stood a moment in surprise and concern, looking about him, and then at her.

The little room was as it had been perhaps three thousand years ago ... with its gaudily-painted walls and mosaic floor. It contained two high-backed chairs, a low Egyptian bed, with side rails exquisitely carved, and a carved chest inlaid with gold and ivory. A single lamp hanging from the ceiling by three chains gave a dim, eerie light. The whole place struck Stephen as being cold and comfortless, although it had a certain austere beauty; that dignity which he always associated with Iris.

And she ... his Love ... was here. She was half sitting, half lying on that ancient couch ... her hair unbound, tangled, hanging across a face that was distorted and wet with tears. Now, seeing him, she sprang up and shook the splendid hair back from her eyes. She reproached him.

'I asked you not to come. You had no right...' but her voice broke into a sob. Instantly Stephen was sitting beside her and

314

she was in his arms, and he was kissing with deep, long kisses that sorrowful mouth and the great pain-filled eyes.

'Iris ... Iris, my darling Love ... what is all this about? Iris ... my dearest one ... for heaven's sake let us put an end to this. Let me take you home. Tell me that this is just a passing madness and that you love me still.'

She lay motionless against him for one pulsating moment ... he could feel her heart beating madly against his ... feel her wet, quivering lips respond to his kiss. He caught a silken strand of her long hair, wound it about his throat and kissed her again.

'Darling, my love ... we can never quarrel ... never, you and I...' he said huskily. 'Look at me ... let me see your wonderful eyes smiling at me again, darling...'

She felt that she was dying, there in his embrace. She wished, indeed, that she might die before he could relinquish his hold of her. She had fled down here, to her little sanctuary ... in utter misery ... hoping that in this entrance to an old tomb she would recover her equilibrium and gain the strength that she seemed to lose every time she saw Stephen. Almost now she told him the truth ... almost ... with the frenzied feeling that he might sufficiently believe what she said to safeguard himself ... to stay out of Usref's reach ... even take her away in the silence of the night to some place where Usref's malice, his murderous intentions, could not touch them.

Almost she spoke...

Then it was as though a blackness descended upon both of them. Silence fell in that lamp-lit Egyptian room. A brooding, sinister silence broken only by their quick breathing. They sat there in each other's arms ... not moving ... not speaking.

From outside, up that little staircase ... there came a sound which sealed Iris's lips as surely as though a physical hand had been laid across her mouth. *The sound of Mikhilo Usref's voice.*

He was here, in the temple. He was speaking with old Siroo. He was here ... the arch-fiend ... he was not going to lose sight of her for long ... nor of Stephen!

Cold as ice, and in complete despair, Iris drew herself out of Stephen's arms.

22

Stephen looked enquiringly at Iris.

'What is it, my darling?'

Her heart was thudding. She shook her head mutely, her ears still straining for the sound of Usref's voice. There was silence now, but she knew, she sensed, that he was still up there. She felt a violent but helpless rage. How could she tolerate this persecution? Once she had been so proud of her supremacy here. Her wish in the 'Little Palace' had always been law. Dully she thought of those dear, half-forgotten days when her father had been alive. What would he have thought of this dreadful fate which had overtaken her? But, of course, had Romney Lowell lived none of this would have happened. She would not even have met Stephen. There was nothing left now but for her to try and be grateful for the few weeks she had known him; when they had loved each other.

Stephen put out a hand and touched her.

'Dear, something frightened you just now, what was it?'

She stood up with a swift movement and began to braid her long, loosened hair. In the dim light of the oil-lamp her face was pale and drawn as she said:

'I was mad just now to let you kiss me like that. No, Stephen, don't touch me again. You must realise that this thing can never be … you and I can never go to England together and marry.'

The words were out at last. They half choked her, but she said them. Upstairs there lurked the shadow of death, *waiting for Stephen*. At all costs she must avert it from him. The sound of Mikhilo's voice … the knowledge that he had so coolly and arrogantly walked into the temple to spy on her had convinced her there was no escape from him. She acted now with the calmness of complete despair. The sooner it was over the better. She was only prolonging the agony.

She dared not look at the man she loved with all her soul. But she could imagine the stricken expression in those grey eyes which were usually so bright with love for her. She heard his voice, slow and incredulous.

'Iris, you can't mean what you've just said. You can't possibly mean it.'

She continued to braid her hair with slender fingers that trembled and burned as though she had a fever.

'Yes,' she said, 'I do mean it. I have been giving a lot of thought to this association of ours. I have decided that our marriage would be unsuitable. You are an English-man, and your real interest lies in your own country; amongst those conventional people who entertained us in Cairo. It would never suit me. I was bored by them. In time I would be bored by the whole life.'

She broke off. Her lips felt dry and her throat ached with misery. And still she kept her face turned from Stephen.

But now he sprang to his feet, and she felt his strong fingers grip her arm. Without ceremony, roughly, he swung her round and forced her to face him. She was shocked by the sight of him. He looked grey, as though he had received a mortal blow. He spoke to her in a harsh voice unlike his own.

'I never heard such damned rubbish in all my life! Why, it's ridiculous! I won't listen to you. What you have said doesn't make sense. You were perfectly happy with me at those parties in Cairo. You told me so. We both agreed that we prefer country life ... our solitude here, etc ... but it's ludicrous of you to say that you won't marry me because you might get *bored*. How deep is a love that confesses to boredom for so slight a reason?'

Iris shut her eyes and set her teeth. If Stephen meant to argue, fight for her, he would only make things all the harder. Yet deep down in her very heart she adored him for his attitude. It was wonderful to know that he cared so much and that he was not going to give her up easily. Her emotions were painfully in conflict. But there was no turning back now, she decided, and grimly she tried to bring this thing to a final conclusion.

She dragged her arm away from him.

'It's no use, Stephen. I have made up my mind. I know you have found me difficult and moody since we got back and it is because I have been gradually realising the total unsuitability of our union.'

He stared at her, his face reddening. He alternated between feeling stupefied by her announcement and being completely puzzled. Her behaviour was so inconsistent that it was enough to baffle any man. He told her so in a few curt words, and added coldly:

'You can't tell me that you don't love me; I know that you do. I daresay you've had doubts ... you are so young and in-experienced ... it is only natural that you should have a few moments of indecision. God knows I'm not so vain that I haven't wondered at times why you should give me your love. But for the most part you have seemed so convinced that we were right for each other, and just now in my arms ... oh, I refuse to believe that you could have kissed me like that if you did not love me!'

Her breath came rapidly.

'I ... lost my head ... you attract me *that* way...' She broke off, loathing the words she had just spoken, and the reproach on Stephen's thin, sensitive face made her feel hot with shame and misery. He said:

'*That way!* ... ye gods! ... are you trying to tell me that this has just been a physical thing?... Why, I don't believe it. We have led different lives in different worlds, but you have always agreed with me that we have had complete mental union. But if it has only meant the other thing to you...'

He broke off with a gesture which added to her self-loathing. But grimly she went ahead.

'Well, there it is, Stephen. You had better face up to it. I am not going to marry you. It would not be a success. I say it for your sake as well as mine. Go back to *your* world and leave me to mine.'

Still incredulous he stared at her. For a few moments he argued and reasoned. He recalled memories of their great happiness, their understanding, their mutual appreciation of life.

He drew close to her again, caught her hand and put it with a boyish gesture against his cheek ... a gesture of tenderness that almost broke her heart.

'Oh, Iris, my darling, you can't mean this,' he exclaimed, 'you are just tired. That week in Cairo was too much for you. You aren't used to all the noise and rush – the wear and tear of modern life. Rest here for a day or two in your beautiful home, my dearest Love, and I know you will feel different again. You can't seriously be asking me to go away and consider our association at an end.'

She steeled herself to pull her hand from his. Opening her eyes she gave him a long, inscrutable look. And now suddenly Stephen grew chilled and much more unsure of her. There was a coldness, a flint-like quality about her which frightened him. He had an awful sickening sensation that she was telling the truth, and that she had, indeed, decided not to marry him.

His love dream seemed to be crumbling at his feet. He said:

'I can't ... I *won't* believe it!'

'You *must,*' said her inexorable voice. 'I want you to go away, Stephen, and never come back.'

'Good God,' he said stupidly. 'This after all we've been to each other? All we've said and planned ... why, it's incredible! No woman could be so cruel, so fickle!'

Her long lashes veiled the agony in her eyes. When she thought of that menacing shadow awaiting up those curved stone stairs ... her courage almost failed her. Almost she flung herself into Stephen's arms and told him everything. It was so awful to see that look on his face and hear the condemnation in his voice. Awful to be responsible for his hurt, his disillusionment. But remembering that Usref waited not so much for her as for *him* ... she gathered fresh strength. She decided to give Stephen the *coup de grâce*.

'Another thing, Stephen ... I have been thinking that it was wrong of me to come between you and Elizabeth Martyn. But perhaps it is not too late...'

She stopped ... afraid of her own words ... afraid of the look in Stephen's eyes. The lover, fighting to keep his love, was fast becoming a hostile stranger, lashed to resentment by that speech from her which, she fully recognised, was unforgivable.

'That settles it,' he said in a low, icy voice. 'I believe now that your supposed love for me has been a complete myth. But I think your sympathy for Elizabeth is a bit misplaced, and as far as I am concerned it comes much too late.'

She stood mute, slender fingers clenched at her sides. It seemed to her that she was enveloped in a great wave of pain.

'You will go now,' she said, more in the nature of a command than a request.

Then he dismayed her ... took the wind right out of her sails ... by giving a curt laugh and looking at her much as he had done when they first met ... as though she were a spoiled child who must be corrected ... reformed.

'I shall have much pleasure, my dear Iris, in completing the task your father set me,' he said. 'I shall go with you to England as planned, and hand you and Miss Morgan over to your Aunt Olivia.'

Aghast, she said:

'I shall not leave Egypt.'

'Oh, yes you will,' he said; 'you've defied me once too often, my child. Now I'm going to prove who is the master of this situation.'

'But you can't...' she began, her whole body shaking with nervous agitation.

He cut in:

'I can and will. There is going to be no more nonsense. Even if I have to get a couple of chaps to carry you on to a 'plane, you're going to England. The law is on my side. You are under age. Your father wished you to be handed over to your aunt and that's the end of it. As for me ... I can see that I have made a damn fool of myself. You say you lost your head ... well, I lost mine too, so we'll cry quits and start again.'

She did not speak for a moment. Her large dark eyes were dilated. A dozen new fears and problems beset her. She had felt so sure that Stephen, disillusioned in her, would walk out ... make it easy. But if he was going to insist on staying and try to force her to go back to England, it would be the very devil. Mikhilo would lose patience and then ... oh God! ... *she dared not* allow her imagination to carry her further.

He added harshly:

'You go back home and tell Miss Morgan and Ayesha to pack for you. And no doubt Your Excellency won't want to be carried on to the 'plane, so you had better make up your mind to walk on to it in a dignified manner.'

And he looked at her with that hostile, resentful expression that agonised her, but which she knew was only the result of her own conduct. She had made him like this ... she had robbed him of his tenderness and charm. She had wounded him to the depths of his being. She knew it and was filled with an intolerable sense of loss.

For the man, ignorant of the truth, it was a disaster. A disaster of love and misplaced belief in a woman. He had never loved Elizabeth, but to Iris he had given the white-hot, fervent devotion of an idealistic boy rather than the man of the world that he was. He had been sure of her. But he had been wrong. She had not really loved him at all. She had only been momentarily attracted. Then with unbelievable ruthlessness she had decided to cut his life in two and calmly told him to go.

Full of bitterness, he regarded her slender, virginal beauty and told himself that as long as he lived he would never love or believe in another woman.

But he was not going to let her off so easily. She was not going to be allowed to stay here and idle her life away in the company of bounders like that Serbian fellow ... exercise the rights of a queen ... avoid all her obligations. He was determined that she should be forced to carry out her father's wishes.

'Come along, Iris,' he said roughly. 'We are only wasting time here.'

She seemed to shrink away from him. He could not guess that all her fear was for *him*.

Her eyes gleamed at him in the dimness of that small, lamp-lit room, which seemed to Stephen suddenly oppressive, even sinister. He wanted to get up and out into the fresh air and light again. The place smelt of age-old spices, of incense and cedarwood, of some faint, lingering perfume which had been distilled perhaps thousands of years ago for an amorous Egyptian queen.

'Let's get out of here,' he said sullenly.

Iris said:

'Go where you like ... do what you like, but leave me alone.'

'No,' said Stephen, in the same sullen voice. 'I'm not going to be dictated to by you, Iris.'

Feeling at the end of her tether, she turned, and lifting her long linen robe, ran up the staircase out of the catacombs into the twilight of the great marble hall above.

She had but one wish ... to get away from Stephen and his bitter, accusing eyes ... to put her hands over her ears and shut out the sound of his hostile voice. She wondered if, in all the thousands of years gone by ... and the previous dynasties ... any young girl who walked through this same temple had suffered more than Romney Lowell's ill-starred daughter.

She heard Stephen's footsteps behind, knew that he was following. Blindly she ran ... not caring much where she went ... anywhere, she thought, rather than say with *him*, now that she had placed such a barrier of bitter misunderstanding between them.

She stumbled as she ran ... felt a steadying hand on her arm, and looking up saw the calm, smiling, handsome face of Prince Usref. At a respectful distance behind them stood old Siroo, who made an obeisance as he saw Iris, then discreetly faded behind one of the giant pillars.

Usref said.

'My Lady of Moonlight hastens ... and to whom indeed should she run more swiftly than to Mikhilo, her devoted slave?'

She could not answer. She was too over-wrought. Trembling, panting like a hunted gazelle, she stayed in his grasp. Her lovely eyes looked up into the man's agate ones ... with mute appeal. He added softly:

'Has something terrified you? You are

trembling, my Lady. You need my protection.'

Still mute, she shook her head, but she found his words ironical. *His* protection! Good heavens, she would so gladly run away from *him*, but dared not. And now her thought was to keep the two men apart. She found her voice and said feverishly:

'Take me outside, Mikhilo. I ... feel faint. I ... need more air.'

He pressed her arm against his side and led her towards a shaft of light which marked the commencement of the outer courtyard. But he cast a searching glance over his shoulder in the direction of the staircase. He knew perfectly well that Iris had been down there ... with Daltry.

And then, before they had moved two or three steps, the slim, straight figure of Stephen, in his English-looking grey flannels, appeared. He called to them in a curt, angry voice.

'Iris ... come back. I want to talk to you, please.'

Usref glanced swiftly at the girl. She was so pale that he feared that she was about to faint. He put an arm right round her. It was the first time he had ever touched more than the hand of the unapproachable Lady of Moonlight. A wild thrill of passion and triumph shot through the Serbian. *Iris was his now* ... she was learning her lesson ...

and this time Stephen Daltry was going to be given his *congé* ... and for good.

Through colourless lips Iris gasped a few words:

'Mikhilo ... take me ... away...'

'But, of course, at once, most lovely!' he murmured.

But Stephen had caught them up. There was a breathless moment of silence between the three of them. Iris would have fallen if Mikhilo's thin, steel-like fingers were not gripping her, holding her slight body against him. She dared not look at Stephen. She was utterly dismayed because she had failed to get Usref away. She was in a blind agony of fear for Stephen ... knowing what lay in Usref's mind.

Stephen addressed himself to the Serbian with scant ceremony.

'If you don't mind, I'll take Miss Lowell back to the Palace.'

Mikhilo's thin lips wore the usual suave smile the while his eyes were narrowed, dangerous. He bowed with simulated respect.

'Your pardon, Mr Daltry,' he said in his oily, unpleasant voice, 'but my Lady has asked *me* to take her home.'

In the ordinary course of events Stephen, at this juncture of affairs, would have turned and walked away; finished with the pair of them. But he was in a dark mood ... goaded to a bitterness and hostility unusual for him by that blow that Iris had dealt him. Besides, he thought, it was one thing for her to decide that their marriage would not be suitable and another to see her walk straight into the embrace of a fellow like Usref. He was filled with detestation of the fellow and with an anger against Iris which sprang from the most acute jealousy. It was intolerable to him to see her being held intimately like that by Usref. Damn it, did she think he was going to stand by and watch that unconcerned, or just meekly crawl away and leave her to go her spoilt, contrary way?

So he stood his ground, white under his tan, hands clenched.

'I think we'd better come into the open and understand each other, Usref,' he said. 'I am one of Miss Lowell's guardians. She is not yet of age – she is an infant in the eyes of the English law – and I have been detailed by the late Lowell Pasha to take her back to her aunt in London. I intend to do this, so the sooner you realise it and stop hanging around, the better.'

Iris put a hand to her lips. Like one paralysed she leaned against Usref ... her huge, tormented eyes fixed on Stephen's angry face. She then made a movement as though to go toward him and immediately Mikhilo's arm tightened around her. She heard his voice ... ice-cold and menacing.

Dear heaven, she thought ... she knew what that menace meant ... dear heaven ... if only Stephen would go *away*...

'I think *you* are the one who must stop "hanging around", as you put it in your English fashion,' said Usref. 'And I agree, Mr Daltry, that we had best understand each other without delay. Miss Lowell is not willing to accompany you to London. She is staying in Egypt where she belongs ... and in due course she will become my wife.'

Another tense silence. Stephen stared at Usref ... then at Iris. He was dumbfounded. Usref added:

'I realise that my Lady is not yet twenty-one, but out here such laws are not recognised. She shall marry me by the laws of Egypt. With the assistance of the Fahmouds, she can easily become a citizen of this country and obtain an Egyptian passport. Eventually, as I intend to be naturalised in America, she will become American by marriage, and ... you English will be concerned no more with her interests.'

Iris shut her eyes. She was beyond speaking or acting now. But Stephen, with an exclamation, caught her arm and tried to get her away from Usref.

'You must be crazy,' he said in a violent tone. 'You can't want such a thing. You can't *possibly* ... after all you have said to me. And what the devil does Prince Usref mean about you marrying him? Since when have you shown the slightest desire to marry Prince Usref? You must be quite out of your mind, my child. You were talking delightedly about marrying *me* yesterday. You can't change your mind all that quickly. Anyhow, agreed that *our* love affair is over, I'm still damned if I'm going to allow you to hand yourself over to this fellow. No, Iris. You'll see your aunt in London first and let her give her consent before I give mine. Is that understood?'

She did not answer. Usref answered for her, this time snarling, without the smile:

'I have stood enough from you, Mr Daltry ... and so has my Lady. I suggest you pack and leave the "Little Palace." You have out-stayed your welcome here.'

Stephen's face suffused with colour. There were only one or two occasions in his whole life when he had lost his temper. And they were under extreme provocation. He lost it now. With a swift movement he caught Iris's wrist and jerked her out of the Serbian's grasp. With a little moan she sank to the ground.

She did not faint. She just collapsed in a little heap ... feeling too weak to go on standing. Her great eyes burned up at Stephen with a hopeless beseeching in their depths which he missed.

'Oh, don't ... *don't...*' she whispered.

Neither of the men heard her. They stood

with clenched hands, glaring at each other. The gloves were off with a vengeance.

Stephen had boxed well at school and later at Oxford. With a quick rapidity and deftness that took the Serbian off his guard, he hit out at the man.

Usref went down, blood trickling from his lips. Stephen, without seeing Iris's pitiful figure – for by now he was blind with rage – waited, face livid, teeth set, for the Serbian to pick himself up. He stood there panting, watching, wary.

Mikhilo Usref got up. But he had none of the Englishman's liking for sport or honour. His hand went to his hip pocket. Something flashed in the faint sunlight. And Iris saw it. Her dread dream had materialised in its full horror. She managed, somehow, to get to her feet and fling herself at Mikhilo. It was enough to save Stephen from death, but not enough to spare him altogether. The hand that held the knife was brushed a little sideways. It pierced Stephen's side, averted from his heart. He gave a cry and stumbled. His last thought before he lost consciousness. *'Damn him ... typical of the swine to play foul...'* He heard Iris screaming...

Then darkness and silence. The great twilit temple ... Iris's voice ... Mikhilo's face, fiendish with malicious fury ... and old Siroo ... running in answer to his Lady's call ... were all blotted out.

23

Sitting in Iris's bedroom, where the green shutters were closed and only a faint light slanted on to the polished floor, old Miss Morgan sat watching and listening to Iris.

The girl paced up and down the room like a caged creature. Her face bore traces of violent weeping. Her hair was unbound. She was still wearing the white linen dress which she had put on earlier in the afternoon when she first joined Stephen after their siesta. The dress was crumpled now, the whiteness stained with a dull, ominous red... The red of Stephen's blood. Whenever Iris looked at it she shuddered ... remembering how she had seen him fall, knelt beside him and cradled his beloved head on her lap. She had been demented with fear that Mikhilo had managed to carry out his threat and had put an end to Stephen's life. She had called *'Stephen ... Stephen ... my Love'* loudly, bitterly, again and again, but he had not answered her. She had looked up at the Serbian and, like a little fury, called him a murderer. *'You shall not do this ... you shall not ... I shall tell the police,'* she had said with choking sobs.

Then Stephen's eyes had opened. She had heard him give a long sigh before he slipped into unconsciousness again. But at least she knew that he lived. And after that the temple had filled with Egyptians. Siroo ... after the manner of his race, had uttered a high, shrill whistle, the call for help ... and many of the *fellahin* working on the land close by heard and had come running. For that Iris was thankful. She did not want Siroo to go for aid and leave Mikhilo alone with her and the helpless Stephen. And once she was sure that Stephen had not been murdered, she became her old self; the cool, poised autocrat of the 'Little Palace.' She gave swift orders to one and all. Siroo was dispatched to the Palace to warn Miss Morgan and tell her to send for a doctor. Two men lifted Stephen carefully on to a hastily improvised stretcher and carried him out into the sunlight. Iris walked by his side. Usref, his face sullen, was close behind them. Whilst they were being rowed across the river they did not speak to each other. With his black, malicious gaze Usref had noted the tenderness with which Iris touched Stephen ... already she had torn a strip of linen from her robe, wrung it out in water and held it under his shirt against the wound to staunch the blood.

Once at the other side of the river, while two of the *fellahin* carefully lifted the unconscious man from the boat, Iris addressed Mikhilo.

'If he dies,' she said. 'If he dies ... you shall be handed to the police as his murderer.'

'You have no proof,' Mikhilo had muttered.

'Siroo will be a witness,' she had said.

'Siroo was not present...'

'I shall be believed...'

Usref had shrugged his shoulders.

'And if he lives ... what then, my Lady ... for I do not think his wound a serious one.'

'Thanks to my hand averting the blow...' she had reminded him. Again he shrugged and repeated:

'And if he lives?'

And Iris had answered:

'Even then I shall hand you to the police for attempted murder. I shall do so the instant we reach the Palace.'

Then he had snarled at her:

'Do so and I kill him. He shall not live to see me in a prison, my Lady. I warn you. Our bargain was made. It is marriage and peace between us ... or I strike again, and *this time I swear I shall not fail.*'

And then she had realised that Usref still had the upper hand. In despair she had watched the red patch widening on the white linen pad against Stephen's side. She had suffered agonies for and with him. She knew that she was defeated again. Brokenly she had said:

'Very well, when he is well he will go. I have already told him that I wish him to go. That is why I was running away from him in the temple. Let him alone now for God's sake!...'

Mikhilo had then bowed and become his oily, obsequious self again.

'Your wish is mine, my Lady of Moonlight...'

She had looked at him in horror, wondering how it was possible to hate any living being so much.

And Stephen lived.

But the dark shadow of Usref's threat remained, and still Iris dared not speak; dared not so much as breathe a word of the truth to old Morga or a living soul.

It was agreed between Usref and herself that they tell the world an unknown assassin had attacked Stephen for the money he carried but had escaped.

Now, pacing up and down her lovely room, Iris repeated this story. And Miss Morgan listened, her face wrinkled with worry and a good deal of astonishment.

Frankly the whole thing puzzled her. Iris's behaviour was so odd ... even granted that she was concerned about Stephen. The doctor had declared he was in no danger. The wound was superficial. He had dressed it and ordered complete rest and quiet for

Stephen ... and for the last hour he had been in bed in one of the guest-rooms, sleeping under the influence of a drug, watched by the devoted Ayesha who adored the grey-eyed Englishman.

Why then was Iris in quite so wild a state? Morga wondered. And how was it possible, if Stephen had been attacked in the temple by a thief, that the latter had got away ... when Prince Usref had been there to give chase to him?

Iris was so incoherent on the subject it surprised and alarmed the old governess. She was certainly not herself. She kept repeating that Mikhilo ran after the man, but that he had vanished into the depths of the temple and they could not find him.

Old Morgan could not guess at the desperate condition of the girl's mind ... or know that she was existing now in perpetual fear that Stephen would be assassinated again ... not by an unknown thief ... but by Usref's own hand. She could not guess that Iris had had to steel herself to try to send Stephen away from her earlier that afternoon ... and that once he recovered consciousness she must deal him a similar blow.

Morga kept saying:

'Calm down and go to your bed, my child. Please ... I implore you. You look ill and exhausted. It has been a great shock. But it

338

is over. Surely you need not work yourself up into a fever like this?'

Iris paused and looked at the old woman, her eyes full of anguish. Then she glanced down at the stain on her robe and shivered. She whispered:

'I cannot rest. Do not ask me to.'

'But, darling child ... Stephen is not in any danger. Dr Rufatt has said so ... and is he not the finest of all the physicians in Upper Egypt?'

Iris's eyes filled with tears. She felt so tired, so sick at heart, she wished she could have thrown herself down on the floor at Old Morga's feet, hidden her face in that kindly lap and burst into weeping. *Not in any danger!* Oh, if only that were true!

'Go to bed, please, my darling,' besought the old woman.

Iris shook her head.

'I must wait ... until Stephen wakes. I must be the first to speak to him.'

Miss Morgan sighed and rose.

'Oh, well, if that is your wish...'

Iris nodded. There was so much more in this than old Morga knew, of course. But when Stephen was able to listen, to speak to her, she, Iris, must tell him to keep silence about the attack ... she must lower her pride and *beg him* not to denounce Usref as his would-be murderer. *Otherwise he might sign his own death warrant.* Usref might strike again ... before the police put him in safe custody. She dared not risk it. She must say: 'I am going to marry Mikhilo. For my sake, please do not denounce him...'

But heaven alone knew what Stephen's answer would be. He might be stubborn and refuse to placate her. She was filled with foreboding. Little wonder she could not rest.

Left alone by old Morga, Iris calmed down sufficiently to bathe and change her robe; get out of that torn, pathetic dress stained with the blood of the man she loved more than life. She folded it, placed it in a drawer and locked it. Then she put on clean, fresh, snowy linen, braided her hair and walked down the cool marble corridor into the east wing of the Palace. She had left not only the old Arab nurse in charge of Stephen, but placed two of her most faithful *suffragis* on guard outside his door. Another watched in the garden near his windows. She was taking no chances tonight. She had said to them all: '*Watch His Excellency ... guard him with your lives, for he may be attacked again...*'

She knew they would not fail her. Most of the Sudanese here had served with her father and her mother. And with all the Egyptians' natural love for children, they had waited on and worshipped the baby Iris ... watched her grow into the beautiful girl who was like a queen to them now.

They would allow no assassin to attack Stephen Daltry tonight.

But there was tomorrow ... *and tomorrow* ... and Usref was waiting... Iris knew there was no escape for her.

She entered the darkened room in which Stephen lay. It was fresh – even cool – a great electric fan whirred noiselessly overhead. The atmosphere was redolent with lemon-perfumed lotion which Ayesha continually sprayed around the bed. There wasn't a fly in here to worry the injured man. Ayesha watched, keeping the ice-cold bandages across Stephen's hot forehead.

She rose as her young mistress entered.

'He sleeps, my little Lady ... fear not,' she whispered in her own language.

Iris answered, also in Arabic.

'Will he recover, Ayesha?'

'Of a certainty, my little goddess of the Nile. He has no fever. It has abated. His wound is not dangerous. He will be himself in a week, or even less maybe.'

Iris's gaze rested gloomily on the man in the big low bed, which was caged in the finest mosquito netting. Opening the cage, she entered, closed it again and sat down beside Stephen. She took one of his inert hands and held it against her cheek. In an instant it was wet with the tears that began to flow down her hollowed cheeks. She whispered:

'Oh ... my Beloved ... oh, Stephen, my Love!'

He slept like a boy. His lashes were bronzed and thick against his brown cheeks. His lips smiled. Once more, so close to him, watching him like this, Iris felt a modicum of the happiness that had once been hers. He looked young and almost happy, she thought, lying there, breathing so quietly and easily. He seemed to be her lover again ... instead of the bitter, disillusioned man who had spoken so harshly to her in the temple.

Ayesha whispered – watching them through the fine net.

'Do not grieve, my Dove ... he does not suffer. He will be up and well quickly ... I promise you. Ayesha knows these things.'

Iris drew a long sigh from the depths of her being.

She would have Stephen here, in her Palace ... for a week or so more. But after that ... no more. *No more* ... for her there could be only pain and separation ... while life endured.

Ayesha whispered again:

'I have thought much of the attempted murder, my little queen. It is strange ... with Prince Usref there to protect the *Effendi*. *Is it not strange?*'

Iris turned and regarded her old nurse. A long, significant look passed from one to the other.

'*Aiwah* ... it is strange,' Iris agreed.

Ayesha mumbled with her lips. A peculiar expression twisted her nut-brown face. She nodded repeatedly.

'Very strange, O my Dove, my little goddess of the Nile. The Prince was there. He looked strange, too, and his hand shook, for I saw it.'

Iris shuddered. Old Ayesha was psychic. At certain phases of the moon she had extraordinary gifts of divination. Iris knew that well enough. She whispered:

'Go, Ayesha ... brood no more ... for it is not your concern. Allah will surely punish the wicked one. Have no fear...'

Ayesha made an obeisance. Her eyes, bright black like little shining buttons, snapped. She gave a crooked smile as she regarded Iris's haggard young face.

'*Aiwah*... Allah will punish him, O Pearl of the Nile valley...'

And she departed, giving a little muffled chuckling sound. Iris, watching her exit, knew that Ayesha *knew* ... yes, she alone of all of them here was aware of the truth.

Iris looked at Stephen again. For several hours she sat immovable, watching him; only stirring now and again to touch his wrist, to make sure he had no more fever ... or to change the iced bandages on his brow.

The sun had set when Stephen again opened his eyes. Outside had fallen the purple darkness of the warm, still night ... pierced by the pure radiance of the moon.

The Nile flowed past like a mighty ribbon of dark green oiled silk. The 'Little Palace' seemed to be buried in a strange and sinister silence. The white peacocks were restless tonight, screaming plaintively, fit-fully, to each other.

Stephen became conscious of a great shadow on the high ceiling, cast by a small shaded lamp which burned on the table beside him. He moved, and, feeling his side stiff and painful, lay still on his pillow again. Then he saw Iris ... the lovely, sad face bending over him. He heard her voice:

'You are ... all right? Do you desire any-thing that I can give you? A drink perhaps ... here is some iced water and orange...'

Her arm went round him, supporting him ... a goblet was raised to his lips. Half awake, still drowsy with narcotic, he drank and found the liquid very refreshing, for his lips were dry and his throat felt parched.

For several moments he could not think ... could scarcely recall what had happened in the Isis Temple. He was aware only of the nearness of Iris ... of her soft arm around his shoulders ... of the exquisite tenderness of her voice. Feebly he put out a hand and rested it on her hair.

'Sweet...' he whispered. 'Iris ... my darling...'

Her heart almost broke ... it was such bitterness and yet such bliss to hear him speak to her like that again. She could not speak, but sat quiet, supporting him, the tears rolling down her cheeks. And yet she knew she must not respond to his half-awakened passion ... that she must go on playing that grim, remorseless part that was her terrible destiny.

Before she could think again Stephen had pulled her head down on to his pillow. Eagerly he claimed her lips. And as he kissed her he whispered:

'You are mine ... I love you ... we belong to each other. Tell me it is so ... darling, darling ... tell me that you love me still...'

Silence ... only the sound of her quickened breathing and his own ... the harsh cry of the peacocks down in the moonlit garden.

For one pulsating instant Iris gave vent to her own feelings. She responded passionately, desperately to that kiss, lying there beside Stephen, her arms about him. Then in terror she dragged herself away and stumbled out of the room. She could not, dared not, remain there. She called brokenly to the old Arab woman.

'Ayesha ... Ayesha ... go back to him ... Ayesha!'

The nurse appeared in answer to the call. She looked at her young mistress's retreating form, then took her place by the sick man. Many ideas were formulating in her queer old mind. Many thoughts. And over them all loomed the detested memory of the Serbian ... who had knocked her over, not so long ago, and whose unworthy foot had kicked at her old bones as she lay groaning on the floor.

She stared through narrowed eyes at the Englishman. He stared back at her. He muttered:

'Iris ... Iris...'

Ayesha took his hot wrist between her fingers.

'Hush, *Effendi* ... keep calm ... do not move, or you will develop a high fever. Her Excellency is indisposed. She has asked me to sit beside you.'

Stephen groaned. He was fully awake now. He remembered everything. His unhappy scene with Iris ... his quarrel with Usref ... and the knife, dishonouring that fight.

Ayesha's voice implored him.

'Patience, *Effendi* ... rest ... and all will be well...'

'Perhaps,' muttered Stephen, 'and perhaps not.'

'It shall be well,' said the old nurse, nodding. 'Ayesha is the devoted slave of my Little Lady and of the *Effendi*. Their friends are hers ... *their enemies, too, are hers...*'

Stephen, his heart rocketing and his whole

body bathed now in sweat, stirred restlessly. He was not quite sure what lay behind that speech of Ayesha's. He did not really mind. He wanted Iris back ... wanted to find out which was the truth ... her dismissal of him in the temple ... or that long kiss which she had just given him, that long, passionate, revealing kiss. He felt feverish and confused.

Ayesha continued to mutter to herself. She saw the handsome, cruel features of Usref. And she nodded her veiled head.

'*Aiwah* ... *aiwah*,' she whispered, again and again. 'Your enemies, *Effendi* ... and the enemies of my beloved mistress ... *are also mine.*'

24

Later that night ... the 'Little Palace' was shrouded in the mystery and velvet darkness of that strange, silent hour before the dawn.

Iris was not asleep. She had not even attempted to go to bed. Ever since she had torn herself from Stephen's side she had locked herself in her rooms and refused admission to anybody. More than at any time in her life she needed to be alone. She had one of those deep, rare natures which can draw strength and fortitude from solitude. Joy she could share with others, but her suffering she wished to hide. She would not even let Ayesha in to see her. Once or twice the old nurse had come outside the door, knocked and called to her:

'Will you come back to the *Effendi?* He cries your name. He asks for you, my little Rose of Egypt.'

But Iris had answered:

'Go back to him, Ayesha, and tell him that he must sleep and that I wish to be alone.'

So Ayesha departed, muttering that the Evil Eye had been cast upon her Dove, and that the Palace was bewitched.

Old Miss Morgan came too, and tried to

induce Iris to unlock her door.

'You have eaten nothing, and quite frankly, my dear child, you are doing more harm than good by acting in this fashion. Come out and talk to me. Don't shut yourself away like this.'

But even to her dear Morga Iris had but one reply:

'Let me alone.'

Miss Morgan continued to argue:

'You'll make yourself ill and to what purpose? Use your intelligence, my dearest Iris. You are not living up to the philosophies which you have studied and loved. You have always said that to allow the emotions to master the mind is the conduct of the weak and foolish.'

To which Iris had answered bitterly:

'Then I am weak and foolish. Do not remind me of the past, Morga, and of the Iris-that-was ... all that is changed.'

'But at least it would be sensible to have food and rest,' the practical old woman said drily.

To please her, and to save further dispute, Iris unlocked her door and permitted Mandulis to bring her a tray with some cold chicken and a French loaf and red wine, and one of the ripe, sweet mangoes which were her favourite fruit.

Worn out by weeping, distracted by grief, by longing for Stephen ... a longing which it seemed could never now be assuaged ... she tried to follow her governess's advice. The chicken she left, but she dipped some of the crisply-baked bread into the wine and ate it. She had to confess later that she felt better for the food and stimulant.

Through pain-blurred eyes she stared at the familiar beauty of her lamp-lit room ... at the purple night and the stars and the eternal splendour of the flowing Nile ... and she could see nothing but Stephen's face, haggard, pleading for her love. To go back to his room ... to feel again his hands on her hair ... his hungry lips drawing the very soul from hers ... that seemed the most desirable thing in the world. But not while Mikhilo Usref lurked in the background. She had her lesson in the Isis Temple. Next time that wicked blade flashed in Usref's hand it would be the end of Stephen.

She must go on to the bitter end.

Now in the early hours of the morning she seemed to have reached a pitch when the strength to endure had once more returned to her. Body and spirit were calmed. Pain was transcended by love. She told herself that she must hurt and anger Stephen for a while ... that she must send him away disappointed and unfulfilled but that he would live to forget her ... or, if not to forget, to remember her and their love only as a charming episode. As for herself ... her thoughts would not carry her further into *that* dark void for there was too much horror in it.

She stood out on the balcony, a solitary young figure in her white wrapper, dark hair falling like a silken cloud past her waist. The steady murmur of the crickets had ceased. There was no sound even from those wild, forlorn creatures, the pie-dogs of the desert, who slink like shadows around the dwellings of the poor, and cry hungrily to the moon.

Iris had never known so intense a stillness. And for some strange reason it had the profound effect of creating that same sense of stillness – almost of peace – within herself.

The night passed. The Eastern sky flushed suddenly with orange light, changing the face of the desert. The grave, sculptured beauty of the temple was suffused with a glow almost of pure violet. Down in the garden, trees and flowers and the white marble of the terraces came into focus again. A little cool wind sprang up and touched the face of the girl who was still standing there silently watching and thinking. And she thought she had never known a lovelier sunrise, and that never had she felt more closely a part of Egypt. An immense sadness enveloped her and yet peace remained. She thought:

'Many thousands of years ago people like

351

Stephen and I loved and suffered and died. This present existence is of little account. In thousands of years to come Stephen and I will live and love again.'

Suddenly she had a great desire to see him and, without being able to explain frankly the reason why she was sending him from her, try to make the parting less bitter so that they should remember their love with happiness. He must not leave Egypt hating her; that would be too great a price to pay!

She unlocked her door and moved swiftly and noiselessly on her sandalled feet through the cool, dim corridors to Stephen's wing.

She entered his room and closed the door behind her.

Ayesha rose. She had been nodding and dozing by the bedside but was easily roused. She put her skinny finger to her lips, pointed at the man whom she had watched and whispered.

'He sleeps ... he revives ... have no fear, my little Lady.'

'It is five o'clock,' said Iris; 'go you and sleep for two hours and I will stay with the *Effendi.'*

In the dimness of the shuttered room the old nurse peered up into the girl's face. How pale she was, with lilac stains under the great dark eyes. Yet there was a tranquility about her that Ayesha recognised. She said:

'Is it not you who need rest, my Dove?'

'No,' said Iris abruptly. 'Go you, Ayesha.'

After the old woman had made her exit Iris gently unfastened the shutters of one tall window. The faint amber light of the exquisite morning filled the room; and with it came the breeze. Stephen needed a breath of that pure air blowing from the desert, Iris thought.

She took her place at his side and regarded him with great tenderness and yearning. He had been hot and feverish all night, but now he was quiet and rather pale. His silk pyjama-jacket was unbuttoned, showing a strong column of throat. His disordered chestnut hair was curly, like a boy's. He seemed to be sleeping peacefully, and yet, even as Iris watched, his brows knit and he stirred restlessly and muttered something under his breath, flinging an arm above his head.

Iris bent over him.

'I am here, Stephen. What can I do for you?' she asked.

His grey eyes opened widely and he looked straight up into her face.

'Iris,' he whispered. *'Iris.'*

She retained her composure, that strength of spirit which she had gained during the long, inner struggle of the night.

She laid a cool hand on his forehead.

'Lie quiet,' she said. 'It is essential that you

should keep very still until your wound is healed.'

For the moment he did not move or speak again, but his searching gaze rested upon her. He, too, was stronger and fresher after his night's rest. But he was still unutterably puzzled by Iris's odd behaviour. For a moment he had a passionate desire to thread his fingers through that wonderful long hair which so fascinated him: to pull her down into his arms, hold her there and never let her go, but something stopped him from doing this ... a curiously remote expression which he had not seen before on that beautiful young face. She made him feel that he must not on any account touch her. Yet there was nothing whatsoever about her of the spoiled goddess or the wayward child. She was just inaccessible ... almost a stranger.

He said in a puzzled voice:

'Iris, what is happening between us? What does all this mean?'

She drew her hand away from his forehead and answered calmly:

'Do not talk for a few moments...'

She went into the bathroom next door, fetched a bowl and some cold water into which she poured eau-de-Cologne, then came back and sponged his face and hands.

'You will feel better after this,' she said. 'And then I will send for tea... Mandulis

354

can make it the English way that my father liked. He always drank a cup when he first awakened.'

Stephen was reduced to silence. Baffled, he lay and watched, and let her do as she wished. He had never seen her look more lovely or tender. How gently she bathed his face and wiped it with a soft linen towel. She was the most extraordinary person, he thought ... the things she did and said were strange and unpredictable, and she carried with her always that intriguing air of mystery, that glamour of a unique personality which had first attracted him.

More than ever this morning he felt that that attraction was fatal ... that once having known and loved this girl, a man could not retract, could never forget. Especially once he had known the rapture of response from her. He realised also that when he had first fallen in love with Iris and considered breaking with Elizabeth it was because he had been certain that she was his true destiny, just as he was hers. There had flowed between them a sympathy and understanding as sure as it was incomprehensible.

Her announcement in the temple that she wished to marry Usref was just a nightmare, Stephen told himself this morning. And now suddenly he felt an immense longing to hear her say so ... tell him that she was still utterly his. When she came back to sit beside him again, having ordered his tea, he said:

'Will you light a cigarette for me, Iris?'

She did so with that grace of movement which was always a joy to him to watch. As he took the cigarette from her slender hand he gave the ghost of a smile and said:

'*"Pale hands I loved"* … do you remember, Iris?'

She folded the exquisite hands in her lap and smiled back at him.

'Yes, I remember, Stephen. You quoted that to me on the night when Elizabeth came here first.'

'That was a damned awful dinner-party,' he said with another crooked smile. 'Awful in spite of its magnificence.'

She looked at him inscrutably.

'Yes … it was a bad night for us all.'

'And yet a good one. It made Elizabeth realise that it was best for us to make a break. It brought me … so I thought … freedom to marry you.'

He uttered that line significantly. She did not flinch. Coolly she nodded.

'It seemed so.'

'Then what has happened between us, Iris?' he asked, repeating the question she had left unanswered.

'Many things, Stephen.'

He lay smoking, frowning, still watching her closely.

'Well, whatever it is, you are not going to make me believe again that you want to stay here and marry Usref,' he said.

Still unflinching, she returned his gaze, but the points of her long, polished nails hurt the soft palms of her hands, so tightly did she keep them clenched.

'You are wrong, Stephen,' she said in her calm, sweet voice. 'You must not forget that *you* changed your mind ... about Elizabeth. Why should it seem curious to you that I have changed mine about you?'

That hit him like a blow. The blood flowed to his cheeks darkly. He drew a long breath of his cigarette. So they were back to *that*, and the news she had given him in the temple was no nightmare but reality. Her general behaviour was beyond him ...he just could not begin to understand. In a few brief words he told her so. He added:

'I broke with Elizabeth because I fell deeply in love with you, Iris, and you appeared to feel the same way about me. I do not see how you can make a parallel of your feelings for Usref. You have not really seen anything of him lately. Why should you suddenly decide you prefer him to me?'

A pause. Iris thought:

'Oh, God! It is difficult. It is difficult, and yet I must go on!'

Aloud she said:

'Do not ask me to explain. Human beings

cannot always analyse emotions or motives, and passion can be as ephemeral as the life of the rose which opens in the morning and scatters its petals before night.'

Stephen's gaze narrowed. He said:

'But our love was not just passion, Iris. You know that. You yourself became aware of the spiritual significance of the feelings we shared long before I did. It was you who first said that our love was no transient thing; that it had existed in the past and was as eternal as those desert sands which lie there across the Nile. Or have I just imagined that you said these things?'

The old sharp pain threatened to rob her of composure, but with an effort she answered:

'I may have said them, but I was wrong.'

He stared at her.

'You really mean it? You really want to marry the man who stuck a knife into me – tried to kill me?'

Her teeth clenched over her lower lip. She began to shiver.

'Why drag up these things ... why discuss them? Why not accept what I have said? When you are well again I want you to go. We must never meet again, Stephen.'

He ignored this and said slowly:

'Am I right or wrong in thinking that you saved my life in the temple yesterday? If you had not thrown yourself at Usref he might have got me ... got me altogether.'

'Maybe,' she said, swallowing hard.

'You would not have done that if you had stopped loving me, Iris.'

'Oh yes, Stephen ... I would have done the same ... for any friend ... for any ordinary friend. Usref is a dangerous man when he loses his temper. I was momentarily afraid for you.'

Stephen's lips twisted. His heart began to pound with the old hot resentment.

'So you forgive him quite easily. And you want to marry this dangerous type?'

'Yes,' her voice was almost inaudible.

'You seem to forget, my dear, that I can charge him with assault.'

Now her dark, brooding gaze rested on him with a mixture of agony and appeal.

'Do not do it, Stephen. Let things rest, I implore. Go from my house in peace, and leave peace behind you.'

He stared, then gave a curt laugh.

'You are crazy ... right out of your mind, my child.'

Now she rose and turned from him, unable to bear his scrutiny any longer.

'Leave it at that ... that I am mad.'

He looked at the slim, white-clad figure and the long, lovely hair.

'No, I'm damned if I'm going to leave it at that,' he said violently. 'I'd as soon see you surround yourself with snakes for the rest of your life as married to Usref.'

'Will you not do as I ask and leave me quietly and without bitterness?' she asked in a choked voice.

'Come here, Iris,' he said harshly. 'Come and take my hands and look into my eyes and swear that that is what you really want.'

The strain was too great for her. In a suffocated voice she said:

'Oh, stop, stop! You are killing me!'

And she left him, moving quickly out of the room without a backward glance at him.

And then Stephen Daltry knew ... guessed at last that there was more to this thing than mere caprice on Iris's part. Something deeper and more obscure than an ordinary change of affection. She did not love Mikhilo Usref. She loved *him.* He had seen it in her eyes ... felt it in her hands ... known it when he had heard her frenzied scream, and seen her fling herself at the hand that held the knife.

What then did it all mean? Usref had some hold over her. *What was it?*

Mandulis came with the tea, followed by Ayesha, who filled a cup and raised it to Stephen's lips, supporting him with pillows. He drank thirstily. The fragrant China tea, flavoured with lemon, was most refreshing. He felt stronger and better, and his side was not so sore. His spirits were rising higher every moment. He was completely puzzled, trying to work out in his mind what had happened between Iris and Usref. But whatever it was, one poignant fact stood out and filled him with renewed hope: *Iris was still his.* And now nothing would induce him to leave her or the 'Little Palace' until he had discovered the truth.

25

In the Fahmouds' handsome villa on the banks of the Nile – from which they could see the blue flashing dome of the 'Little Palace' – Nila was giving a cocktail party.

There were many luxurious cars outside the gates and on the terrace a crowd of the Fahmouds' friends, of all nationalities, were gathered drinking *apéritifs* and eating the many delicacies which – despite six years of war – were procurable in this country.

It was a warm, moonlit night. Lights sparkled on the terrace and from the wide open windows of the villa, Nila, as smart as ever in pale yellow, with a yellow flower in her sleek black hair, flitted among her guests chattering in many languages. But her pretty, vivacious face was downcast. She was quite frankly puzzled by the things which were going on in the Palace, and bitterly disappointed because the most beautiful and glamorous of all her friends was absent from the party. It was not Iris Lowell's habit to attend parties, but some time ago she had promised to come to the next one. Half the guests were disappointed at not meeting the 'Daughter of Earth and Sky' tonight.

Nila, of course, made the excuse that Iris was indisposed. But she knew perfectly well that this was not the case, and that the person who lay ill in the 'Little Palace' was the English diplomat, Stephen Daltry.

Mikhilo had come home with the amazing news that an attempt on Stephen's life had been made in the ruined temple. He had suggested that he personally had made a heroic attempt to save Mr Daltry's life, but that the assassin had escaped. On the other hand, there were whisperings and noddings and shakings of heads going on among the servants. Nila had lived long enough in Egypt to know the Sudanese servants. They had an uncanny knack of getting first-hand information about people and things and passing it on, one to another. Maybe the Fahmouds' head *suffragi* was cousin to Mandulis, or the Lowells' second house-boy was a nephew of the Fahmouds' cook. But news spread rapidly out here and eventually everybody heard it.

Nila had heard this afternoon, before Mikhilo told her, of the incident in the temple. Hassan, the grey-headed, trusted *suffragi* who had carried Nila about in his arms when she was born in Alexandria, had told her that there were 'queer goings-on' in the Lowell home: *he* had it on the best authority that Siroo, the old custodian of the temple had actually witnessed a fight between Prince Usref and the Englishman.

Nila, for all her frivolity and tactlessness, sometimes knew when it was best to keep silence, and this, she thought, was one of them. She said nothing to her parents. Fahmoud Bey, her father, was blind and never appeared in public. Nila's mother was deeply religious and spent most of her time with her infirm husband or on her knees, praying. So Nila and her brother, Atta, more or less ran the household alone, and did as they chose; both of them spoilt and with wealth at their fingertips.

Atta had just returned to New York on business. Mikhilo should have accompanied him but had asked to be allowed to stay on in Upper Egypt for another month.

Once Nila had hoped that Mikhilo, with his handsome face and smooth manners, would win Iris. Nila had no personal interest in the Prince; her heart at the moment belonged to a young French pilot working on the Suez Canal. She genuinely loved Iris and wanted her to marry Mikhilo. She had been willing to help Mikhilo in every way. She had genuinely believed that Stephen was an outsider who had no right to interfere in her friend's life or trifle with her affections.

But now Nila's butterfly mind was working on different lines and she had begun to probe quite seriously into the whys and wherefores of the whole thing. She was not sure that she either liked or trusted the Serbian Prince any more, and she was not a little horrified by all the ugly rumours. She asked herself many disturbing questions.

Could it be true that the Englishman had been injured in a fight between himself and Mikhilo? Had the latter lied about it? And why was Iris behaving so strangely? Another rumour was spreading from the staff of the 'Little Palace' to Nila's domestics, that Iris shut herself in her room day and night, and when seen was always weeping, and that there was great trouble at the Palace.

For a whole week it had been like that. It was a week since the Englishman had returned from Cairo with Iris and Miss Morgan, and every day Hassan had said, 'The doctor called at the Palace.'

Every day Prince Usref called there also, and he had hinted strongly to Nila that he was making great headway at last with the late Lowell Pasha's daughter and hoped soon to give Nila the best of news.

The pretty Nila, so friendly and amiable and stupid, accepted this information in her usual gay fashion, but deep down within her she began to wonder if after all it would be the 'best of news.' She could not regard her brother's bosom friend with the old admiration. One cannot like a person one cannot trust, Nila told herself, and Usref was changing ... he was becoming arrogant, even here in the villa in which he was merely a guest.

Nila had had a conversation on the subject with her latest *amour*, the young canal pilot from Ismailia who had come to attend her party and spend a few days in Upper Egypt.

'I shall be glad when Mikhilo returns to America,' she said. 'And it troubles me, *mon cher*, that Iris will not see me any more and that no one save Mikhilo is allowed through those gates. I have told you all that is being said. What do you think is going on?'

The pilot, blond, charming and deeply enamoured of the dark-eyed Egyptian girl, was not interested in the 'goings-on' in her neighbour's home. He was interested only in the colour of Nila's eyes and the shape of her lips, and he told her so. But Nila was not to be flattered into a state of forgetting Iris. She was also nettled because twice today already she had asked Mikhilo to take her to see Iris, and he had refused. With his new arrogance, he had said that he could not comply with her wishes. Iris wished to see nobody but himself.

And when Nila had enquired after the health of Mr Daltry, Usref had smiled in what Nila thought a rather unpleasant fashion and said that he was 'making such good progress that he was now allowed up.' The assassin's knife had merely glanced off

366

one of his ribs, and he had suffered from shock and some fever due to loss of blood, but was now almost himself again.

'In fact, he will be well enough to travel back to Cairo and start his new job next week, we hope,' Mikhilo had ended with that unpleasant smile.

That was all very well, Nila thought, but what did Iris think about it? What had caused her complete reversion of feelings towards the Prince? For when the girls were friends and had talked of these things, Iris had made it quite plain that she could never fall in love with the Serbian.

So filled was she with curiosity and also resentment because she was being ignored, Nila decided to take matters into her own hands. She made use of the presence of Pierre, her adoring Frenchman.

When her cocktail party was over she said to him:

'Pierrot, *mon cher*, we will drive in your car to the "Little Palace".'

Humbly, Pierre got his Citroën out of the garage and complied with his pretty Nila's request.

'And now, Pierrot,' said Nila, as they drove through the wonderful night, 'you will act a part. You will cease to be a pilot of the Suez Canal Company. You will become a doctor. I have been refused admittance so many times to the Palace, but now I shall be refused no more.'

The young Frenchman meekly enquired as to why he should become a doctor, and what he should do.

'For thee, my Angel, I would do much, but do not ask something too difficult,' he pleaded.

Nila gave a tinkling laugh, and touching his cheek with a provocative hand she gave him further instructions.

The keeper of the lodge gates must not be blamed when he opened those gates that night for Mlle Fahmoud, who in perfect Arabic informed him that Her Excellency had sent for a second opinion on the health of the Englishman and that she, Mlle Fahmoud, had brought at her request a French doctor from Alexandria.

Once through those gates, Nila laughed at her Frenchman's embarrassed face. He would die of nerves, he said, if he was asked so much as to take the temperature of the Englishman. He was a good pilot, but he was *not* a doctor.

But Nila assured him that his job was over and that he could now remain in the car and wait for her. She was going to see her friend Iris alone. A determined woman, no matter how stupid, can always get her way. Nila got hers.

It was about nine o'clock that she practised her little deception. And once in the gardens she decided that she was not going to be seen by that old watch-dog Mandulis either. But as she tiptoed up the steps of the terrace she was startled by the unexpected sight of Stephen Daltry himself. He wore a silk dressing-gown and leaned on a stick. In the moonlight his face looked pale and grave. He seemed equally surprised to see her.

'Mlle Fahmoud!' he exclaimed. 'So it was your car that I heard. I came down from my room to test my strength. I am tired of being treated as a sick man. It has all been a fuss about nothing. But I did not expect to find *you* here.'

'No, Mr Daltry,' said Nila, 'for nobody has been allowed here lately except Prince Usref.'

'That is only too true,' said Stephen with a sardonic smile.

Nila drew closer to him.

'You have noticed that?'

'Obviously.'

Nila waxed confidential.

'Well, I am going to tell you straight away that I am annoyed because Iris no longer seems to need my friendship.'

Stephen, leaning on his stick, looked across Nila's pretty head with narrowed gaze.

'You are wrong, mademoiselle. She has never needed it more.'

Nila's pulses thrilled. So she had not come in vain. Something was very wrong.

'Oh, tell me ... where is she? How is she?'

'I have not seen her for a week,' said Stephen. 'I have merely received notes from Miss Morgan telling me that Her Excellency would find it convenient if I returned to Cairo as soon as the doctor would permit me to travel.'

'But I thought she was going to England with you and Miss Morgan.'

'She is,' said Stephen grimly, 'once I have made up my mind how to get her there. I have every intention of keeping my promise to the late Pasha, mademoiselle, despite the efforts of your charming friend the Prince to keep her here. But, of course, you are a friend of his and—'

But here Nila cut in excitedly.

'But I am not, I am not, now. I have reason to suspect that he has not been honest with me and that things are not as they should be. I have changed my mind about Iris and the Prince.'

Stephen looked a little less grim. He stood still a moment tapping his shoe thoughtfully with his stick.

This last week had been very unpleasant. He had not enjoyed his enforced solitude in a sickroom, with only the servants to talk to. None of the notes he had sent to Iris appealing her to see him had met with success. He had one conversation with Miss Morgan which had been unsatisfactory, as the old woman had seemed confused and worried about her pupil but unwilling to act as a go-between. Obviously she was influenced by Iris. And Iris received nobody except Mikhilo Usref, who, Miss Morgan had told him, was allowed to see her daily in her private salon. But even Usref never stayed long. Iris for most of the time shut herself in her own rooms. It was all most disquieting – and, for Stephen, infuriating. For despite Ayesha, who was so obviously anti-Mikhilo and on *his* side, and despite Stephen's inner convictions that Iris still loved him, he did not seem able to regain her confidence or friendship.

But he was not going to leave the 'Little Palace' without a fight; even, he told himself grimly, it if meant another stand up fight with Usref.

After a moment he said to Nila, 'How did you get into the grounds?'

Nila smiled and told him proudly of her little ruse, and the young pilot who was patiently waiting for her in his car.

'I insist on seeing Iris,' she added. 'Once we were friends. I do not believe that she has altered so completely.'

Stephen gave a hollow laugh.

'But I believe it,' he said, 'she has given me every reason to do so.'

'I shall go up to her room and remain outside her door until she lets me in,' said Nila dramatically.

Then a clear, cold voice broke in on this conversation.

'You need not go up to my rooms, Nila. I am here. You have resorted to trickery in order to enter my house, but I forgive you for that, as you did it in the name of friendship. Say what you wish and then go back to your own home and leave me alone. You will none of you leave me alone.'

The ice-coldness of that voice cracked a little on the last few words.

Both Stephen and Nila turned to see Iris standing in the archway which led into the hall of the Palace. The light fell upon her, illuminating her young, graceful figure. She wore a long black chiffon dress with a girdle of silver, inlaid with cornelian. Her dark hair was wound with a single silken plait around her head. Her face was camellia-pale and she looked ill. She had put on no jewellery. She was like a figure of mourning. Nila, who had not seen her for some time, received quite a shock. Stephen's feelings were indescribable. A long look passed between them. An inscrutable look.

'Oh, Iris, *ma chérie,* you look dreadful! What has happened? Why have you shut me away? What is all this mystery?' Nila broke out in her rapid voluble fashion.

Iris scarcely moved. Her veiled eyes looked neither at Stephen nor at Nila now, but at the shadow of the temple over the river. Stephen, watching her, became conscious of great unease. This was not the Iris he had known and loved. *What was wrong?* He was going to get to the bottom of this mystery soon, or go crazy, he thought.

'Won't you even speak to me, Iris?' Nila asked.

Iris looked at her friend.

'I have asked for peace and to be allowed to go my own way without interference,' she said.

Nila peered at her. With sharp feminine, discernment she saw that Iris was neither as cold nor immovable as she would have them think. Her hands were clenched at her sides and her lower lip trembled.

'But look here,' said Nila in an aggrieved voice, 'why should you see only Mikhilo? Why must your other friends steal like thieves into your grounds?'

'Because,' Iris answered, 'it is my wish.'

'That isn't altogether true,' came from Stephen suddenly and harshly, and his hand clenched over the top of his stick.

She turned to him. It was Nila rather than the man who saw Iris shiver.

'You should not be here like this,' Iris said to Stephen, with a note of anxiety in her voice which she could not conceal; 'you are

373

not yet strong enough.'

He gave a curt laugh.

'My dear child, you are so anxious to throw me out of the place it's just as well that I make an effort to get on to my feet again.'

Iris made no answer. She wondered if either of these two could guess at her sickness of soul, her loneliness, her secret dread.

Then suddenly there came the sound of a motor-horn ... of a car coming up the drive on the other side of the Palace. The three of them stood listening. Iris drew a sharp breath.

'I will not have people coming here disturbing me like this!' she exclaimed in a nervous, agitated voice. 'How dare they let through another car tonight? Mandulis told me Nila had come with a doctor. They considered it only right that you should be allowed in ... but this time—'

But now she broke off, for Mandulis came out of the Palace, his brown face worried and apologetic. He was followed by two ladies in European dress. Iris, Stephen and Nila stared at them in astonishment. One was an elderly woman with a smartly waved grey head. She wore a linen suit and hat. The other was young and slim, and good-looking. Her hair fell in brown curls to her neck.

Rapidly Iris interrogated her *suffragi*. The

man answered in Arabic.

Then Iris gave a low cry and turned to Stephen.

'It is my father's sister ... my Aunt Olivia and my cousin, Daphne.'

Nila stood by, inquisitive as usual. Iris looked as though she was completely unnerved by this sudden appearance of her relatives and as though fresh tragedy rather than good fortune had befallen her. But Stephen came forward, his grey eyes lighting up with undisguised relief.

Mrs Cornwall, the late Pasha's sister! What a wonderful stroke of luck; nothing short of a miracle ... that she should have chosen to come out here instead of waiting for her niece to go to her.

Olivia Cornwall advanced upon them. She was a very big woman ... a woman of authority ... with a deep, authoritative voice. She had none of her brother Romney's poetical nature, or love of scientific and historical study. She was and always had been a 'social light' and a realist. She completely dominated everybody, including her daughter. Daphne was obviously a trifle subdued and overshadowed by her monumental mother.

The Cornwalls had had a long and tiring journey by air, and their 'plane had arrived three hours late. It was their first visit to Egypt. They were both so hot that they could scarcely breathe. The Egyptian driver who had brought them in a hired car to the 'Little Palace' had driven much too fast. Aunt Olivia was therefore not in the best of humours. She looked first at Nila, so *chic* and pretty in her smart yellow dress, then at the beautiful girl in the long black chiffon robe which seemed to her singularly out of place. She bore down upon Nila.

'Iris, my brother's child!' she said in her booming voice. 'My poor Iris!'

Nila retreated, smothering a laugh. Then Stephen said:

'No – that is Mlle Fahmoud. This' – he indicated Iris – 'is your niece.'

Aunt Olivia seized the stricken Iris in her embrace.

'Romney's daughter! Well, well, my dear ... I shall be a mother to you in future. This is your cousin Daphne. You are the same age. Daphne was born twenty-four hours after you made your appearance ... you two should be great friends...'

Daphne, exhausted and dazed, put in a polite word.

'Yes, it will be awfully nice, won't it?'

Then Nila said:

'I think perhaps I had better come and see Iris another day...'

On the side she whispered to Stephen:

'Ring me up or come and see me, Mr Daltry. Believe me, I am your friend.'

376

He whispered back:

'I reckon things will be all right now. Nothing could be better than this...'

Mrs Cornwall was explaining how she had received Stephen's letter and had first of all thought of waiting to see Iris in London, then had decided that a change of air and scene would be good for dear Daphne, who had just had her appendix out. So she had cabled to Iris, telling her that they had been lucky enough to book seats on a flying-boat which should have arrived at Assuan early this evening.

'You don't seem to have had my cable, I'm told things go astray out here,' she said. 'I had great difficulty in making these black men of yours understand that I am your aunt, and allow us into the place. I presume you did *not* expect me?'

Iris stared at her aunt, completely bewildered. She could see nothing in this big dominant woman to remind her of her handsome father, but her gaze softened as she looked at her cousin, for Daphne had inherited quite a few of Uncle Romney's physical traits. She said:

'No – I received no cable, Aunt Olivia.'

Stephen added:

'But you have arrived at a very opportune moment, Mrs Cornwall.'

'And who are you, young man?' she demanded.

'I am Stephen Daltry.'

'Ah!' exclaimed Mrs Cornwall. 'It was *you* who met my poor brother and afterwards wrote to me. Now I understand.'

'Shall we go in?' Stephen suggested.

'There is nothing I would like better than a long drink, some food and a rest,' said Olivia Cornwall, fanning herself vigorously with a copy of *The Times* which she had clutched and never let go during the whole journey from London.

As they moved into the Palace Mrs Cornwall whispered to her daughter:

'My dear, I always told you your uncle Romney was a bit mad. Have you ever seen anything like your cousin Iris's get-up? And goodness knows what Mr Daltry is doing in a dressing-gown, and with a stick. I am certainly needed here.'

Daphne nodded. But secretly she was entranced by the beauty of her cousin. She thought Mr Daltry very good-looking and the 'Little Palace' a fabulously lovely and exciting place. She was glad they had come here. It certainly was a change after her conventional London home.

But Stephen caught Iris's arm just as she was about to follow her aunt and cousin into the Palace, and drew her back to the terrace.

'Well, my sweet,' he said, with a touch of irony in his voice, 'now you are going to find it a little more difficult to shut yourself away from us all and pretend that you want to marry Prince Usref ... is it not?'

He heard her sharp, indrawn breath, and looking down at her caught the expression of indescribable misery in her eyes.

She did not answer, but she thought:

'I love you so ... I love you so! But what am I going to do now? With my aunt here ... how am I going to protect you, Stephen? *What can I do about Mikhilo?*'

26

The next morning three people, Mrs Cornwall, her daughter and Stephen, breakfasted together under the striped canopy on the terrace of the 'Little Palace.'

It was one of those perfect mornings in the hour before the real heat of the day begins. The grounds were still sparkling with the heavy dews of the humid night, and looked fresh and verdant. The Nile was a clear deep green. The jacaranda trees made a patch of exquisite colour against the yellowish green of the mango trees. Hundreds of small coloured birds darted in and out the foliage. The Palace grounds were a charming contrast to the sombre shadow of the Isis Temple on the other side of the river and the pitiless monotony of the sunbaked desert.

Stephen saw it all with the aching eyes of a man who had not slept. He had walked his rooms most of the night, torn with all the old wild fever of longing for Iris, and with the fear that she had, indeed, ceased to love him, and was going to ask her aunt's permission to marry Prince Usref. He had already made up his mind that Olivia

Cornwall, with her air of authority and domination of her young daughter, was a good and worthy lady ... without a touch of romance in her make-up. She had Daphne to 'marry off' ... she might not wish to be bothered with Iris in England ... she might be stupid enough to be dazzled by the sound of a title and agree to hand her niece over to the Prince. And in Stephen's opinion such a thing would be a terrible disaster. Quite apart from his own loss, he could not bear to see Iris waste her exquisite self on a man like Usref. No, Stephen had not slept all night.

Daphne Cornwall gazed upon the wonderful scene around her with the young and enraptured gaze of one who had never travelled before and to whom all this was enchanting. What a breakfast she was eating, after the rationing at home! Pilak had served grapefruit, omelettes, fresh-baked rolls, honey, any amount of creamy butter and the most delicious French coffee. She had slept soundly all night in a bed-room more luxurious than she had ever imagined one could be. She anticipated having a good swim this morning and she was quite happy.

The other member of the breakfast party, Aunt Olivia herself, was neither happy nor unhappy. She was not a woman given to mercurial changes of mood. But she was frankly puzzled and a little shaken by what she had found in her late brother's Egyptian home.

She had so little to do with Romney and Helena in the years gone by and had not approved of the way he had shut himself up in this place, never returning to England, scarcely ever communicating with her, and – so she had heard from friends who came out to Egypt – bringing his young daughter up in such a fantastic fashion.

Now she knew her disapproval was justified. She had arrived too late last night to enquire much into the state of affairs, but had seen enough of Iris to convince her that the girl was, as she put it to Daphne later on, *'most peculiar.'* She was sure that something 'queer' was going on in the Palace.

She admired what she had seen of Stephen Daltry. He seemed a charming young man, and most intelligent. He had a good position and some money, and was, in fact, the sort of man whom Mrs Cornwall cordially liked. She quite understood why Romney had placed his trust in the boy. But even Stephen Daltry seemed a bit *'peculiar'* ... he was, for instance, reluctant to talk much about Iris; and the girl herself hardly opened her mouth and seemed nervy and (so Mrs Cornwall decided) afraid of her own shadow. It was all rather gloomy and mysterious, and Mrs Cornwall did not like it.

Then there was the old governess, Miss Morgan. A nice old thing but doddery and far too inclined to fawn upon Iris. Mrs Cornwall didn't agree with fawning. She had never allowed anybody to turn Daphne's head. In fact, everyone in the Palace treated Iris as though she were a goddess. All a lot of nonsense, in Aunt Olivia's estimation. But what she was going to do with this extraordinary niece of hers she did not know. Iris was quite obviously going to be an unwelcome responsibility.

Last night when mother and daughter retired Daphne had burst into unstinted praise of her beautiful cousin, but Aunt Olivia had interrupted sharply:

'You may be taken in by all this nonsense that your crazy uncle encouraged, but it doesn't amuse me,' she had said, 'and the sooner I get your cousin Iris into sensible clothes and find her a suitable husband the better. And don't you go imagining that you can put on chiffon négligés and throw orders around, because I won't have it.'

Daphne had replied meekly:

'No, Mummy.'

But she had found both Iris and her environment very exciting.

When breakfast was over Mrs Cornwall said to Stephen:

'Well, my dear Mr Daltry. I think we had better start looking through my brother's papers and decide what had best be done. I suggest that my niece be sent for and we will have a conference.'

Stephen twisted his lips in a faint smile.

'Your niece, Mrs Cornwall, has been brought up to give orders rather than to take them. She does not as a rule come down from her rooms until midday.'

Aunt Olivia seized a whisk and brushed away the flies which were irritating her.

'Nonsense!' she said. 'Tell one of these black creatures to go up and call her down.'

Stephen's smile broadened. He could see plainly that Aunt Olivia was not going to understand Iris. She rather amused him.

'Look here, Mrs Cornwall,' he said, 'you'll forgive me, won't you, if I suggest that you deal gently with Iris. She has had a strange upbringing, and is finding it hard to attune herself to the change brought about by her father's death. Quite frankly, I have begun to wonder what on earth will happen to her in London.'

Mrs Cornwall looked at Stephen doubtfully.

'I am beginning to wonder myself.'

Then Stephen said bluntly:

'You might as well know the truth right away. You are her aunt and have a right to know. There are two men who want to marry your niece. Myself, for one, and a foreign prince for another. At one time I hoped that Iris was going to marry me and that I could ask your permission to arrange an immediate marriage.'

Mrs Cornwall's eyes brightened. She looked at Stephen Daltry with new interest. She saw an immediate solution to her problems.

'Well, now, how very nice!' she exclaimed.

'Unfortunately, though, your niece has other views,' Stephen added drily. 'She wishes to stay here and marry the other man.'

Aunt Olivia looked disappointed.

'What's he like?' she asked dubiously.

Stephen bit his lip. He stood a moment looking at the wing of the Palace in which he knew Iris's rooms were situated. He said:

'I think you had better let her tell you about Prince Usref herself. It is her affair and not mine.'

'You are quite right, Stephen. It is my affair and not yours...' The cool, clear voice of Iris cut in on the discussion and made the three at the breakfast-table look up.

Stephen rose.

So Iris had come down early this morning! And – he did not know whether she had done it just to be perverse or not – she was more Egyptian in appearance than usual. She wore one of her straight linen tunics caught on one bare shoulder with a blue scarab brooch. The long dark hair was turned under, like a black helmet curving to the neck. The dark eyes were shadowed, the lids stained with blue. Her cheekbones stood out in a face that was as white as milk. Stephen had never seen her look more fascinating or more un-English ... as though there could be no possible relationship between her and her aunt and cousin in thoroughly British cotton frocks and straw hats.

Mrs Cornwall had had a slight shock when she had seen her niece last night. Now she received another. It was on the tip of her tongue to greet her niece with an acid comment on her appearance. But somehow words failed her. Gracious! she thought, what an extraordinarily intense way the child had of looking at one ... and there was decided dignity in the way she moved and spoke.

Mrs Cornwall gulped:

'Good morning, my dear. I am glad you are down. I was going to send for you. You and I and Mr Daltry must have a conference without delay. We wish to discuss your future.'

Iris avoided Stephen's gaze.

'I have decided upon my future, Aunt Olivia, and nothing will change my mind.'

'Oh, heavens!' thought Stephen. 'Now what does she mean?'

Mrs Cornwall coughed and said:

'Now, my dear, you mustn't be difficult. Your poor dear father has asked me to take care of you and...'

She stopped. As the three of them walked into the house they were confronted by a tall, dark-haired man with what Aunt Olivia called 'a foreign face'... His shoulders were too wide, his shoes too pointed and his smile too glittering, she decided at once.

But Iris held out her hand to the new arrival. Usref kissed it ceremoniously. Stephen, watching, stiffened and felt suddenly sick. And it was a sickness which intensified when he saw Iris draw closer to the man and confront them with a defiant look on her face. She said in a high, clear voice:

'Aunt Olivia, cousin Daphne, I would like to introduce you to my future husband, Prince Usref...'

Mrs Cornwall blinked. One shock after another in this place. Daphne looked disappointed. She had already concocted a wonderful romance in her mind between Iris and Stephen.

Mikhilo Usref bowed and clicked his heels together.

'I am delighted to meet you,' he said.

'Well, really,' said Aunt Olivia, 'I didn't know that you were engaged, Iris. We haven't discussed anything yet. Mr Daltry, don't you think...?'

But to her dismay Stephen suddenly turned and walked away, looking neither to the right nor left.

Iris took an involuntary step forward with an expression of unbearable pain in her eyes. But Mikhilo's long, flexible fingers caught her wrist and drew her back.

'*Malêsh*, let him go,' he whispered in Arabic, 'you have done well to introduce me like this to your aunt. It is useless for Stephen Daltry to interfere further. You are mine, Iris, and you know it. Let us now convince the good aunt that we shall find it agreeable if she will consent to our immediate marriage.'

Iris swallowed hard. Stephen had left the room. Perhaps he meant to leave the 'Little Palace' altogether. She did not know. She was too dazed. She could not loose her wrist from Mikhilo's pitiless grasp. She stood there like a trapped creature. Like one in a trance she heard her aunt and Mikhilo talking together and then allowed herself to be drawn towards the library. She caught something that her aunt was saying:

'It is really most trying of Mr Daltry to go away just at this moment,' and then Usref's voice:

'Perhaps we shall not need Mr Daltry. I am hoping that you will allow your niece to become Princess Usref, and I, as her husband, can then possibly relieve you of the charming responsibility.'

The dark waters of despair swirled around Iris's head. She drowned in them as she walked like an automaton between Usref and her aunt. She was thinking:

'Good bye, Stephen my Love … good-bye, for ever … you will never know how much I have loved you and that I have done this thing for you…'

Stephen walked with a set white face up the great staircase and through the cool, marble corridors to his rooms. This seemed to him the end. That Iris should so flagrantly introduce that fellow as her future husband was more than he could bear. His one wish was to get away from her … from all of them.

Like a drunken man, without seeing, he stumbled into the bulky figure of Iris's nurse. He put out a hand to steady the old Arab woman, and apologised.

She touched her forehead in homage, rearranged the veil about her head, and then peered at him with her knowing little eyes.

'Your Excellency hurries away?'

'Yes, Ayesha,' he said unsteadily. 'I want to go as soon as possible. Your mistress has just announced that she is to marry Prince Usref.

The old woman recoiled as though she had received a mortal blow. Then, muttering to herself in her own language, she put up a wrinkled brown hand and seized Stephen's coat sleeve.

'Excellency, do not go. Do not leave this house,' she whispered.

'I am sorry, Ayesha. I can no longer stay.'

'But you must – oh, my master! For I say to you that my little Lady will never wed with this man. It is written that her destiny is woven with yours.'

Stephen gave a bitter laugh.

'*She* said that once, but the words, if they were ever written, have been blotted out.'

'No, no! She is not for the Serbian, she is for you.'

Stephen, his nerves frayed, his whole body and soul burning with resentment and frustration, shook himself free from the old nurse's grasp.

'Let me alone, Ayesha. You don't know what you are talking about,' he said harshly.

He started to walk away from her and she wailed after him softly:

'*Aie-e-e!* do not go, my lord Stephen ... for it is you whom she loves...'

But Stephen shut his ears to the sound of that cry. He was going to his rooms to pack. For a few hours more he would stay in the 'Little Palace' in order to hand over Romney Lowell's effects to Mrs Cornwall, and then he would go. He never wanted to see Iris again. He was defeated. She and

Usref between them had defeated him.

But Ayesha went hurrying down the staircase as fast as her old limbs would carry her. Through the heat of the morning she walked out of the gates of the 'Little Palace' and into a small Arab village a mile away … the village in which she had been born.

There, in one of the flat-roofed mud houses built in the shade of two date-palms, dwelt a woman older than herself – Ayesha's sister, who was once the medicine-woman of the village, and still consulted by the sick. She sat outside the door of her hut. A goat was tethered near by nibbling at dry grass. Chickens pecked in the dirt at her feet. Near by a camel squatted, munching. A little grey donkey, tethered by the wall, twitched his tail against the onslaught of a million flies.

The atmosphere was odorous, and nothing was clean. Ayesha squatted by her sister and they gabbled together and nodded their heads in understanding of each other. After a moment the older sister rose and hobbled into the hut and came out with a twist of paper which she handed to Ayesha. The old nurse took it.

'You are sure that this does not bring death?' she asked a trifle fearfully.

The other old native cackled.

'Not death, but worse, my sister. All shall be well for the little Lady. All will be well for your Dove. *Inshallah!*'

A short while later Ayesha left the fly-plagued village and went back to the spotless luxury of the 'Little Palace,' the twist of paper tucked in her bosom and a cunning smile upon her brown face. She made her way into the kitchen and found Mandulis there, getting ice from the refrigerator.

'They call for drinks in the library,' he told the old nurse. 'The Prince is here and there are many discussions. The Prince smiles, but Her Excellency is like a frozen image. What is it, think you, Ayesha?'

'Ask no questions, but wait and see,' she said, then added slowly, 'Do you give wine to the guests, Mandulis?'

'*Aiwah.*'

'Do you wish to see the Prince Usref married to Her Excellency?'

Mandulis uttered an exclamation of horror.

'Her revered father would turn in his grave!'

'You do not like the Prince, Mandulis?'

'Has Siroo not said that he struck a knife into my lord Stephen? Has he not brought misery to our Lady? Has he not kicked you, Ayesha, widow of my cousin and the mother of many sons?'

Ayesha drew the twist of paper from her bosom.

'Shake this into a goblet and tell me if it

can be seen, Mandulis.'

The old *suffragi* tapped the paper with his finger. A pinch of what seemed the finest dust settled in the bottom of the glass. He lifted it to the light.

'It cannot be seen, Ayesha.'

'But you, Mandulis, know that it is there.'

'*Aiwah.*'

'And it is your custom to pour out the wine and hand it to the guests?'

'*Aiwah.*'

Ayesha chuckled under her breath.

'Go carefully, Mandulis. It is written that Her Excellency shall marry my lord Stephen,' she said. '*Ya salem.*'

Two brown hands, loyal hands which had served Romney and Helena Lowell and then their child, met and clasped in confidence and understanding. A shaft of sunlight caught the goblet which stood on the table beside them, glittering; empty, save for that fine dust.

27

The hot, bright day was ending.

Mrs Cornwall and her daughter had been sleeping peacefully most of the afternoon.

Iris lay on her bed in a darkened room, alone as usual with her horrifying thoughts. Not only was she mentally exhausted now, but her head ached violently. She felt ill. The whole day had been a nightmare; that conference in the library, after Stephen had walked out; the discussion that had followed ... the questions Aunt Olivia had asked her ... and always the sinister grip of Mikhilo's fingers reminding her that she dared not tell the truth.

She hardly knew what she answered to all the questioning. She only knew that in the end Mandulis brought drinks and the exhausting discussion was over. But not the nightmare. She had managed somehow to convince her aunt that she wished to marry Prince Usref. But Aunt Olivia had by no means given her final consent. She had told Mikhilo frankly that she was quite sure her brother would have wished his daughter to marry a man of her own race, but that since Iris seemed set on marriage with him she would discuss it with her, and let Mikhilo know the result.

'I must also discuss it with Mr Daltry,' she had ended.

Iris had not failed to catch the ugly look in the Serbian's eye. Hastily she had said:

'But Mr Daltry has nothing to do with it...'

When her aunt had reminded her that Stephen was one of her guardians she had continued to protest. She wanted to marry Prince Usref, she said. Nothing would change her mind. But nothing would change Aunt Olivia's either. She had taken a violent dislike to the oily Mikhilo, and was aggravated by Iris's obstinacy.

Stephen, she said, must be consulted. After that the meeting broke up, and Mikhilo went home. But not before he had whispered to Iris:

'You will be firm about this, my Lady of Moonlight, *you understand.*'

She understood well enough, and was frantic with ânxiety. Stephen appeared for lunch, but was cold and remote and hardly looked at her. He announced that he intended to leave Assuan that same night. Then followed fresh misery for Iris. For Mrs Cornwall was unwilling for Stephen to go, and used every wile she could think of to keep him here.

She was independent and resourceful, but

she did the 'weak woman act' on Stephen.

'I really cannot cope without you at the moment, Stephen ... I must call you Stephen,' she said. 'I don't think we girls ought to be left here alone with all these foreigners and natives, and no Englishman amongst us. Besides, we have by no means settled this question of Iris's marriage...'

Iris cast an anguished look at Stephen, but he avoided her gaze. He answered icily:

'I would prefer to have nothing to do with your niece's marriage.'

But Mrs Cornwall managed to persuade him to remain at least until tomorrow morning. That to Iris seemed bad enough, when she knew how essential it was that he should go. She felt that matters were worse still when her aunt intimated that she was fast making up her mind to forbid the marriage and take Iris back to England with her at once.

Now, alone in her bedroom, Iris faced up to the awful fact that in order to save Stephen there was only one thing left for her to do. She must run away from everybody in the Palace and go to Mikhilo, so that her aunt – and Stephen – would be forced to consent to the marriage.

In her overwrought condition she came to the conclusion that the sooner she went, the better. She could not face another conference with her aunt, or another hour with

Stephen. She could not endure his bitterness.

From her window she could see her aunt, armed with her fly-whisk and wearing an enormous hat, chatting with old Morga. Yes, thought Iris, even the old governess was joining hands with her aunt. They would all endeavour to get her away from Egypt and Mikhilo. Everybody was against her ... and, indeed, she could quite understand why, but was powerless to let them know it. It seemed to her that the shadow of complete disaster hung over the 'Little Palace.' She must go at once to the Fahmouds and ask Nila to help her ... help her to run away with Mikhilo.

With these wild, terrible feelings tearing her to pieces, the girl acted on her impulses and began to prepare for her flight.

She changed from her beloved linen tunic into modern dress. She did not even bother to call Ayesha, but packed a few of her newly bought clothes, pinned up her long lovely hair and tied a scarf around her head. She could still see her aunt and Miss Morgan in the garden, and now Daphne, who had been bathing, joined them. She stood there drying her wet curls in the sun. With envy, the miserable Iris looked at her cousin. How lucky Daphne was! ... the cheerful, happy go-lucky Daphne who had led such a normal life and would, no doubt, one day choose a nice husband, marry him and produce a family – and enjoy an ordinary, uncomplicated existence.

With all her heart and soul Iris longed for Stephen; realised how much she was about to lose. But he was the one person on earth whom she must not see again.

Taking her bag, she walked out of her room. She would find Mandulis, order the car and drive at once to the Fahmouds' house.

But Stephen happened to come out of his room at the same time. He saw the unexpected sight of Iris in her grey linen suit with a pale yellow scarf about her hair and the suitcase in her hand. Quickly he came to her side.

'Where are you going, Iris?'

She began to tremble.

'Leave me alone ... let me go ... do not interfere!' she stammered.

But Stephen, after a long deep look at her, took the bag from her fingers.

'Oh no, my dear, you're not going to run away like this. I have said that what you do does not concern me. And that may be true. But even as a disinterested spectator I don't care to see you make a complete mess of your young life. In that much I am your aunt's firm ally. You were, I presume, about to run off with your charming Prince?'

Iris could not answer for a moment. She felt as though she were going to fall down, there at Stephen's very feet. She wished that the ground would open and swallow her up so that she could suffer no more.

He was watching her intently. All his bitterness evaporated. Once again he was seized with the strong suspicion that Iris was acting like this against her will; that the wily and treacherous Serbian had some strong hold over her. He put down her suitcase and caught both her hands roughly in his.

'Iris,' he said. 'Look at me. Tell me ... what is all this? For heaven's sake tell me the truth this time. I don't believe any woman on earth could lie as you have lied to me ... be so much in love with me, then so ready and anxious to run away with another man. *I don't believe it.* Usref is forcing you to do it. How ... why? Answer me, Iris...'

With terror-stricken eyes she looked up at him. Her teeth began to chatter.

'No ... no ... let me go, Stephen...'

'I'm damned if I will!' he said violently. And now he, too, was shaking; the strongest passion of his life possessing him. He loved this girl. He had always loved her. Once she had loved him, too. They had been utterly, completely happy together. He was not going to let her creep out of the Palace to Mikhilo Usref like a frightened, runaway child who is being terrorised. He felt her fingers trembling cold in his own ... saw the fear in those great, tortured eyes, and this time he was so far carried away by his own strong feelings as to ignore her appeals – even her repeated assurance that she no longer cared for him and wanted to marry Usref. He picked her up in his arms. She was light; much too light and thin, he thought. He carried her back to the suite from which she had just emerged. He took a swift survey of the big, beautiful rooms, the disorder of clothes ... hastily opened cupboards and drawers ... chiffons, silks, delicate lace ... a variety of shoes ... and that faint, elusive perfume that was essentially *hers* ... pervading all. He laid Iris, limp now, and unresisting in his arms, on the richly brocaded *chaise-longue* which stood at right angles to one of the tall, arched windows. The room was dim ... the green shutters excluded the strong, hot sunlight. But Stephen could plainly see that Iris was on the verge of fainting. Her eyes were shut, her breathing laboured, her face colourless.

He slid a cushion under her head and, turning, ran from the room and down the corridors to Miss Morgan's rooms. He found them empty. He called for Ayesha but nobody came. The place seemed deserted. He ran back to his own room, fetched a flask of brandy which he kept in his cupboard for emergencies, and returned to Iris's room. The girl lay motionless where he had left her. He knelt down, slid an arm

400

under her shoulders and raised her head.

'Iris,' he said. 'Darling ... darling ... drink some of this ... you'll be better in a moment ... drink, darling ... then let us get this thing settled once and for all. Come along ... please...'

Her long, heavy lashes lifted. He saw great tears in her eyes. They brimmed over and rolled down her cheeks. His heart ached for her. He drew her closer to him.

'Iris, my beloved ... my darling,' he said huskily. 'What is it? Drink some of this *cognac* ... please...'

She did not resist when he lifted the flask to her lips. The strong, stimulating drink brought a little colour back into her face. She gave a long sigh. She could not speak, but the tears rolled desolately down her cheeks.

Stephen kept an arm around the girl. With his other hand he drew off her yellow scarf. The beautiful black hair which he loved so much tumbled down, covering her like a mantle. He brushed a strand gently back from her forehead, leaned down and kissed her between the exquisite brows. It was a kiss without passion ... a kiss of pure, un-adulterated tenderness.

'Iris ... Iris...' he whispered. 'You are still mine, aren't you? You always have been. This is a nightmare ... Iris, tell me that it is!'

It was his tenderness that broke her down.

401

Her resistance broke ... her courage to endure what Stephen had so justly termed a nightmare ... failed at last. She gave a sudden heartbroken cry and collapsed in his arms. With her hands locked about his throat, her face pressed against his shoulder, she cried and cried and cried. Her slim body was convulsed, shaken with that terrible weeping.

Stephen held her without speaking. His hand automatically smoothed the dark, precious head. Without words he tried to comfort her. But the sound of that bitter sobbing would haunt him for ever, he thought. And yet ... his heart beat fast with renewed hope and his narrowed eyes were curiously content. Iris had answered his question. He knew now, beyond all doubt, that she was still his. And now there remained only the necessity to find out why she had ever played that other part.

For a long time he waited, kneeling there by the *chaise-longue*, holding, caressing her. For a long time she wept out her surcharged young heart. And when that storm of grief had passed and she was quiet again, her eyelids swollen, her face wet and ravaged, he looked down at her and saw nothing but beauty ... her sorrow he could not yet understand, but he yearned to assuage it.

Gently he said:

'Tell me the truth now, darling.'

She was spent and exhausted. But in her unhappy mind still lingered the fear of Usref and his threats against Stephen's much-loved life. She whispered:

'I ... do love you ... I ... admit it ... but I must go.'

Stephen laughed aloud.

'What nonsense! Do you imagine for a moment that I'd let you go to that swine of a fellow if you still love *me?*'

She buried her face against his shoulder again.

'You must. I ... can't explain ... don't ask me to ... just let me go.'

'Darling,' said Stephen, 'you must think me a lunatic. Listen. Usref has some hold over you. I've known it for some time. I guessed it once we got back from Cairo. Old Ayesha knows it, too.'

Iris lifted her head and stared at him with her hurt, blurred eyes.

'*Ayesha?*'

'Yes.'

'She can't know ... nobody knows...'

'Nevertheless she guesses. She has second sight, the old thing. She told me so...'

Iris drew a sharp breath. Fear returned, gnawing at her. Yes, the old Egyptian nurse had second sight. That was true. There had been many proofs of it in the past. Iris's small, hot hands gripped Stephen's arms hard.

'Ayesha mustn't be allowed to interfere. Nobody must... It is my wish ... that we should say good-bye, Stephen,' she said, in a strangled voice.

He laughed again ... and put his hard, sun-browned cheek against hers.

'My adorable darling ... don't begin that again. Do you think I believe you ... after your tears ... after *this?*'

And suddenly he turned his head and kissed her on the mouth ... a long, deep kiss. And once again Iris's resistance snapped. Passionately she clung to him. There was a long silence in the warm, perfumed room. And for these two the world was lost ... shut out... They knew only the renewed heaven of a mutual, ecstatic love.

The long kiss ended only when they heard voices and footsteps outside in the corridor. Stephen stood up, smoothing back his hair. Iris lay motionless, exhausted, looking up at him with eyes that had begun to shine again. For these few moments she had forgotten even Usref and his threats. She belonged completely to Stephen.

Somebody knocked at the door.

Stephen opened it. Old Ayesha stood there, blinking at him with her beady eyes, clutching her black veil about her head. Behind her stood Mandulis, who made an obeisance of respect as he saw the Englishman.

'*Effendi*,' he said, 'we seek Her Excellency.'

'Her Excellency is not well...' began Stephen.

But the old nurse had shuffled forward and reached the side of her adored mistress.

'My little Lady ... grave news,' she said.

Iris sat up, pushing the heavy dark hair back from her flushed face. The room seemed to be spinning a little around her.

'What is it, Ayesha?'

'His Excellency Prince Usref...' began the nurse.

Now Stephen, his face darkening, came forward.

'Your Lady cannot be disturbed. Tell the Prince to go immediately,' he said.

Ayesha's eyes seemed to disappear into the back of her head, but her lips smiled. She bowed low.

'*Effendi* ... there is no need to tell him to go. News has reached us from Fahmoud Bey's dwelling. The Prince has been seized with a terrible illness. Too terrible to describe, *Effendi*. He lies stricken, totally paralysed, in the Bey's house, *Effendi*. They are coming with an ambulance to take him to the hospital.'

Iris – white to the lips – her large eyes staring incredulously at her old nurse – could not find words. Stephen said:

'What is this, Ayesha? Are you sure of your facts?'

The old woman bowed and mumbled.

'Very sure, *Effendi*. They say he is unable to move or speak, but only stares.'

Stephen shot a rapid glance at Iris. Then he ran to her side.

'Your Lady has fainted,' he said brusquely. Then he left Iris to the old nurse and walked downstairs. Miss Morgan and Mrs Cornwall came out of the gardens into the hall. Miss Morgan began:

'Have you heard what has happened to the Prince? They say the poor man has had a stroke or something and is totally paralysed.'

'Yes, I have heard it,' said Stephen, 'and I'm going to drive down to the Fahmouds' villa to see Nila and find out exactly what has happened. Look after Iris. She is ill.'

Aunt Olivia gave an exclamation.

'The poor child! What a disaster for her, though I must say for myself—'

But Stephen broke in, his face and voice grim.

'I don't think it is a disaster for Iris, Mrs Cornwall, if something terrible has happened to Prince Usref. On the contrary, it may be the end of her miseries.'

'What *do* you mean?' demanded Mrs Cornwall.

But Stephen had gone. The two English ladies walked up the stairs together, speculating upon what he had said.

In the kitchen Ayesha and Mandulis

retired to order hot coffee for their Lady. The whole staff was talking excitedly of the sudden 'stroke' which had seized Prince Usref.

Ayesha and the old *suffragi* eyed each other furtively. Then said Mandulis:

'Will he recover, think you, Ayesha?'

The old nurse shook her head.

'He will not recover, Mandulis. I have consulted my sister. She says it is an incurable malady and that for the rest of his life he will lie helpless as a babe, powerless to move or talk, with only his thoughts to keep him company. She says, Mandulis, that it is a rare disease which no physician can cure. *Inshallah,* it is a fearful thing!'

'*Aiwah!*' said Mandulis, nodding.

'Allah has willed it.'

'*Aiwah.*'

Then nurse and *suffragi* smiled at each other ... a long smile ... but Ayesha's smile turned to a low, satisfied chuckling sound, terrible to hear.

That night Iris lay on a low divan piled with cushions, on the terrace, overlooking her Nile garden.

The evening meal was over. Aunt Olivia, Daphne and old Morga were in the library with Nila Fahmoud, who had come over to see her friend. The four were playing cards.

Stephen sat beside Iris, one hand in hers,

while he smoked his after-dinner cigar. The night was velvet, luminous with stars, filled with the scent of a thousand flowers. And for the first time for long weeks the hearts of these two were completely at rest.

For at last the terrible truth had been told. Stephen now knew why Iris had 'changed her mind' and decided to marry Mikhilo. Aunt Olivia and the others knew it, too. Stephen had returned from the Fahmouds', confirming the news that Usref had been taken ill soon after he left the Palace this morning; that he had fallen down and been picked up, unconscious, his face grotesquely twisted. The hastily summoned doctor could do nothing for him. He said that it was a bad stroke from which the Prince might never recover … and an ambulance had driven Mikhilo away to Assuan within a few hours.

Then and then only … relieved of the ghastly dread that Stephen's life was in danger … Iris poured out her story.

Stephen, an arm round her, had listened, his face working. When she finished he had lifted one of her slender hands to his lips and kissed it reverently.

'My darling,' he had said, in a voice full of emotion, 'how I'm ever going to thank you, heaven alone knows. I'm shaken to the core. I don't know what I've done to deserve such a heroic effort on your part. Your courage … your endurance … oh, Iris, darling … that

408

you of all people should have been so terrorised and bullied because of me ... it makes my blood run cold!'

'As for me ... I am remorseful that I *ever* introduced Mikhilo Usref into my home and to you, Iris. It is too awful,' Nila Fahmoud had put in with passion.

Mrs Cornwall had gazed at her niece with a growing admiration and added:

'Jolly good show ... well done, my dear. Plucky of you. Daphne ... your cousin is a little heroine.'

And Daphne had added her usual humble, 'Yes, Mummy' – this time with enthusiasm.

But Iris – a great weight lifted from her mind – could only hold one of Stephen's hands against her cheek and whisper:

'It's all been so worth while ... to save your life, my beloved.'

And that is what she said to him again tonight as they sat together, talking ... making their plans for the future.

'Your life is all that mattered to me,' she said. And Stephen answered:

'It's an unworthy life, darling, but it's all yours ... dedicated to you ... for as long as it lasts.'

She had only one fear left ... that Usref might recover and return to threaten Stephen's life. But this he soon drove from her mind.

'There is no further need for you to be anxious about me, my sweet. To begin with, Nila 'phoned the hospital this evening and the report is that Usref's case is incurable ... and to end with ... should he ever get back his ability to speak or move, I shall see that you go with me to the police and steps shall be taken to evict that young gentleman from Egypt. You alone have enough power – and so has Fahmoud Bey – to arrange that. Egypt doesn't want visitors of Usref's *genre*. As it is, Nila has cabled her brother and told him to ask Usref's father to come over here and take charge of him. *If* he survives that long.'

Iris shuddered.

'It is a terrible thing ... to be struck down like that in the prime of life, Stephen.'

'Do you pity him?' asked Stephen incredulously.

'No,' she said in a low voice. 'I ought to, I suppose, but I cannot.'

'He made you suffer, blackmailed you and damn' nearly murdered me. That, apart from the fact that he hurt you so badly, is enough to make me feel that a long, lingering paralysis cannot be bad enough for him,' said Stephen shortly.

Iris shuddered again and reached both arms up to her lover. He came and sat on the divan beside her. She was still looking pale and fragile in her black chiffon gown, with her wonderful hair braided about her small head. But there was a new light in her eyes ... a new happiness curving her rich, pouting mouth which he loved to see.

For Iris – for them both – the clouds had lifted. Aunt Olivia, only too gladly, had given her consent to their marriage. There would be no need for Iris to go to England now. Later, when Stephen had done some work at the Legation, he would get leave, he said, and take her to visit the country of her birth. But for the present they planned to stay in Egypt ... and spend their honeymoon here in the glorious home which Romney Lowell had built for his wife, and which Iris loved so much.

They were to be married quietly by special licence next week. Aunt Olivia and Daphne would be here to attend and celebrate... After that, they were going home. But Iris and Stephen would stay in the 'Little Palace' ... together as man and wife ... never to be separated again. It was an intoxicating thought for them both.

Stephen held Iris close against his heart.

Dreamily she lifted a hand and touched his cheek. Her eyes were lifted to the stars.

'My love ... my beloved,' she whispered. 'Allah has been good to us. I never dreamed of such a solution to all my terrible problems. Nothing, nothing can part us again.'

'Nothing, my darling,' he said.

'So, after all, old Ayesha was right ... and it was written,' she said.

He bent to kiss her. They clung in breathless silence. And suddenly the moon flooded the enchanted gardens with light. A bird called – piercingly, sweetly – from the shadow of the jacaranda trees. The Isis Temple shimmered proudly in that all-revealing moonlight.

But the Nile flowed on its mysterious way ... deep, strong, full of rich fertility ... bearing with it all the history of the ages ... the things that have been ... the things that are yet to come ... the knowledge of good and evil ... the secret of life, and of death, and, over all, the eternal mystery of love.

The publishers hope that this book has given you enjoyable reading. Large Print Books are especially designed to be as easy to see and hold as possible. If you wish a complete list of our books please ask at your local library or write directly to:

Magna Large Print Books
Magna House, Long Preston,
Skipton, North Yorkshire.
BD23 4ND

This Large Print Book for the partially sighted, who cannot otherwise read normal print, is published under the auspices of

THE ULVERSCROFT FOUNDATION

... we hope that you have enjoyed this Large Print Book. Please think for a moment about those people who have worse eyesight problems than you ... and are unable to even read or enjoy Large Print, without great difficulty.

You can help them by sending a donation, large or small, to:

**The Ulverscroft Foundation,
1, The Green, Bradgate Road,
Anstey, Leicestershire, LE7 7FU,
England.**

or request a copy of our brochure for more details.

The Foundation will use all your help to assist those people who are handicapped by various sight problems and need special attention.

Thank you very much for your help.